FOR HA...
ALWAY... ...EN FOR
THE TRUTH

LIE CATCHERS

A PAGAN & RANDALL INQUISITION

PAUL BISHOP

Bishop

2019

WOLFPACK PUBLISHING
— EST 2013 —

PRAISE FOR PAUL BISHOP

AND LIE CATCHERS

LIE CATCHERS

"Paul Bishop is the real deal – real cop, real writer. You never go wrong with a Bishop novel." – Max Allan Collins, bestselling author of *Road to Perdition*

"Lie Catchers crackles with authenticity. Bishop's thirty-five years as an LAPD Top Cop fuels a turbo-charged novel." – Robert Crais, bestselling author of the Elvis Cole novels.

"Paul Bishop's experience as a top-shelf interrogator shines through the pages of Lie Catchers, a fascinating emotional story of truth, redemption, and justice. Bishop presents an intriguing cornucopia of characters, each with their own secrets, motivations, and desires – including the dedicated detectives who use avant-garde techniques to sort through deception and lies. Lie Catchers is an outstanding debut to the series featuring top LAPD interrogators Ray Pagan and Calamity Jane Randall." – Kathy Bennett, author of the LAPD Detective Maddie Divine series

"Paul Bishop weaves a fictional account so vivid you feel as if you're riding shotgun with the investigating officers. A crackling good story, you'll love Pagan and Randall, Bishop's latest dynamic duo." – Robin Burcell, bestselling author of *The Last Good Place*

"Through the narrative of Lie Catchers, Paul Bishop opens the door to the secrets of police interrogation, giving us a unique take on LA crime. With dynamics worthy of Sherlock Holmes, Ray Pagan and 'Calamity' Jane Randall are unlike any detectives you've seen before...their methods are entirely fresh." – Sam Hawken, *The Night Charter*

"Lie Catchers is a remarkable journey into police interrogation tactics and the study of criminal psychology. Bishop has been there and knows all the intimate details. Authenticity simply spills across the pages." – O'Neil De Noux, author of the LaStanza novels

Lie Catchers
Paul Bishop

Paperback Edition
© Copyright 2018 (as revised) Paul Bishop

Wolfpack Publishing
6032 Wheat Penny Avenue
Las Vegas, NV 89122

ISBN: 978-1-64119-262-0

LIE CATCHERS

CHAPTER 1

"Liar, liar, pants on fire. Nose as long as a telephone wire."
- Unknown

When I first crossed swords with Rycovic *Ray* Pagan, he was already an LAPD legend in the interrogation room. Detectives would take bets on how long it would take Pagan to break a suspect wide open. It was said, he never missed – always coming out of *the box* with something to advance an investigation.

He was revered, feared, and jealousy being what it is, despised.

I was a bit of a legend myself. Twelve years on the job, five as a detective, currently assigned to Robbery Homicide's elite Rape Special unit, and I still couldn't get away from the *Calamity* Jane Randall moniker hung on me during my rookie year.

I'd solved my share of major cases, putting various

villains in prison for more years than they had left on earth, but *Calamity* I'd been tagged, and *Calamity* I remained. A series of escalating coincidences while I was still in uniform – involving the accidental discharge of a shotgun, a sergeant's squad car with a blown tire, and a urine soaked PCP suspect – were hard to live down.

My latest debacle – a suspect's bullet taking a chunk out of my leg while my bullet took a chunk out of his vitals – hadn't helped much. Nobody was saying the suspect didn't get what he deserved and the shooting was clean. Nobody was saying the human smuggling ring we smashed wasn't great police work. But the essence of calamity still hung over everything like a cheap celebrity perfume.

Ray Pagan was going to change that perception – not by changing me, but by allowing me to find my *truth-self*. Ray was big on truth, or at least his definition of truth. He was going to become more than my mentor. He was going to become my friend, despite me fighting him every step of the way.

However, I knew none of this as I used a black Malacca cane to stiffly walk my left leg into Chief Bullard's office at the new Police Administration Building. Geographically only three blocks away from where LAPD's old headquarters – the revered Parker Center – awaited demolition, the new PAB was a soulless warren of narrow hallways and bureaucratic oppression.

The chief stood up when I entered and came around his desk, walking through the shafts of sunlight unmuted by the tint covering the offices' large windows.

"Jane, how are you? How's the leg?" Chief Bullard asked as he attempted to corral me toward one of the two chairs in a small sitting area off to one side of his desk. I sat, ungracefully, which is to say I plopped down the last six inches into the leather chair, my leg stuck out in front of me like a fallen redwood.

"It's coming along," I said. "Physical therapy is helping."

"You look great," the chief said.

I gave an unladylike snort, which made him look uncomfortable.

I'd spent the three months since the shooting in sweat pants and t-shirts. Depression had killed my appetite and the physical therapy had burned through whatever calories wine provided. I'd lost weight and the gray Ann Taylor pant suit I was wearing would have looked better on a scarecrow.

"I look like hell, Chief, and I know it,"

He nodded as if deciding something. "What's the prognosis?" he asked, pointing to my leg. Both of us were relieved to be getting to the point. No more small talk.

"The doctor said I should be certified full-duty in another month, but I can come back light-duty effective immediately." My voice went up a notch with desperation and I hated the sound.

The chief looked at me. After a pause, he asked, "Want to try again?"

I fidgeted with my cane. I wanted to cross my legs, but that wasn't happening.

The chief reached a long arm over and picked up a file from his desk. He opened it in his lap and looked down at it. "The doctors say you'll always have a limp. Apparently, your right leg is now an inch shorter than your left."

"Half-inch," I said. Actually, I blurted the words and could feel myself blush when the chief looked up at me. *Calamity, Calamity, Calamity!* I couldn't shake the curse.

I tilted my head down letting my dark hair fall forward to hide my eyes. I'd always used my hair as a defense ever since I'd been the tallest girl in my middle-school class. I paid it little attention beyond brushing and the occasional trim, yet somehow it had stayed rich and full.

The chief closed the file. I waited for the guillotine to fall.

"They are suggesting a full medical pension."

Whack! Head into the hand basket and on the way to Hell...

"Chief..." I started.

"Relax," the chief said. He tossed my medical file onto his desktop and sat back comfortably in his chair. "If I listened to doctors, I would have been dead from cancer ten years ago. It's going to take a lot more than a pessimistic prognosis to kill this old war horse, or to make me give up on a potentially great detective."

Potentially?

I brought my head up and looked directly at Chief Bullard. He smiled, knowing his word had hit its bull's-eye.

"*Calamity* Jane Randall," he said. "A pretty harsh handle to live with, especially as it isn't true."

I took a deep breath. "It kind of is," I said, then tapped my cane against my leg. I was not going to cry. I would not cry.

"No, it's not." The chief's voice was kind, but there was some steel in it. "I know your record. I know the cases you've cracked since you've been with RHD. You were shot in the leg, but you kept on going. Not only did you put your attacker down, but you crawled across the floor and, before he died, got him to tell you where twenty-six women were who were locked up in a storage container. They would have died if it wasn't for you. I don't call that a calamity. I call it being a hero."

I didn't know what to say, so I kept my mouth shut.

"I've got a special assignment for you."

"I don't want a desk job." I heard the defensive whine in my voice and cringed inside.

"Have I said it's a desk job?" There was the tinge of exasperation in Bullard's tone. "You may be a wizard in the field, but I understand the term *calamity* is actually appropriate when applied to your paperwork and organizational skills."

I swallowed.

"Do you know Ray Pagan?"

"I know who he is, but I've never actually met him."

"I'm surprised. Other than his *wolves*, he's managed to meet and piss off almost every other detective in this department at one time or another."

"That's one of the things I've heard."

"Ray's a brilliant guy. The best interrogator this department has ever seen. I'd put him up against any interrogator anywhere. He's that good, but he's also a loose cannon."

"I've heard rumors he screwed up big time a few years ago."

The chief gave me a level look. "He did his job. He didn't screw up. Sometimes bad things happen. You should be familiar with the pattern."

Ouch.

"What else have you heard?"

I shrugged. "Not much. He was buried in *deep freeze* – working cases so stone-dead even the Cold Case Unit won't touch them for fear of frostbite."

"Ray's choice, not mine, but I'm putting an end to his self-imposed exile. I want him back in *the box*, and I want you in there with him."

"Why me?"

"Because he needs a minder. Ray is at his absolute best when he is freelancing. His *wolves* would follow Pagan to the gates of Hell. However, everybody else wishes he would go there."

I wasn't quite sure who these *wolves* were, but I guess I was going to find out. "What's our assignment?"

"You will both be attached to RHD under Captain North. You're going to be the *go to* interrogation team in major cases."

"Who decides when we go in?"

"It will be case by case on direct orders from myself or North. Since Ray sees things others don't, he can also decide to take a case. He'll decide if you simply hit and run – do the interrogation and cut loose – or if you work the case further. I'll make sure you get resources and the cooperation."

"What's my role?"

"You have the most important job. You keep Pagan in line and on track."

"I'm sorry, chief, but I don't think being the albatross around Pagan's neck is something for which I'm cut out."

The chief indicated my cane and leg. "Do you want back on the job, or do you want to be medically pensioned?"

"I want back, but I know a *calamity* when I see one coming."

"Exactly," the chief said. "So, you should be well prepared for the brewing storm. Jealousy is a funny thing. You'd think having a guy who can open up any suspect like a can of cheap tuna would be someone you'd want on your side. But detectives are very territorial. Nobody likes Pagan coming in and making them look foolish by actually getting *blood* out of a stone suspect. He doesn't purposely make people look bad. He just has what he himself dismisses as *a knack.*"

"You're saying nobody is going to make this easy," I said.

"Hear me clearly, Randall. I don't care about fragile egos. I care about results. Ray gets results...and so do you."

I felt stunned. "What does Pagan think about this set-up?"

"It doesn't matter." The chief paused before asking, "You in?"

There was only one answer. "Where do I find this paragon of truth and justice?"

"Court. He's being cross-examined about an interrogation in one of his cold cases. It should be entertaining."

CHAPTER 2

**"She entered the territory of lies
without a passport for return."**
- Graham Greene, The Heart of the Matter

L.A.'s Airport Superior Courthouse on South La Cienega
was always a hive of activity. I took the elevator up to
Department 'S' and took a seat in the back. I noticed two
Los Angeles Times reporters, a jerk from the LA Weekly
who had burned me twice, and several stand-up talking
heads for the networks and cable channels in the audience.
This was unusual, especially for a thirty year-old case with
an octogenarian murder suspect and a total non-celebrity
victim.

The draw had to be Ray Pagan.

It was a deep freeze case he'd been working. He'd
apparently found something in the old case file and then
gone on to obtain the confession, which was currently the
main evidence against the suspect.

The defense was preparing to start cross-examination as Pagan reentered the witness box after the lunch break. I could see he was very tall and looked to be wiry under a well-cut suit in a style I'd never seen before. It had a silver-blue sheen and he wore it over a black shirt and silver tie. His shoes were muted, but the same basic color as the suit. *Who was this guy?* I knew a few detectives on the department who were sharp, but conservative dressers. Pagan was from a whole different fashion show.

When he took his seat on the witness stand every eye in the room was riveted upon him. The jury members were leaning forward as were all the reporters in the audience. Even Judge Rita Billings, as hard-bitten as they come, had turned her chair and was looking at Pagan intently. I couldn't believe it, but there was a trace of a smile on her thin lips.

"Do I need to remind you about being under oath, Detective Pagan?" the judge asked.

"No, your honor. I've done this once or twice." Pagan's voice was honey over spikes, and I swear he turned up the wattage on the sly, brilliantly white-toothed smile, he sent her way.

Pagan's straight black hair was brushed back from a devil's peak on his forehead, dropping over his collar at the back. As he turned to face the defense attorney, Pagan ran his hands back through his hair, securing it behind his ears, and sobered his expression. No crew-cut or department regulation tapered back and sides for this guy.

His features were dark. High cheekbones, hooded eyes. His thin aquiline nose had been broken in some distant fracas. From the amount of time he had on the job, I knew he must be in his early forties, but he looked ten years younger.

Gerald Raines was a big time hired gun defense attorney. Tennis fit and coiffed to within an inch of his life, his dark blue suit cost three times more than any other suit in the courtroom – including Pagan's. He rarely had difficulty handling even experienced prosecutors like Peter Simmons, whom he was facing today. However, I got the feeling even Raines was intimidated by Pagan.

Next to Raines sat the defendant, Arthur Howell. In his eighties, Howell was bent with age. The black suit he wore bagged at elbows and knees. He was accused of stabbing and killing an-ex army buddy thirty years ago. Howell had served with the victim in the Pacific during World War II, and had survived POW camp in the Philippines with him. After returning stateside, they had lived close and remained best friends. None of the detectives in the original investigation had even looked at Howell as a suspect. Even now, the only real evidence against him was the confession Pagan had elicited after reopening the case.

"Detective Pagan." Raines paused to clear his throat, excused himself, and started over. "Detective Pagan, isn't it your job to convict my client?"

Pagan sat comfortably upright in the hard wooden witness chair, not moving forward to speak into the microphone in front of him as almost everybody did. "My job is to search for the truth."

"Isn't it true you would do anything to convict my client?"

"I would use all legal means at my disposal to uncover the facts in this case and reveal who committed the crime." Pagan's voice was sincere and unruffled.

Raines touched a file on the table in front of him. "I see in the transcript of the interrogation, you told my client after thirty years his DNA had been recovered from the murder weapon, when in fact it had not. Wasn't that a lie?"

Ray looked directly at Raines, his gaze unwavering, his voice not changing. "Yes it was."

"Do you lie to all the people you interrogate?"

"On occasion, I use deception as a technique to test the response of some people I question."

"But you admit you lied to my client."

"Yes." Pagan's voice held no trace of irritation or guilt.

"Then how can we possibly believe anything you tell us now?"

"I lied to the defendant during my interrogation of him. It was an interrogation technique to test his response and to help me determine what the truth was. I acted within California law in doing so and never tried to hide any of my actions. However, today, I am under oath and have sworn to tell the truth. I take my oaths as a witness and a peace officer seriously and I would never violate them."

Raines didn't like the answer. Nor the condescending tone in which it was delivered. He moved papers around in front of him, seemingly searching for a new questioning direction, but couldn't move past what had worked for him so often in the past when trying to get under the skin of a detective on the stand.

Nobody likes to be called a liar – except, apparently, Ray Pagan.

"Isn't it true to be a good interrogator, you have to be a good liar?" Raines snapped his question.

"No. To be a good interrogator, you have to be good at measuring verbal and non-verbal responses."

"Isn't it true you would say anything to get a suspect to confess? Please answer yes or no."

"I apologize, I cannot answer the question yes or no."

Pagan turned his head toward the judge. "May I explain, your honor?" He followed this up with a smile as if he and the judge were sharing a private joke Raines wasn't in on.

"Please do," Judge Billings said.

Pagan turned back to make eye contact with the defense attorney. "First, my job is to find the truth, not to get a confession. I am a gatherer of facts. I do not have the power to make any promises to a defendant and I have been specifically trained to avoid even implying I can grant things like a reduced sentence."

I chuckled inwardly. Every professional in the courtroom knew the Supreme Court has ruled a confession to be *the most damning of all evidence*. Defense attorneys will do everything they can to stop a confession from getting into evidence. If it does get into the record, then they must at all costs discredit it. Most often this is done by attacking the integrity of the investigating detective.

I'd been cross-examined by Raines in the past. It wasn't pleasant. He was an expert at bringing a detective's tactics under scrutiny and making them look bad in front a jury, but Pagan was totally unruffled.

Raines was the one looking put out. He dug in and tried again. "In the interrogation, you told my client it would be better for him to tell the truth. What did you mean?"

"Isn't it always better to tell the truth? I wanted him to unburden himself from the guilt of his actions and not compound what he had done with more lies."

Raines walked to the side of the podium where he was standing in a clear attempt to assert his authority.

"You told my client remorse was good. You told him judges and prosecutors look more favorably on people who show remorse. What did you mean?"

Pagan didn't hesitate. His voice was soothing, somehow

implying Raines' question was simplistic. "Since we were children we've been taught if you admitted a bad thing and expressed sorrow you were a better person for having done so. You were an even better person if you promised not to do the bad thing again, as opposed to being unremorseful after being caught in lies."

"Objection, your honor!" Raines snapped. "Detective Pagan is going far beyond the scope of my questions and is verbally assuming my client's guilt."

Judge Billings smiled. She'd obviously seen Pagan play this game before. "These are your questions, Mr. Raines. Detective Pagan's answers are responsive and reasonable. If you are not prepared for his answers then don't ask the questions. Overruled."

Raines turned pale under his sunlamp tan. He probably couldn't remember the last time he'd been put in his place by a judge.

Flustered, Raines grasped at a straw. "Did you know my client had been a prisoner of war, incarcerated by the Japanese in the Philippines during World War Two?"

"Yes."

"Is that why you mentioned the film *King Rat* to him? To attack him with cruel mental images in order to get him to confess."

When Raines said the words *King Rat*, I saw the elderly defendant sitting next to him flinch.

Again, Pagan was smooth. "*King Rat* is a powerful story about redemption. It is about survival. It is about doing what you have to do to survive, which I believe was the motivation for your client's actions thirty years ago when he stabbed and killed the victim. A man who had been a POW with him, and whom he eventually found out had collaborated with the enemy causing the death of other POWs."

Pagan's words tumbled out like a waterfall. He was a Shakespearean actor delivering a soliloquy, which nobody dared to interrupt. The stunned silence following his last sentence was invaded by the sound of sobbing.

"Look at your client, counselor," Pagan said quietly. "He has been in a prison of his own making for thirty years. He may be facing actual incarceration, but his acknowledgment of his actions to me set him free."

Raines turned to face the elderly man next to him. I couldn't see Howell's face, but I had no doubt tears were streaming down as he sat rocking slightly.

"Any further questions, Mr. Raines?" The judge asked.

CHAPTER 3

"I do not mind lying, but I hate inaccuracy."
- Samuel Butler's Notebooks

"*KING RAT*?" I asked.

"James Clavell's first novel," Pagan said, unhelpfully.

"I know what it is," I said, "I even saw the George Segal movie. But what made you think to use it in the interrogation room?"

We were standing outside the courtroom near the building's glass exterior wall, watching as planes swooped in toward LAX. After Pagan's bombshell, Raines had immediately asked for a recess and a meeting with the judge. We were waiting on the outcome.

"I needed an appropriate *trigger phrase*," Pagan said. "Something which wouldn't come up in normal conversation. If Raines hadn't mentioned *King Rat*, I would have had to do so myself, but Raines is very predictable."

"*Trigger phrase*?" My mind was racing. "Wait...Are you saying, you made the defendant cry on cue?"

"Absolutely." Pagan was unashamed. "Just like he did

when I said it during the interrogation. Oldest mentalist trick in the book. Once a suspect begins to cry, you own them."

I was astonished. "You planted a subconscious sugges- tion during the interrogation and waited until now to trigger it?"

Pagan shrugged. "Not in the *box*, but when I was escorting Howell from the station lobby to the interrogation room."

"Is that legal?"

"Most people will tell you it can't be done, so you tell me," Pagan said. "You watched a tape of the interrogation."

"How do you know?"

Pagan shrugged. I would come to realize, his shrugs carried a variety of meanings. This one was off-hand and dismissive. "After you left the chief's office, you couldn't help yourself," he said. "You were curious. You wanted to know what you were getting into."

I could feel myself blushing, so I dropped my head and let my hair fall forward.

"Was Howell telling the truth in the interrogation when he admitted to stabbing the victim?" Pagan asked me.

"Yes," I said without hesitation.

"How do you know?"

This time I did hesitate. I looked up and shook my head slightly.

Pagan smiled. His tone changed, becoming almost gentle. "Just tell me if a subconscious suggestion, telling Howell to cry every time he hears the phrase *King Rat*, forced him in any way to admit to his actions?"

I thought about what I'd seen in the tape of the interro- gation and what I'd seen in the courtroom. "No, it didn't.

But it sure had a huge manipulative impact on the jury in the courtroom. It convinced them of his guilt."

Before I could say more, the courtroom door opened and Peter Simmons, the prosecutor, came out and approached us. He was smiling.

"Raines is digging in his feet on the terms of a plea bargain, but he'll cave. He can't go to jury and he knows it. Great job." Simmons stuck out his hand and Pagan shook it. "Handball next week?" Simmons asked.

"Wednesday, regular time?" Pagan replied.

"Absolutely," Simmons said. Nodding in my direction he headed back into the courtroom.

Pagan looked at me. "So, Howell told the truth and the jury believed him. Our work here is done."

CHAPTER 4

**"And after all, what is a lie?
'Tis but the truth in masquerade."**
- Lord Byron, Don Juan

I STUMBLED AND SWORE.

We were walking out of the courthouse, toward the parking structure, and Pagan's foot had clipped my cane. I would have gone to the ground if he hadn't caught my arm.

"Sorry," he said, but I knew he didn't mean it. *What the hell?* Did he do it on purpose?

I pulled my arm out of his and steadied myself. I didn't want to answer any questions about my leg, but surprisingly Pagan didn't ask, which made me angrier.

Pagan's phone buzzed and we stopped while he answered it. He listened, looked at his watch and said into the receiver, "We'll be there in thirty minutes." He disconnected and looked at me. "And so it starts. West L.A. has a trio of gang members in custody. They're suspects in a drive-by shooting from last night in which a rival gang member was shot."

"Who called you?" I asked.

"Amanda Tyler. She's the *homicide-three* at West L.A."

Pagan had started walking. I pushed off on my cane and struggled to catch up. "You know her?"

"I trained her," Pagan said.

I still wasn't ready to go charging off. I needed to stop, catch a breath, and talk to Pagan about the whole situation. Apparently, I wasn't going to get the chance. As we entered the parking structure, the gate guard stepped out of his booth and sketched a salute toward Pagan.

"You driving your personal vehicle or a department sedan?" Pagan asked me.

"I've got one of the RHD pool cars."

"You need anything out of it?"

"Just my war bag," I said, using a catch-all term for a large duffel bag filled with work related gear.

"Get it and then give the car keys to Marco." Pagan indicated the gate guard. "He'll take care of getting the unit back to RHD."

Pagan shook hands with Marco, and I could have sworn I saw a bill change palms.

"What about my personal vehicle?" I asked. The last thing I wanted to be was stranded.

"Give those keys to Marco as well. Tell him where you parked. He'll leave it at *The Hacienda*."

"The Hacienda?"

As he was walking away, Pagan spoke over his shoulder. "You're going to have to trust me, Randall. It's only going to get stranger from here. I'll meet you back at the gate."

I didn't know if I was ready to trust Pagan yet, but it looked like I didn't have a choice if I didn't want to come across as a spoiled child.

I still couldn't help asking Marco. "What if I don't want to give you my keys?"

He was a skinny black man of indeterminate age. His uniform was clean and pressed and his black shoes shined.

"Be best if you did," Marco said with a wide smile. His Caribbean accent was pronounced. "You don't want to buck Mr. Pagan."

Interesting...*Mr. Pagan* not *Detective Pagan*.

"You always do what *Mr.* Pagan says?"

"Yes, ma'am," Marco said. "He got me this here job. Mr. Pagan is a good man."

Hmmmm. I wondered if Arthur Howell felt the same way. Somehow, I thought he might, despite the years in prison he was facing. However, I doubted Gerald Raines, the defense attorney, would be as generous.

My plain colored detective sedan, a beat up piece of trash that wasn't freeway safe, was in a handicap spot next to the guard booth. I got my war bag out of the trunk and gave the keys to Marco. As I dug out the keys to my personal car and gave them with instructions to Marco, Pagan pulled up in a late model black Escalade.

Marco opened the door for me and, as I clambered ungracefully into the passenger seat, he took my war bag and put it on the back seat.

I looked over and realized Pagan had changed clothes. The flashy suit was gone, replaced by black jeans, a black roll-necked sweater, and soft black leather half boots. He had the sleeves of the sweater pulled up to his forearms. A wide silver bracelet was wrapped around his right wrist, a black-faced watch on a black leather band was on his left. The face of the watch was turned to the inside of his wrist. His black hair had slipped from behind his ears and swung loosely as he turned his head to check traffic and pulled smoothly away. *Who was this guy?*

I looked into the back of the large SUV. The rear seat was empty except for my bag, but I could see the rear cargo section had been customized. Everything was clean and precise – almost sterile.

"Rycovic?" I asked, turning front again and referring to Pagan's given name. "Eastern European?"

"Romani," Pagan said glancing over at me.

"Gypsy?"

"For lack of a better term." With his eyes on the road, he changed the subject. "What do you think?"

"About?"

Pagan looked over at me, but didn't speak.

Somehow, I knew what he wanted to hear. "Chief Bullard lied," I said.

"About everything?"

"No. About all this being his idea...About you being forced to accept me as a minder."

Watching Pagan's profile, I saw his features transform into a wide grin.

"And how do you know he was lying?"

"Are you saying I'm wrong?"

"No. I'm asking how you knew he was lying."

After a pause, I said, "I'm not sure."

"Yes, you are," Pagan said. "You just don't want to tell me yet."

"If you say so."

How could he know?

Pagan continued blithely on, "When we get to West L.A., Tyler will have the suspects isolated in separate inter-rogation rooms. First thing we'll need to do is figure out which one is the alpha wolf."

"Don't you want to know who the weakest sheep is?"

Pagan smiled again. "One thing you and I will never do in an interrogation is *the expected.*"

The West Los Angeles Area headquarters was on Butler Avenue, a side street a couple of blocks down Santa Monica Boulevard off the 405 Freeway. It was an unremarkable bunker-style building. I knew the detective squadroom was housed on its windowless second floor.

After we pulled into the parking lot, Pagan bounded out of the car, slamming the door behind him. I didn't try to keep up with him. My leg was aching. He ran his ID card through the electronic lock on the station's backdoor, pulling the door open for me. I knew he was mentally tapping his foot as he waited.

Inside, Pagan turned left and walked briskly down a short hallway to a stairwell. He didn't wait for me, taking the stairs two at a time to the second floor. I didn't know if he was doing things on purpose to tick me off, but I figured he couldn't be that clueless.

I thought about stopping at the drinking fountain to take a pain pill, but I was feeling unreasonably angry and just kept stumping. The stairs had a landing halfway up where I stopped to catch my breath.

I could hear a commotion coming from above and, when I finally reached the entrance to the second floor detective squadroom, I saw Pagan surrounded by a half-dozen detectives. He said something and they all laughed. Then he turned and looked toward me, waving me over with a smile and a flash of his dark eyes.

I decided he was a condescending bastard and even a desk job would be better than working with him. However, the thought of being shunted off on a medical pension got me across the room.

The woman standing next to Pagan took her hand off his arm and extended it toward me. She was short and busty. She wore her thirties well under close-cropped auburn hair. A pair of retro cats-eye reading glasses hung on a chain around her neck. "Amanda Tyler," she said by way of introduction. "Thanks for coming."

I shook her hand. "Jane Randall."

Tyler gave me a probing look then smiled. It was as if she had picked up exactly what I was thinking via the contact with my hand, which she was still holding. She glanced back at Pagan who had moved slightly away with the other group of detectives.

"How long have you known Ray?"

"An hour."

Tyler chuckled. "It's best just to accept he's always two moves ahead."

"Is he always insufferable?"

"Some days are worse than others, but you'll never be bored."

"Boring might be nice."

Tyler gripped my hand a bit tighter. "Liar," she said. "You're no different than Ray or any of his *wolves*. We'd all rather be dead than bored."

I took sole custody of my hand. "Who the hell are these *wolves* I keep hearing about?

"For lack of a better term, we're Ray's acolytes. Over the years, he's hand-picked and trained several dozen of us. None of us would be where we are personally or career-wise if it wasn't for Ray."

"So, he's Svengali incarnate?"

The expression on Tyler's face went cold. "Ray is the most selfless person you'll ever meet. If he's picked you then he sees not only someone of value, but someone who isn't living up to their potential. If he's being an ass there's a reason."

"Sorry."

Tyler flapped a hand and softened her expression. "No, I'm sorry. I sometimes forget how often he pissed me off in the beginning. Ray is a hell of a detective and the best interrogator I've ever seen. If the truth is out there, Ray will find it. But Ray's depths run deep. He's far more than the sum of his parts."

We both turned our heads when we heard Pagan call my name. He was standing by a cluster of long desks shoved together in the corner of the squadroom claimed by the Homicide unit. Tyler and I moved over to join him and the other homicide detectives who were grouped around.

"Drive-by shooting," Ray said, pointing at a cluster of crime scene photos scattered across the desk. "No witnesses who can ID. Two wits say there were three males in the suspects' car, but we don't know which one was the shooter. These guys were stopped six blocks from the scene. No gun recovered yet."

"How do we know they're the suspects," I asked.

"Good work by the first officers on the scene," Tyler said. "They put out an immediate crime broadcast with a description of the suspect vehicle. Another responding patrol unit saw these guys in a car matching the color from the crime broadcast. Pulled them over and recognized them as members of a rival gang with a grudge."

"Rival gang?"

Tyler nodded. "Victim, Sander Ruiz, was the main suspect in an ADW against them two days ago. No hits, but it wasn't for lack of trying. Apparently, they found Ruiz before we did."

"He dead?" I asked.

"Circling the drain," Tyler said. "But he's a hardcore gang-banger, so I have no doubt he'll pull through. If he'd been an innocent, he'd be toes up by now."

"Do you have the reports from the prior incident?" Pagan asked.

Tyler handed him a sheaf of papers, which Pagan quickly scanned.

"Gunshot residue tests?" I asked.

Tyler indicated some other forms on the desk. "Nothing. We swabbed all three, but their hands came up clean."

"What about their forearms or their shirts?" Pagan asked.

"Gavin?" Tyler asked, glancing over at one of the other detectives. He was a heavy-set guy wearing a shoulder-holstered .45 over a sweat stained white dress shirt, his stained tie at half-mast. He immediately blushed. "I just did the back of the hands."

His words were met with brief silence and ice-dagger looks from Tyler before Pagan graciously came to the rescue saying, "Not a problem. Gives us somewhere to go. These guys watch CSI on TV. They know about gunshot residue. The shooter was probably wearing gloves and threw them out along with the gun. He's confident his hands are clean and isn't worried. Going back in and swabbing his arms and shirt will make his sphincter pucker, which is exactly what we want."

I stepped up to the desk and riffled through the suspects' rap sheets. Cesar *Fallo* Toma, Carlos *Payaso* Cruz, and Antonio Marino were all members of *Los Locos*, a small and – to this point – relatively low level local gang. Marino was sixteen. Cruz and Toma were eighteen.

"Who was driving when they were stopped?" I asked.

"Cruz," Tyler said.

"Any of you have prior contact with any of the suspects?" Pagan asked.

"I popped Fallo twice for dope when I worked gangs," a skinny younger detective said. "He's the hard-ass of the bunch. You won't get anything out of him. I'd start with Antonio Marino. He's more wanna-be than member."

"You think he pulled the trigger?" Pagan asked.

"Maybe. If Fallo goaded him into it to prove himself."

Pagan picked up Fallo's rap sheet. "Have they been advised of their rights?"

"Not yet," Tyler said. "I know you like it left up to you."

Pagan looked up and smiled at her. "Thanks." He shuffled through the other rap sheets. "I want to look at them."

Tyler moved back. "The video cameras are running."

"Okay," Pagan said. Moving past Tyler, he put a hand on my shoulder and directed me along with him. "Give us a minute," he said to the detectives. "Then we'll start with Fallo."

"I told you," the younger detective said. "Fallo won't tell you anything. You should start with Marino."

"Shut it, Pierce," Tyler said with steel in her voice. "Maybe you'll learn something and be able to sit at the adults' table come Thanksgiving."

Pagan continued on as if he hadn't heard the exchange. In his wake, I could see the set of his shoulders had changed. He was charged, electric, a closed force unto himself.

CHAPTER 5

*"Of course I lie to people. But I lie altruistically,
for our mutual good."*
- Quentin Crisp, Manners from Heaven

We entered the small video room. I started to flip on the lights, but Pagan stayed my hand. He was staring intently at the three video screens, each one showing a different suspect in their individual interrogation rooms. The rooms were stark, several hard wooden chairs, a very small table pushed into one corner. On the wall of each room was a battered white board.

I recognized each of the suspects from the booking photos on their rap sheets. Carlos Cruz was sitting in one chair, his feet resting on another. Marino was pacing back and forth. Fallo Toma was sitting, slumped in a chair, which he had scooted over to the small table. He was resting his head on his arms, eyes closed.

"Since Cruz was driving, chances are either Fallo or Antonio was the shooter." I ventured.

"Possibly," Pagan said, but I could see he was only humoring me.

Pointing at Fallo's screen, he said, "Tell me why he's guilty."

"He's asleep. Put a guilty man in an interrogation room and he'll go to sleep."

"Yes, an old detective axiom, but tell me why?"

I felt my ire begin to rise. I was an experienced detective, not some rookie being worked over by a training officer.

Pagan turned his head to look at me. The back glow from the video screens hid his features in shadow, however, I didn't need to see him to read him.

"I know this isn't your first rodeo," he said suddenly. It was disconcerting – as if he knew exactly what I'd been thinking. "But to become an extraordinary detective, you have to go beyond axioms and understand the reasons underlying the behavior."

I didn't reply because I was processing the bit about becoming an extraordinary detective. Plus, I could see he was telling the truth.

His teeth flashed in the shadows hiding his face. "Everybody lies, Randall," he said. "But very, very few can see the truth."

I felt my stomach clench. *How could he know? Nobody knew...*

"Anxiety," I said, trying to keep my voice steady – backing up the conversation. "When anxiety gets elevated it begins shutting down non-essential body functions. Anxiety overload can cause fainting. If a suspect's anxiety gets high enough, his body will put him to sleep if left alone."

"Exactly," Pagan said. I could see his white smile widen. "So, let's go wake him up and drive his anxiety even higher."

As he moved past me to exit the video room, Pagan again caught the point of my cane with his foot. I did not have my complete weight on it, but I still almost went down as I was forced to put unexpected weight on my injured leg.

"Sorry, sorry," he said, but he hadn't even stumbled as he'd done it.

I was getting more and more pissed, but I stuffed the feeling down and followed in his wake, determined to keep up.

Pagan made a beeline for Tyler who held out a yellow legal pad and a black Sharpie. Pagan nodded his head toward me and Tyler turned to give me her offering. Pagan was already moving on, determination oozing from him.

He didn't hesitate outside the door to the interrogation room where Fallo was being held. He popped the door open sharply and moved inside in a rush. By the time I'd entered, Pagan was already sitting down in a hard backed chair directly to the side of where Fallo sat with his head down on the table. I could now see the table was secured to the walls in the corner.

Pagan reached out and grabbed a leg of Fallo's chair and, seemingly without effort, pulled the chair around so Fallo was facing him. He smoothly reached up and pulled the hoodie off Fallo's head and dropped it down his back.

"Hey!" Fallo said, startled out of his sleepy state.

"Relax," Pagan said, as I was closing the door behind me.

"I want my..."

Pagan got his hand up in front of Fallo's face and spoke sharply, cutting Fallo off in mid-sentence.

"What you *want* is to listen to me, Fallo," Pagan said,

surprising both Fallo and me with his rapid Spanish. "I know you are going to tell me you didn't do anything."

Fallo was clearly caught off guard. "Yeah. I didn't do anything."

He was leaning back in his chair, uncomfortable with Pagan sitting so close to him. Pagan, clearly recognizing this, scooted forward to the edge of his chair – placing one of his legs on the floor between Fallo's legs and the other outside Fallo's left leg. He leaned forward and placed his hand on Fallo's shoulder.

"You didn't do anything. That's the truth." Again his rapid Spanish seemed to befuddle Fallo. Again his sentences were declarative, not questions.

"Yeah."

"Then you won't mind signing a statement saying you've told the truth." It wasn't a question, but a command. Pagan held out his hand and I passed him the legal pad and Sharpie. Pagan placed the pad on the table next to Fallo. He took the cap off the Sharpie and held it out to Fallo.

"Just write you told the truth, sign your name, and we're done."

Fallo looked confused. "All I got to write is I told the truth?"

"And sign your name."

"Then I can go?"

"You told me the truth. Write it down and sign your name."

Fallo hesitated for a moment, but then reached out and took the Sharpie from Pagan. He turned toward the table and began to laboriously print on the pad. Then, more quickly, he scribbled his name in juvenile handwriting under the printed sentence.

Pagan looked at what was written. "You're Los Locos. You should be proud. Put your tag and gang sign."

Fallo didn't even hesitate. He leaned forward and used the Sharpie to decorate the paper with his personal graffiti.

"Thank you," Pagan said when Fallo was done. He took the Sharpie back and picked up the pad. He stood up. "Sit tight," he said, and signaled me to lead the way out of the room.

Outside the room, he closed the door and we moved away.

"What about the Miranda admonition?" I said.

"What about it?" Pagan said, while scribbling something on the yellow legal pad. "You need three things for Miranda, right?"

"Police, custody, and accusatory questions," I said by rote, seeing where this was going and answering my own question. "And you didn't ask anything accusatory about the crime, so Miranda doesn't come into play."

"I didn't even mention the crime. All I did was agree he was telling the truth. He says so right here..." Pagan wagged the legal pad.

"Okay, so what?"

Pagan smiled. It was his go-to expression. "Come on," he said. "Let's see what Antonio has to say."

Moving down the hall, Pagan opened the door to another interrogation room and we slipped inside.

Antonio Marino looked up like a startled squirrel. He was light-skinned, acne-cheeked, and scrawny. He wore a dirty t-shirt over baggy khakis and oversized Nikes. He was trying to look cool, but his whole body language screamed fear.

Pagan pulled two chairs away from the wall, sat in one,

and pointed to the other. "Please sit down," Pagan said. No Spanish this time.

Antonio sat crossing his arms. Pagan scooted his chair forward, violating Antonio's personal space. He reached out and gently pulled Antonio's arms loose. Pagan's expression was petulant.

"It's over, Antonio."

"What's over?"

"Fallo has told us the truth about what happened. He doesn't want you to go down for attempted murder."

"Fallo didn't tell you nothing." The sneer in Antonio's voice and on his face was anxiety-fueled bravado.

"I don't speak Spanish," Pagan said. "So I need you to read this and tell me exactly what it says." He held the legal pad out in front of Antonio.

Antonio's eyes dropped to the choppy scrawl on the front page.

"Read it for me," Pagan said, his voice engaging.

Antonio hesitated then, in a dull voice, read, "*Payaso hizo los disparos. Le dije la verdad.*"

"What does it mean in English?"

"*Payaso* did the shooting. I told the truth."

I was thrown for a second, knowing Fallo hadn't written anything about Carlos *Payaso* Cruz doing the shooting. Then I remembered Pagan scribbling on the yellow pad in the hallway.

Pagan began to press. "Who told the truth? Whose handwriting is it? Who signed it?"

"Fallo."

"Okay," Pagan said, standing up. "Let's go for a ride."

"A ride?" Antonio sounded more scared than ever.

"Sure," Pagan's voice was back at its most engaging. "I

told you Fallo didn't want you to go down for the shooting. He said you could show us where the gun was dumped."

"Why didn't he tell you?"

"He told us the hard part. He told us about Carlos. But he knows how the system works. He knew you would have to have something to tell us, so he said you'd show us where the gun was dumped."

Antonio looked at the yellow legal pad again. Then stood up slowly.

An hour later, we had fished the gun and a pair of latex gloves out of a storm drain near Santa Monica Boulevard.

Two hours later, after waiving his rights and having his arms and shirt swabbed by Pagan for gunshot residue, Carlos *Payaso* Cruz copped to pulling the trigger. Once Cruz admitted, Fallo cracked open like a bad melon. Antonio was already cooked.

All three of the suspects were booked for attempted murder. Tyler and her crew were happy to handle all the paperwork.

It was kudos all around. However, I still wasn't any closer to figuring out how Pagan knew from the start Cruz was the culprit.

CHAPTER 6

*"When you commit a crime it tells me about
what you did. When you lie about it, it tells me
about who you are."*
- Rebecca Stincelli, Victims From Both Sides of the Badge

I didn't know where we were going when we left West L.A.
It was dusk as Pagan pointed the Escalade onto the 405
freeway north and into the heavy early evening traffic. He
was humming infuriatingly, as if he was the only one in the
vehicle. He had gone interior, thriving on his own central
energy which was burning off him in waves.

"Where are we going?" I asked, breaking down almost
immediately after vowing to myself I wouldn't ask.

"Heading for The Hacienda." Pagan's lips twitched in
what I had to assume was amusement. He knew he hadn't
given me an answer...knew I had no idea what or where
The Hacienda was.

I let it go for the moment. I'd just have to figure it out when we arrived. There was a more pressing question.

"How did you know Cruz was the shooter?"

"Did I?"

"You know damn well you did...right from the start. Can we please stop playing games?"

"Are we playing games?"

"Damn it, Pagan!"

"All right...all right," he said, making a tamping down gesture with his right hand. "Bad habit. I always get on *the jazz* after an interrogation and turn into a pain in the ass."

I could see he was sincere, but I still couldn't help myself. "Like you weren't a pain in the ass before the interrogation?"

Pagan laughed, a deep rumble from the back of his throat. "You are absolutely priceless, Randall."

"So, how much is it going to cost me to find out how you knew it was Cruz?"

Pagan sighed, releasing pent up tension I had been unaware was in him till that moment. "People *look*, but they either don't *see* or see just what they want to see. Objective observation is like a muscle. If it isn't used it atrophies. If you consciously apply BPEs it becomes second nature."

"BPEs?"

"Behavior. Personality. Environment."

"And this applies to Cruz how?"

"The victim of the ADW committed by Sander Ruiz – the drive-by victim – had the same last name and address as Carlos *Payaso* Cruz. Also his moniker was *Little Payaso*."

"His brother?"

Pagan shrugged. "Who knows...Brother, cousin, nephew...It doesn't matter. What matters is if you apply BPE to those facts, who would you think was the shooter?"

"Okay...I get Cruz would want to pull the trigger, but he was driving."

"Behavior again – It's standard gang behavior after a drive-by. They stop the car a couple of blocks away and everybody inside does a Chinese fire drill to switch up their positions and throw the cops off if they get stopped."

"Why didn't you say anything before we started the interrogations?"

"If you reveal the trick, the magic goes away."

"Then why are you telling me now? Why not explain it to the young guy, Pierce?"

"You asked. He didn't. Anyway, Tyler will explain it to him. That's her job."

"Are you saying Tyler knew?"

"Absolutely."

"Then why call us?"

"Because she needed to teach her people a lesson and she would rather have them resent us than her. She has to work with them every day."

We had crested the Sepulveda pass and were dropping down into the San Fernando Valley. Pagan smoothly changed lanes and picked up the 101 Freeway north, which meant we were actually going west across the Valley toward Ventura County. Sometimes in L.A. do you have to go north to go west.

The traffic began to flow and we shortly passed the Topanga Canyon Boulevard off-ramp, which was the exit I used to get to my apartment complex. I still didn't ask where The Hacienda was, but ten minutes later Pagan took the Kanan Road exit in Agoura Hills – an upscale bedroom community just outside the LA County line.

He turned left from the freeway exit and back over the

freeway. He passed Roadside Drive, which ran parallel to the freeway, turning right at the next light – Agoura Road.

A half mile later, he pulled into a clearly upscale collection of shops, restaurants and offices all sharing the same Spanish Mediterranean architecture. There was a large, well-maintained gravel parking lot, which was almost full. People talked, drank coffee or simply sat in unique socializing areas – some connected to the restaurants while others had a park like feel.

"The Hacienda," Pagan said, parking in a well-marked reserved section at one end. My Honda Accord was parked one spot over. Beyond it there was a red and gold Airstream coach parked along one of the stucco boundary walls.

I craned my neck looking around. The small shopping and restaurant arcade appeared self-contained, as if we had entered a separate country. In the early evening darkness the buildings looked surprisingly pretty. The signage for each of the businesses was muted and consistent. The beige stucco walls were covered in vines, fragrant blooming honeysuckle, and twinkling lights leading up to the windows of the second story and the red tiled multi-level roof above. Numerous trees, bushes, and several fountains gave the whole collection the feel of a palazzo. I was surprised nobody asked me for my passport.

The mix of shops, offices, and restaurants had an interesting natural flow. The island style of the Tiki Joe's coffee bar at the far end somehow blended into Sophia's Italian Trattoria next door, which itself blended into the next retail establishment, a row of non-descript offices, what appeared to be a British pub called The Raven, several more retail stores, a Spanish flamenco themed restaurant, and several more offices before being capped by what was clearly a martial arts dojo called Sunzu. The mix of cultures was bizarre, yet seamless.

There was a second story extending across the length of the collection, displaying numerous round and rectangular windows – more offices perhaps. In the center of the building was a clock tower. It extended a story higher to accommodate a spotlighted, clock face with Roman numerals and black curlicue hands.

A large detached building on my right had the same Spanish Mediterranean styling and was clearly part of the overall collection. I could hear brass and piano driven jazz floating out of open double doors covered in blue leather. The words Blue Cat Jazz and the outline of a stylized feline were depicted in blue and gold neon above a large window, through which I could see an intimate darkened bar and dinner club – a spotlighted stage featuring a six-piece ensemble.

"Okay. Why are we here?"

"This is where I live."

"Here? In a glorified strip mall?"

Pagan nodded. "Apartment on the second floor. And we prefer *upscale collective* to strip mall."

"You say tomato..." I sniped simply to be caustic, but I looked around again – interested despite myself. "How did you find this place?"

"I helped build it."

"What?"

"You've seen *Field of Dreams*?"

"What are you saying? *Build it and they will come*?"

"Exactly. The countess and I took a gamble on everyone who has a business here or a studio or an office...and they all took a gamble on us."

It was my turn to sigh. My head was beginning to hurt as much as my leg. "Countess? I'm confused."

"I can imagine," Pagan said. He reached under his seat and removed a thick manila envelope. He held it out toward me. "Review this tonight. It will explain why I put myself into Siberia for two years. Meet me here at eight tomorrow morning. You'll probably be even more confused, but I promise to explain further."

I took the envelope and then opened the door of the Escalade, turning to slide out.

Pagan's voice stopped me cold.

"I know who you are, Randall. It's time to stop hiding."

I turned to look back. I could feel my heart pounding, the blood coursing through my veins.

"I also know *what* you are," Pagan said. His voice was soft, mesmerizing, yet his words were like hammer blows.

"Am I supposed to gamble on you?" I asked, dry mouthed.

"You don't gamble on a sure thing," Pagan said – and I saw truth.

CHAPTER 7

"Every violation of the truth is not only a sort of suicide in the liar, but a stab to the heart of human society."
- Ralph Waldo Emerson

I'D STOPPED SHAKING by the time I drove the ten miles back to my non-descript apartment. However, as I unlocked the door and stepped in, it washed over me just how non-descript, anonymous, and bland the place containing my off-duty life remained. I couldn't call it home because it wasn't a home. It was a place where I slept – alone.

I moved in almost eighteen months ago after my last personal relationship went south, taking all my trust and self-esteem along with it. The only thing in the apartment to which I had any attachment was a collection of photographs and old cameras which had once belonged to my father – an Army combat photographer killed in the line of duty on his last attachment in Afghanistan. I was sixteen when the letter arrived.

My mother died a year later of cancer. We had three weeks between diagnosis and death. I finished out high school living with a family friend and trying to avoid the tentacles of Children's Services.

Now I was twenty-eight years old, beat up emotionally, shot physically – figuratively and literally – a career on the skids, and precious few options. All my little pity party needed to be complete was a half-dozen cats.

I threw my keys on the kitchen table, plugged in the coffee maker, and moved into the bedroom. I still carried Pagan's envelope with me, weighing heavily in my hand. I tossed it on the bed where it waited while I stripped, showered, washed my hair, and dressed in an ancient pair of gray sweats I still had from my time in the police academy. My name was stenciled across the front and rear of the shirt.

The sweats harkened back to a time when I could run a mile in under five minutes and break three hours in a marathon. Now, I had trouble walking up stairs. In the shower, I had gingerly washed the purple inflamed-looking skin puckering around the bullet's entry and exit holes in my left leg. There had been some nerve damage, leaving the numbness which made walking difficult. It was ugly, and I hated it.

Toweling my hair dry and shaking it out, I grabbed Pagan's envelope from the bed and went to get coffee. I didn't want to eat, but forced myself to take a yogurt and a prepackaged salad out of the fridge.

I unclipped the envelope and slid the contents out onto the kitchen table. There was a stack of official reports topped by a DVD in a plastic case. I picked up the top report – a Preliminary Investigation Report of a murder from three years earlier. Alexis Walker, a seventeen-year old white female, had been found strangled and tossed behind a dumpster to the rear of the Barnes & Noble bookstore where she worked the coffee bar. The store was located in a busy mall on Roscoe Boulevard in Panorama City, a suburb of the San Fernando Valley covered by LAPD's Van Nuys Area.

I scanned through the report, barely noticing the food I was ingesting. Michael Thomas Horner, another bookstore employee was quickly identified as a possible suspect. Several of his coworkers reported Horner had been fixated on Alexis, who had not returned his attentions.

Horner had been brought to the station and a call had gone out for Pagan to do the interrogation. I felt queasy. I somehow knew this wasn't going to end well. I ignored the rest of the reports, along with my makeshift dinner, opting to pick up the DVD – which I realized had to be a recording of Pagan's interrogation.

I booted up my computer, which sat on a small desk in what passed in my apartment for a living room. When the screen came to life, I slipped the DVD into its slot. Within moments, the familiar environs of an interrogation room came into view – blank urine colored walls, a small scarred table in one corner, two hard backed chairs – all of it looking like a two-page photo spread out of *House & Jail Magazine*.

The individual I assumed to be Michael Thomas Horner slumped in the chair closest to the back wall, perfectly placed to be picked up by the camera secreted in one corner of the ceiling.

Horner was scrawny and unattractive. His long, stringy, brown hair looked like it had been hacked instead of cut. He wore a black Mortal Kombat t-shirt, generic jeans held up by a too long belt with a metal marijuana leaf buckle, and black combat boots sans laces. He sat with his arms wrapped around himself, his skinny legs twisted so they crossed at the knees and again at the ankles – dead meat for somebody like Pagan.

Pagan entered the room and introduced himself. He held out his hand, keeping it out until Horner responded by unwrapping one of his arms from his chest and presenting the hand at the end of it like a limp fish, accepting Pagan's grip. The resolution of the camera lens was good enough for me to see Horner's fingernails were long and jagged – all dirt and sharp edges.

Due to the camera angle, I could only see Pagan's back and the top of his head. He pulled up the second chair in the room and sat down very close to Horner, still holding Horner's hand.

"Michael, I appreciate you voluntarily coming to the station with the uniformed officers. You do understand you are not under arrest and are free to leave at any time?" Pagan's voice was soothing, intimate, friendly – not the coldly professional tone of most cops who have watched too much television.

"Yes." Horner's voice held defeat and despite his affirmative word, I could see he didn't believe what he'd just said.

Pagan was between Horner and the door to the interrogation room. I could tell from Pagan's body language the only way Horner was leaving the room would be in handcuffs after Pagan had wrung a confession out of him.

I could pick up the falsehood in Horner's statement. He didn't believe he was free to leave, but the video and audio would say he did believe he was free to leave when it was played back in court. Legally, it only mattered what Horner believed – and he'd just admitted he believed he was free to leave.

What I saw, nobody else would see. My stomach was beginning to churn.

"How old are you, Michael?"

"Twenty-two."

"And how long have you worked at the bookstore?"

"Two years."

I Knew Pagan didn't care how old Horner was, or how long he'd worked at the bookstore. He already knew. He was establishing a truth baseline based on questions Horner most likely would not lie about.

Pagan released Horner's hand. Horner immediately began to pick at invisible blemishes on his arm. He fidgeted in the chair, which wobbled on an uneven leg, reminding me of my own physical shortcoming. Pagan had most likely shortened the leg himself – controlling everything going on in the room.

Ten minutes had passed in innocuous chit chat. Horner's legs were still crossed, but he had unfolded both his arms and was running his nails along his thighs, sharpening the jagged edges. I sensed it was a comfortable habit. He was loosening up.

Pagan moved on.

"Who are your friends at the bookstore?" Pagan asked

"Don't have no friends. Who'd be friends with me?"

Good question. Horner might be twenty-two, but he was clearly socially inept. He wasn't mentally handicapped, just a very dim bulb – a goofball, with a skinny, pimply, awkward body, and greasy hair falling into his eyes. He was one of life's unfortunates.

"How about Alexis Walker?"

I saw Horner's eyes move rapidly from side to side as if looking for an escape. I was sure the *tell* hadn't escaped Pagan's notice.

"She's nice. Talks to me sometimes."

"Talk to you last night?"

"No." The answer was immediate. Too immediate. He had anticipated the question, prepared his lie, letting it burst from his lips in an exploding mist of spittle.

Again, even watching the video, I saw the falsehood.

Pagan sat very still and quiet. Waiting. Horner's chair skittered back and forth as he fidgeted. "She said, 'hi,' when I took out the trash," Horner finally filled the silence.

"You take out the trash from the café area? I thought your job was to shelve books?"

"I take the trash out, too."

"Do you only take out the trash when Alexis works the coffee counter?"

"No."

Pagan sighed aloud. "Michael, we were doing so well, but I don't think you are being completely honest with me now. It upsets me when you belittle yourself, Michael."

With somebody like Horner, you keep using their first name, personalizing the conversation, working on emotions of friendship they don't know how to control or understand.

"You're a good person, aren't you, Michael?"

"Yes."

The original crime report stated Alexis Walker's father had reported her missing when she didn't return home after her shift ended at 11pm.

Two hours later, uniformed officers refereeing a dispute between two homeless men collecting aluminum cans had noticed her strangled body behind the bookstore dumpster. Her bra had been taken – a souvenir.

Responding homicide detectives quickly cleared the homeless men, and just as quickly established Horner, the store's weirdo employee, as being seen skulking around Alexis' car after closing.

The detectives were no doubt understandably upset when their captain told them to call Pagan. I was sure they believed they could crack an egg like Horner as easily as Pagan, but their captain wanted the clearance on his record and didn't want to take any chances. Pagan didn't miss. Get Pagan.

Detectives door-knocked Horner's house and got him to agree to come to the station voluntarily. The second he was out of sight in a patrol car, the detectives had produced a warrant to search the residence where Horner lived with his father.

I watched Pagan, seeing him get ready to change focus. He held up what I assumed was Horner's rap sheet.

"Tell me about the time you were arrested," Pagan said.

"It was stupid," Horner replied. I could see he was actually embarrassed.

Pagan gently shook the rap sheet. "You think being arrested for burglary is stupid?"

"It was kicked down to trespass."

"Tell me about it."

"What do you want to know? They made me mad."

"Who? The people you burglarized?"

"Yeah. They was always messing up the store."

Pagan looked at Horner. Waiting.

Horner uncrossed his legs at the ankles. I could see the urge to justify himself bubbling inside him.

"The guy was always coming in the bookstore, taking out books, reading them in the chairs and then not putting them back. It wasn't just one or two books. It was ten, fifteen, twenty books – every day. I had to follow around behind him all the time putting the books back. He didn't care."

"There was somebody else, too," Pagan said.

Horner nodded. "Yeah. A woman. She was always buying lattes and leaving the cups on the bookshelves. She left stains everywhere – didn't care."

"What did you do?"

A slight smile touched Horner's lips. "I went into the guy's house and moved everything around. I didn't take nothing, just moved everything so he had to find it and put it back, just like he did to me."

"And the woman?"

"I stored up a week's worth of empty coffee cups and put 'em all over her house."

If Pagan was amused, he didn't show it, not varying the tone of his voice at all. "Did you go through her underwear drawer while you were in the house, Michael?"

"No. I don't do stuff like that."

I saw the lie.

"Of course you do," Pagan said. "I would have gone through her underwear drawer."

Horner uncrossed his legs completely and looked at Pagan.

Bingo.

"You would have?" Horner asked

"Sure," Pagan said confidentially, guy to guy.

With only two exceptions, there is nothing in the rules saying an interrogator can't lie to a suspect. You can't tell a suspect you'll cut them a deal with the judge, and there is case law saying you can't use the specific phrase, *the truth will set you free*. Any other lie is fair game.

I knew the quickest way to get a suspect to confess is to present them with what they believe is a socially acceptable manner to explain their behavior. Blaming the victim is one way to do this – a woman was asking to be raped because of what she was wearing...five year-olds can be sexually precocious...if the victim just hadn't pushed the suspect's buttons...

An interrogator doesn't believe the justifications, but if a suspect believes they will be judged less harshly because of a lame excuse, they will confess more readily.

If Horner thought Pagan was an understanding kindred spirit, he'd spill his guts. I could see Pagan was lying – he wouldn't have gone through the woman's underwear drawer.

I, however, might have left dirty coffee cups all over her house.

On the video, Pagan was moving on. "You told the truth when the officers arrested you back then?"

"Yes."

"That's good, Michael, because I need you to tell me the truth."

Horner had turned his face away, but his body remained open.

"Michael?"

"What?"

"I need you to tell me the truth."

Pagan waited.

"About what?" Horner asked eventually. He was stalling. He knew the answer. Guilt builds inside a guilty suspect like a geyser ready to explode. The more a suspect tries not to think about the truth, the more the truth forces its way to the forefront of his consciousness, and the harder it becomes not to talk about it.

Pagan waited. Horner waited.

A minute passed before Pagan said, "About Alexis," as if there had been no pause.

"She was nice," Horner said.

"Tell me about her."

Horner's face turned toward Pagan again. "She came here from Houston. She worked in a Starbucks there. Her dad lives here with her stepmom. He promised her a job in his insurance firm, but it didn't work out."

He was tapering his story down, but Pagan kept him talking. "Why didn't it work out?"

Horner shrugged. "She said her dad moved offices. The new office came with a secretary a bunch of the people shared. Her salary came out of the rent. He didn't need Alexis anymore."

"Tough break."

Horner only nodded. Pagan needed him verbal. "What did she do?" he asked.

Horner gave another shrug. "She came to work at the bookstore making coffee."

"Heck of a career – barista for hire," Pagan said. "Was she mad at her dad?"

"What do you think?"

Oh, oh. Hostility.

"I think she had every right to be mad," Pagan said. "And I think you took out her trash to try and make her feel better." Pagan paused. "Right?"

"Yeah. She said she was going to fix her dad for screwing her over."

"Bet you wanted to help her?"

"No. I'm not good at stuff like helping."

I saw the truth of the statement as bright as the dawning sun.

Pagan waited. A minute passed. Another minute passed.

A tear rolled down Horner's cheek.

"You know Alexis is dead, don't you, Michael?" Pagan's voice was quiet, soothing. He had formed the questions to only require a one-word answer.

"Yes," Horner said, providing the word Pagan was waiting for.

"You killed her, didn't you, Michael?"

Horner's eyes widened. "No. I found her when I took out the trash. I was scared. I didn't know what to do. I just left her there."

I believed him. I could see he was telling the truth. But I could also see Pagan believed he'd just heard a lie.

"Michael, it upsets me when you lie. I'd rather you not tell me anything than lie to me. Do you understand?"

Horner's tears were flowing faster now. "Yes."

There was the soft bong of a bell outside the interrogation room. I knew it was a signal to Pagan. Horner didn't even hear it. Nobody would interrupt an interrogation, but if they had important information for the interrogator they sounded the bell. The interrogator responded only if it felt appropriate.

Pagan stood. "You sit here and think about the truth, Michael. When I come back, we'll talk about the truth. I know you want to tell me, don't you?"

"Yes."

Pagan opened the door and slid out.

I later learned from the file Nick Baxter, one of the homicide dicks on the case was waiting for Pagan. He'd just returned from serving the search warrant at Horner's house.

They had found the victim's bra in Horner's closet along with a stack of photos of Alexis, clearly taken without her knowing.

There were even some photos of Alexis that Horner had managed to take in the bookstore's woman's' restroom. And there were some taken through the window of Alexis' residence bedroom. Horner had drawn the usual juvenile sexual crudities across the photos.

On the video, Pagan returned to the interrogation room, bringing the photos with him. He moved over to stand next to Michael, his body close to touching him.

When Horner looked up, Pagan dribbled the photos to spill down over Horner's lap and onto the floor. Each one fell like a guillotine blade chopping the head off a lie.

"Tell. Me. The. Truth. Michael."

"You won't believe me."

"I will believe you, Michael. I know the truth already. I just want you to tell me. You killed Alexis, didn't you?"

"No."

It was not the answer Pagan wanted.

But I could see it was the truth. Watching what was happening in the room was like watching a train wreck in slow motion and being helpless to stop it. My stomach kept clenching over and over, the yogurt I'd ingested souring and regurgitating bile into my throat.

Pagan continued speeding down the railroad tracks. "What happened, Michael? Did you try to kiss her? Did she catch you taking photos? Did she make you mad like those customers?"

"No, no."

"You took her bra, Michael. I know you did. It was in your closet. Please don't lie to me."

"Yes, I took her bra, but she was already dead."

"I know she was dead *before* you took the bra, Michael. You took it after you killed her. You needed something to remember her by, she was your friend."

"She was nice to me."

Pagan sat down, reaching out to put his hand on Michael's shoulder. "Michael, don't do this to yourself. Don't disappoint me. I know you know the truth. I know the truth. Truth is even better if it's shared."

"She said she was going to get back at her dad. She said she had files. He was taking people's money, but not paying their insurance stuff."

Pagan was silent. His fingers now stroking the back of Michael's neck.

"She was going to tell," Michael said.

"I know she was, Michael. She was going to tell about you." With his other hand, Pagan tapped the photos remaining in Michael's lap. "She was going to tell about the photos, wasn't she Michael. I know you were ashamed. I would have been as well. It wasn't nice was it, Michael?"

"No." Michael was blubbering slightly.

"You killed her didn't you, Michael?"

Pagan's hand was now on Michael's shoulder, rocking him softly back and forth, making Michael's head begin to nod in the affirmative. "Tell me the truth, Michael. It's easy once it's out. Don't cut us with lies."

Pagan leant forward placing one hand on Michael's thigh, the other hand rubbing Michael's back. "Tell me the truth, Michael," Pagan said in a whisper. "You killed Alexis didn't you?"

There was a pause as silent tears fell – then, "Yes."

I saw the bottomless purple of a dense lie. Bile rose in my throat.

On the DVD, the interrogation room door opened.

Pagan looked up, angry. Baxter saw Pagan comforting Michael and smirked as if he'd caught two kids making love in the back of a car.

"Captain wants you," Baxter said.

"Get out," Pagan said flatly.

"Now," Baxter said, but he closed the door.

Pagan rubbed Michael's back again.

"It's okay. Thank you for telling me the truth."

"What will happen? Will I go to jail?"

"Yes," Pagan said.

"I don't want to go to jail."

"I'm sorry," Pagan said. His words were the light blue of truth.

Pagan got to his feet. "I'll be back," he said, and left the room, closing the door behind him.

The DVD kept playing showing Horner crying softly. I pressed the pause button and scrambled for the reports I'd left in the kitchen, desperate to know what was going on while Horner sat in the room. Why had Pagan been abruptly summoned? I found a *follow-up* report and scanned it.

The official statement was brief and to the point. The victim's stepmother had called in. Her husband, the victim's dad, had committed suicide. Stepmom found him in his car in the garage with the engine still running – carbon monoxide poisoning.

My heart began to thump around in my chest like a bat trying to escape a cage.

Alexis' dad had left a note confessing to getting furious with his daughter because she had some files of his showing he wasn't paying his customers' insurance premiums. He'd gone to confront her at the bookstore. She had led him to where the dumpsters were to avoid a scene inside. Their verbal arguing had turned physical. They fought, he strangled her, didn't know he was killing her until too late. He left the body behind the dumpster, then went home and killed himself.

I fumbled my way back to my computer screen. I could barely bring myself to watch what I knew was about to happen. I pushed the fast forward button in a silly effort to make the reality less real.

Horner eventually stood, removing his belt. He next took the chair Pagan had been sitting in and wedged it under the door knob. Then he stood on his chair and pushed up the soft acoustic tile in the ceiling. Above the tile, he must have found a pipe.

Getting down from the chair, he dragged over the small table from the corner of the room. He put his chair on top of it and climbed back up. He slipped his belt through the buckle and then reached up into the ceiling to secure one end of the belt.

On the screen, Horner's movements were as inevitable as they were quick and jerky, made even more so by the video being on fast forward. Horner went up on his tip toes to place his head in the loop formed by his belt and the buckle. Without hesitation, he kicked the chair out from beneath him.

His bodyweight fell, tightening the loop impossibly around his scrawny neck.

He hung and kicked.

Then he didn't kick anymore.

His body spun slowly, turning his mottled purple face away from the camera.

I released the fast forward button and stared in horror.

On the screen there was a commotion as the door banged back and forth until the chair dislodged. Finally the door was thrown open and Pagan bolted into the room, moving immediately to Horner's hanging form.

He was too late. I knew he was too late.

I couldn't watch anymore. I hit the stop button, sending the screen blank.

I didn't know when I had started crying.

My stomach clenched again.

I stood up and stumbled awkwardly toward the bathroom, my hand an inadequate dam against the spewing vomit.

CHAPTER 8

"The truth is like a lion. You don't have to defend it. Let it loose. It will defend itself."
- St. Augustine

I'd pulled myself together by the next morning, but it had been a rough night. I'd eventually read all the reports Pagan had put in the envelope, including the transcript of the internal hearing, in which the department cleared him of any wrongdoing. Clearly, Pagan hadn't been as easy on himself, exiling himself to the hidden realms in the furthest corners of the cold case squad. However, judging by the Arthur Howell trial from the day before, even thirty year-old cases couldn't stop Pagan's talents from rising to the surface.

I also spent some time on the Internet checking up on The Hacienda. It appeared Pagan's benefactor was an actual Italian countess – Valentina Brunetti. She'd been exiled by her family from her native Venice when she married a *drylander* – a Tuscan whose landed family was said to have started their vineyard with Rossignola grape vines stolen from the Province of Vicenza centuries earlier. She was quite the character, immigrating to America with her husband where, after settling in California, he founded a new winery, presumably using cuttings from those anciently stolen grapevines. The California soil and the Italian grapevines fell in love and turned the new winery's output into the hottest vintage on the worldwide market.

Four years ago – fifteen years after alighting on sunny west coast shores and with time and money on her hands – the countess had turned philanthropic, building *The Hacienda* collective in the original style of her adopted home, blending it with her European roots, and opening its doors to entrepreneurs and restaurateurs with big dreams, but little capital.

She then sought out artists, writers, and musicians and added them into the eclectic mix in studios located on the collection's second story. Her efforts had met with as much success as her husband's wines.

None of the coverage on the Internet spoke about Pagan's involvement with The Hacienda, but I had the feeling he had been there from the beginning – working behind the scenes during his self-imposed exile. It was there in the mix of businesses and restaurants. I had no way of knowing for sure, but I could sense Pagan's presence in the mix as much as the countess.

The hands of the clock in the tower above the main building registered ten to eight when I pulled into the parking lot of The Hacienda. The area was already busy, with *Tiki Joe's* doing a brisk morning business both inside and via its drive-thru window. Next door, *Sophia's Italian Trattoria* was not open, but several employees were busy cleaning and setting up the outside eating area for the lunch business.

The glass of the next door office was covered with a laminate declaring it the entrance to the studio of *Martini in the Morning* – an Internet radio station featuring lounge music. Then followed what appeared to be an office full of cubicles called *Writers' Haven* – whatever it was.

Fleet Feet, a running and biking store, led on to *The Bookaneer* – a used bookstore – then several other businesses I couldn't identify at first glance led down to *The Raven* pub, the *El Cid* Spanish restaurant, and the *Sunzu* dojo.

Everything was clean and cared for and, despite the eclectic mix, it all seemed to blend into the happy Bohemian mix of cultures I'd felt the night before. Even in the early morning there seemed to be a positive electricity in the air.

I realized I had no idea where I was supposed to meet Pagan. I had half-expected him to be waiting outside, but as I was about to park, I saw a woman step out of the pub and wave. She pointed, and I realized she wanted me to park in the reserved area next to Pagan's Escalade.

I pulled into the same spot my car had been parked in the night before and saw, with a start, *Randall* had been painted on the concrete parking bumper. When had that been done, and why did I feel vaguely pissed off by it?

I opened my car door to find the woman who had waved at me standing near.

"Hello, dear," she said. She was pushing sixty, but holding it at bay with brassy blonde hair and an indiscrete display of plump cleavage. She was unassumingly dressed in too tight black jeans and a plunging red silk blouse with a single string of pearls. Her accent would have done the queen proud.

"I'm Rose Parker," she said, extending a hand for me to shake. "His nibs is inside having his breakfast. Asked me to guide you in."

Rose's eyes took in my lack of makeup, my hair hastily pulled back into a ponytail, and the black shell I'd thrown on over grey slacks and low-heeled shoes. She didn't comment on the gun strapped to my hip, but I still grabbed a lightweight windbreaker off the backseat of my Honda, pulling it on to cover the armament.

"You look like you've been put through the ringer, dearie," Rose said, smiling to take the insult out of the words. "And I've a feeling it won't be the last time if you're going to be working with Mr. Pagan."

There it was again...*Mr. Pagan*.

It had taken me longer than normal to stretch out my leg after getting up because I hadn't stretched it before falling into an emotionally exhausted sleep on my couch the night before. I was frustrated because the leg seemed to get shorter every day. In reality, the tendons and ligaments were still traumatized by the injury. Rehab was a painful hell, but I'd be damned if I was going to give in and add a half inch thick sole to every left shoe in my closet.

As we crossed the parking lot, I realized I was leaning hard on my cane and forced myself to straighten up. There was soft music coming out of speakers hidden in the planters...something from the Great American Songbook – Summer Wind.

"Sinatra?" I asked.

Rose looked confused for a second then twigged I was talking about the music. "Yes," she said, looking at her watch. "Always a double dose of Sinatra at eight – AM and

PM." She pointed toward the end of the collection of shops anchored by Tiki Joe's. "*Martini in the Morning,* all lounge music, all the time. Standards and modern standards. Always swinging." She sounded slightly rapturous – a convert to the music style.

"Do you own the pub?" I asked, trying to bring Rose back to point.

Rose laughed. "The Raven? Goodness no. My husband Trevor is The Hacienda's caretaker and I am the collection's concierge. We make sure everything is shipshape and runs smoothly."

"Do you like it here?'

"Everybody likes it here, dearie. We have a nice apartment above Tiki Joe's. Helps to be here when needed."

She said no more, opening the door to The Raven and pointing me toward where Pagan was sitting at a table by a window.

"Thank you, Mrs. Parker," he said with a quick raise of his palm. A young waitress was gathering his finished plate.

He was drinking tea from a large mug. A pot with a funny looking knitted hat sat on the table to his right.

A second large mug, this one filled with steaming black coffee, had been placed on the table near the chair opposite Pagan's. "Good morning, Randall." He pointed to the mug of coffee. "Tiki Joe's special blend. Full strength. I think you'll like it."

"How do you know how I drink my coffee?" I sat and took a sip, leaning my cane against the table. I was grateful for the coffee, but was not about to let on. "And what's with my name painted on the parking bumper?"

Pagan simply smiled. "I sent you home with an emotional time bomb and all you want to talk about is how I know stuff about you?"

"And parking bumpers," I said.

When Pagan was silent, I looked down and started again.

"Look...Ray...can we stop jousting. What's going on? What is this all about?" I put the envelope he'd given me down on the table between us.

Pagan put his tea mug down and wiped his mouth with a black linen napkin. I realized there were no other customers in the pub because it wasn't open for business yet, but Pagan was as comfortable as if he were in his own kitchen. The waitress who'd taken his plate appeared to be oblivious to us as she went about setting up shop for the day.

"Ginny?" Pagan got the waitress' attention. "Can you leave us for a while?"

"No worries," she said. Her accent was Australian, her smile filled with perfectly white teeth. She made one last adjustment to the bar and then ducked out through a set of swinging doors, which I assumed led to the kitchen.

I looked after her as the doors swung closed behind her.

"Don't worry," Pagan said. "We're alone. Ginny's a good girl. She'll use this as an excuse to grab her surfboard."

I knew Malibu was only a few miles away down a winding canyon road.

Pagan finished his tea and began messing with the milk and tea pot, building a refill. I took a long draught of my coffee and felt the caffeine run through me like electricity.

When he finished pouring, Pagan looked at me. "I've been searching for you, Randall, or someone like you, for three years."

"What does that mean?" I hated myself for the sound of pleading in my voice.

Pagan pointed at the envelope on the table between us. "When you viewed the video what did you see?"

"I saw a tragedy unfolding, but it wasn't your fault."

"Yes it was, but you didn't answer my question. What specifically did you see?"

I swallowed. I knew what he wanted me to say, but I had kept this hidden for so long. This was my secret...*My secret!*

"It's safe, Randall. You need to trust me." Pagan's voice was gentle and full of warmth.

I wanted to look up at him, but I stubbornly kept my head down – which made me pissed off at myself. I wasn't in middle school. I was an adult...an LAPD detective for Hell's sake...

Pagan got up and came around the table and pulled another chair up next to mine. He sat and took one of my hands in both of his. "You've never talked to anyone about this, have you?"

It was as if through the connection of his hands, I could feel his thought process racing. The emphasis in his voice changed to amazement. "You think your gift is a curse, don't you?"

I looked up sharply. "It is a curse!" I could feel something inside me crumbling.

Pagan shook his head and gripped my hand tighter. Tell me what you saw on the video."

I forced the words out. "Horner lied when he said he did it..."

"You saw the lie?" Pagan was calm, as if he already knew the answer.

"Yes..." I felt tears prick my eyes. I'd lived with this curse for so long.

"You are amazing, Randall!"

It was my turn to shake my head. "You don't understand..."

"I do, Randall. Of course, I do. Everybody lies and you see them do it every time...parents, teachers, boyfriends, lovers, used car salesmen...you've seen them all lie – time and time again. Trust is an alien land to which you've been denied a visa."

I was crying, tears rolling down my face, but I laughed. Pagan's voice had changed as he delivered that last line, cutting me with his truth while balming me with his understanding. I sniffed and took back my hand from his. Pagan handed me a napkin and I wiped my eyes and gently blew my nose.

I knew I looked a wreck, but there was no judgment in Pagan's countenance or body language. Part of me suddenly realized I was seeing Pagan's genius at work up close and personal. He didn't understand my pain, he felt it. I felt his empathy wash over and unburdened me.

"When did you first know you were different?" Pagan asked softly.

I couldn't not answer him. "When I saw my dad lie to my mother when I was four. I called him on it and it created havoc – almost split them up. It was bad enough dad being a career Army officer and gone so often. But I was too young to know any of that."

"Did your parents know you could see lies?"

"No. It scared me, so I kept it hidden."

"And it has caused you no end of problems in relationships ever since."

"You have no idea..."

"Actually, I do. I don't see lies the same way you do, but I always know more about what somebody is saying than is good for any relationship."

"But how do you know about me?"

"First, tell me how you see lies."

"When people talk, I see colors."

"You see auras?"

I shook my head. "No. Streamers connected to words. All pastels, except for lies. Lies are a deep purple." I was feeling both scared and liberated at the same time.

Pagan nodded. "Do you know what you are?"

"Besides a freak?"

"You're not a freak. Randall. You're a *synesthetes*."

"I don't understand."

"Synesthesia means *union of senses*. It is a neurological condition in which stimulation of one sensory or cognitive pathway leads to automatic, involuntary experiences in a second sensory or cognitive pathway. You have a form of synesthesia, known as *grapheme* or color synesthesia."

"How do you know this? Is it common? How did you know about me?" My head was spinning and I could hear myself jabbering. I was also flustered because I saw no purple of any hue tinging Pagan's words.

"Slow down, Randall. Synesthesia is far from common. Color synesthesia is even rarer. As for how I know these things, I've spent a lifetime studying lying. I come from a race of people for whom lying is an art form, an acceptable way of life."

Pagan reached across the table for his tea mug. "Horner's death is on me. I maneuvered him into confessing. I knew his weaknesses and I used it against him without thinking about the consequences. I'm different from you. I have gifts – enhanced skills – but everything I know and do in an interrogation involves experience, information, awareness, knacks, and trickery – it's all smoke and mirrors. I understand people. I can reach them on an empathic basis. But after Horner, I knew that to do what I do, I had to have a touchstone…a safety net to make sure I never make the same mistake again. You are that touchstone."

"I understand what you're saying, but I still don't know how you found me."

"I've studied the videos from hundreds of interrogations conducted by LAPD detectives – and those are aside from the thousands of interrogations I've watched from departments around the country and around the world. I've seen the videos of every interrogation you've done since getting to RHD. I watched them over and over because I could sense there was something different about how you responded when suspects talked to you. I finally realized what it was – you weren't watching the suspect when you talked to them like every other good detective does, you were watching something else…something outside of the suspects. You were watching their words."

I sipped at my half-forgotten coffee. I could feel something odd…I could feel Pagan feeling me – not tactilely, but emotionally.

"You're an empath," I said suddenly. "You say what you do is all smoke and mirrors, but it's not. You're an empath."

Pagan gave a little shrug. "We all have guilty secrets, Randall. I know yours, and now you know mine. I'm not a full blown empath, but I have well over half of the thirty common traits and a good gaggle of the not so common."

"How does that work?"

Pagan shrugged. "One example would be when somebody is angry. All most people hear are the angry words. I feel what is behind the anger, what the person is truly saying: *I am scared, I am frustrated, I am insecure, I feel threatened.*"

"You don't hear those things, you actually *feel* them?"

"If it is indeed what the angry person is feeling. I can also tap into their rage as a physical experience."

I was a little nonplussed. That all sounded a little scary. "So what happened with Horner?"

Pagan sighed. "Do you ever get tired of seeing lies and try to hide from your synesthesia?"

"I didn't know it was called synesthesia, but I know what you're talking about. Sometimes, I get so tired of all the purple lies coming out of people, I force my mind to go cross-eyed and run all the colors together. Sometimes, I don't want to know."

Pagan reached out and took my hand again. It was as if he was picking up my every emotional vibe. "Some days," he said, "I get tired of feeling what everybody else feels. I want to feel what I feel. My own negative emotions are the easiest to feel – anger, depression, discouragement. I was holding on to all those feelings of my own when I went in the room with Horner. I thought I didn't need to feel Horner in order to get him to confess. I thought I'd put him through the paces and he'd roll right over."

"And he did," I said.

"Yes, because I manipulated him into it. He lied and I didn't feel it because I was too burned out from feeling other people's feelings and too busy feeling my own ball of anger."

We were silent for a few moments as I processed. Pagan waited, but there was no weight to his waiting. He held my hand as if we were in some kind of Star Trekkie Vulcan mind meld – it was as if I could feel emotions and thoughts going both ways.

"That's the reason for The Hacienda," I said with dawning realization.

Pagan's lips crept into a grin and his eyes sparked. "Got

it in one, Randall. I am impressed. The Hacienda is a very positive, creative, environment. I can recharge here. The job surrounds us with nothing but angst and negativity. I had to find a balance. The Hacienda – and what we do here – gives me balance."

I set the empty coffee mug in my right hand down on the table. "So, what now?"

Pagan released my left hand and stood up. His eyes were still sparkling and his irritating grin grew wider. "I thought you'd never ask."

CHAPTER 9

*"The best liar is he who makes the
smallest amount of lying go the longest way."*
- Samuel Butler: The Way of All Flesh

"Most of the rooms up here are artist studios with a couple
of soundproof music studios and a communal room
mixed in."

Pagan was giving me the tour of The Hacienda's main
building's second floor. It was bright and airy with explosions of flowers and vines painted on the walls in many
different styles.

"I have rooms on the other side of the clock tower. The
Parkers have rooms over Tiki Joe's. And this..." Pagan was
acting like a magician revealing the startling end of an illu-
sion as he opened the door to the left of the clock tower and
entered a large space with exposed beams, "...is for you, if
you want it..."

I felt my breath rush out of me. The space was larger

than my apartment. There was a small kitchen area with sparkling appliances, a sitting area with a couch and easy chair on a large rug, a wide screen TV in easy viewing distance, and a futon-style mattress was hung like a hammock from the ceiling beams by a chain at each corner. A small set of steps on one side gave access to the bed, which looked uncannily like a flying carpet. Light cans were suspended dramatically here and there, and through an open door to a partitioned off area there was a bathroom. Wide round windows with views of gently rolling hills let in copious amounts of light.

Pagan put a hand on my shoulder, sensing my inability to speak. "This isn't just for you, Randall. I need you close. Right now, we are in a honeymoon period of enlightenment. But we both know the darkness will soon descend. It's the way of *the job*."

I turned to face Pagan. "I can't..." I ducked my head wishing my hair wasn't in a ponytail so it could fall forward and hide me.

"Of course, you can," Pagan said. He reached over and raised my chin with his hand. "You don't have to hide anymore, Randall. You have come home. This is where you belong."

I moved my chin away. "I have a home."

"No. You don't. You have a utility box where you stay. It isn't a home."

I could barely manage a grunt. Pagan's truth pierced me and tore at me in a way the gangster's bullet which tore the chunk out of my leg never could. I felt overwhelmed, yet I was also aware of Pagan reading and feeling my emotions.

"We have too much work ahead of us, Randall, for you to worry about moving. Don't even think about it. It's already in hand. Give me the keys to your apartment and put the rest out of your mind."

"You're quite the control freak," I said. The words came out hasher than I expect, but Pagan appeared to absorb them without impact.

"You have no idea," Pagan said. "You also have so much to learn."

My hackles raised. "What do you mean?"

Pagan's expression was neutral, but there was something shark-like moving beneath the surface. I became aware of the color of his words. The attached streamers waved like pastel ribbons – not a hint of purple.

Pagan was watching. He knew I was *looking* at his words. It was disconcerting. The streamers had been with me all my life. I had learned to keep them hidden from everybody. Pagan's knowledge left me feeling raw and exposed.

"Knowing somebody is lying isn't enough. You have to know what to do with the deceit," Pagan said. "If you let me, I'll teach you."

"And I keep you from making a mistake?"

"From making *another* mistake," Pagan said.

"Semantics," I said.

"Not if you're Michael Horner."

I moved my attention from Pagan's words to his face. There was pain there, but there was also acceptance and patience in the hollows and shadows below his eyes and above the sharp edges of his cheekbones.

"You and I are the same," Pagan said, his gaze intent, his tone a mesmerizing silken caress. "We may come at the nature of truth from different perspectives, but neither of us can hide from it. Everybody lies. On average, seven times a day. Small lies, white lies, guilty lies, cheating lies, spin doctor lies, political lies, poker lies, industrial sized box store lies, and every one of them claws at us, jars us, disgusts us, and fills us with despair. Every lie, even the ones we speak ourselves, affects us. You and I are truth junkies, we crave its purity. We know it doesn't exist, but we keep looking for it, expecting it."

I didn't know what to do with my hands. I felt like an awkward teenager, all elbows and knees and acne. Yesterday, I thought my biggest challenge was fighting back from a physical injury. Now, I felt I'd been dumped into an unwanted, yet somehow cathartic mental therapy. Walls of emotion inside me were raging, transmogrifying, changing too fast. I couldn't keep up.

Pagan's hands were on my shoulders, supporting me and guiding me down on collapsing legs until we were both sitting cross-legged on the floor.

In my head I saw images of Pagan in the interrogation room completely missing the truth of Michael Horner's confession. It made my chest ache.

"There is no truth," I said finally. "Only perceptions of truth."

Pagan surprised me by laughing. His hands shook my shoulders lightly. His touch wasn't romantic or sexual. It was accepting, and understanding, and connecting. I knew it was foolish, but I could feel his strength flowing into me. "Exactly," he said.

There was a part of me wondering how he did it, how empathy flowed out of him, how a man I'd met only yesterday had the ability to bring my world into such an intimate and close focus.

"Society, religion, even science teach us truth is a fixed point from which there is no deviation." Pagan continued. He lowered his hands from my shoulders to my elbows.

"But anyone who believes truth is a constant has never stepped into an interrogation room. Truth as we use it in law enforcement is an abstract. It is battered and banged by limited resources into a recognizable shape easily swallowed by juries to produce an end game fitting a socially acceptable mishmash of plea bargains and negotiations, which we call, for lack of a more precise term, justice."

"Are you saying the pursuit of truth is hopeless?"

"No. I'm saying it is the highest of all callings. Because of the gifts with which you and I have been cursed, we have the ability and the responsibility to pursue the truth. To go wherever the hunt leads. To get the truth, not confessions flawed by the perception of either the subject or the interrogator."

I shook my head. "Isn't that what cops do?"

"You know it isn't," Pagan said. "It's what cops should do, but most don't have the skills. In the academy we train cops to write reports, to shoot guns, to drive in pursuits, to defend themselves physically, to use tasers and batons, to write tickets, and what the letter of the law says. What we don't teach them is how to talk to people, how to relate to different cultures, different values, different upbringings, different moral compasses, yet those are the skills which are required for ninety-nine percent of the job."

Pagan moved his hands into mine. Again there was a part of me that marveled at how I was losing myself in his enthusiasm, his focus, his...humanness.

"There are turning points in all of our lives." Pagan's voice had lowered and taken on a slight rasp. "You and I have a chance to make a difference. To fulfill our potential. To become together something greater than the sum of our partnership. It will be the most demanding thing you have ever done. I will push you, and try you, and make you angry, but I will always rely on you. I will always have your back."

I took a deep breath. I tried a half-smile. "Do you go through this with all your *wolves*?"

Pagan smiled. "I told you I had been looking for you for a long time, long before I went into the interrogation room with Michael Horner. I need you, Randall."

"How do you know it's me you need?"

"Frankly, because you need me as well."

There was a knock on the open door behind us. We both turned to see an emo, twenty-something, male with long hair dyed green and a wisp of a blonde goatee.

"What's up, Arlo?" Pagan asked.

"Sorry to bother you," Arlo said, his voice appeared not to have cracked when he hit puberty. "But you're probably going to want to see this." He held out what looked like and official LAPD crime summary report. Each LAPD area prepared one each morning covering the crimes in their jurisdiction from the day before and sent it in via email to the staff at each bureau HQ.

Pagan stood up in one fluid movement, holding my hands and bringing me up with him. He took the proffered report and scanned it. I could feel a change of focus and determination coming over him.

"Give Arlo the keys to your apartment," he said. "It's game time."

CHAPTER 10

Interview: Getting information from somebody they want to give you.

Interrogation: Getting information from somebody they don't want to give you.

AS WE STEPPED out onto the Hacienda's boardwalk, I had just asked, "Who is Arlo," when I sensed Pagan change his weight. Instinctively I knew what he was going to do.

Time appeared to slow down and I was somehow aware of everything...an Asian man wearing a well-worn *judo gi* sitting on a bench behind us...the soft lounge music coming from the hidden speakers...the crunch of the parking lot gravel as a green Range Rover drove slowly past – and Pagan slightly shifting his weight.

I firmly planted my good leg and transferred my weight off the cane in my left hand. When Pagan shot his toe forward to clip the tip of my cane, I used the momentum and a twist of my wrist to flip the cane up, its ferrule coming to rest in the taught skin under his chin.

Pagan, moving faster than I thought possible, had both his hands wrapped around the cane, his arms frozen like iron bars. I couldn't have stabbed the cane any further upward even if I'd wanted to do so...and on some level I did.

"What the hell, Ray," I snapped.

"I told you she was a fast study," Pagan said, obviously not to me.

The Asian man had moved off the bench and was suddenly feeling my left thigh. I looked down appalled and tried to pull away, but Pagan was still holding my cane and I was too off-balance to let go of it myself.

"Ray!"

"This is Tanaka Sunzu. He is my sensei...my teacher..."

I remembered seeing the sign for the Sunzu dojo at one end of the Hacienda main building. I also realize one sleeve of Tanaka's gi was empty and secured to his side.

"Too skinny," Tanaka said releasing my thigh at the same time Pagan released my cane. I stepped back flustered.

"Need to eat lots of protein. Be at dojo tomorrow morning, five o'clock. We teach you how to use cane. How to get balance back. First, eat." Tanaka smiled, his eyes crinkling so tight they almost closed. He radiated happiness. I couldn't not like him despite feeling like I'd been the victim of a masher.

"Come on, Randall," Pagan said, taking my arm and steering me away before I could reply. "Don't let the old reprobate charm you. This time tomorrow you'll hate him. Trust me, he's a sadist at heart."

Pagan hit the electronic locks on his black Escalade. He released my arm and I half stumbled around to the passenger door.

Pagan opened the rear hatch of the Escalade, reaching into one of the many custom compartments in the rear. When he closed the hatch and slid into the driver's seat, he set two protein bars, a package of nuts, and a surprisingly cold chocolate protein drink in my lap.

"Eat," Pagan said. "Always do what Tanaka says or he'll find a way to make you suffer."

Life had become a whirlwind, twisting through everything in its path. My head was spinning. So many questions, I didn't know where to start anymore.

"Eat," Pagan said again, starting the SUV.

Because I didn't know what else to do, I stripped out a granola energy bar and popped the tab on the protein drink. Pagan looked over and seemed satisfied to see my mouth chewing.

My brain had locked up. I could only focus on the physical act of eating. Bite...Chew...Swallow...Sip...Bite...Chew...Swallow...Sip...

Everything Pagan had said in the pub raced through my thoughts in static bursts. A *synesthetes*...There was a name for what I was...That meant there were others like me...Pagan had said my synesthetes was rare...But still – others like me...Bite...Chew...Swallow...Sip...Bite...Chew...

Pagan an empath...Everything that happened in the interrogation room with Michael Horner...Pagan manipulating the three drive-by shooting suspects...Getting a suspect to cry on cue in the courtroom...

Bite...Chew...Swallow...Sip...

I know he was allowing me time to process, but Pagan was remaining annoyingly silent. He smoothly drove the Escalade away from The Hacienda, accelerating onto the nearby freeway onramp heading toward L.A.

I didn't even know where we were going or what we were doing.

I had to start somewhere. Through a mouthful of protein bar, I asked, "Why don't you wear your gun or your badge?"

Pagan chuckled. "Everything that's happened since yesterday and you want to know why I don't wear a gun and badge?"

I swallowed. "We're cops. It's part of the territory. I have a right to know why my partner is the only cop in the city not wearing his gun on duty."

Pagan slid his left hand into what I assumed was the molded pocket on the interior of the driver's door and pulled out a holstered, stainless steel, Smith and Wesson .38 revolver. He showed it to me and then slid it back. "I also have a two-inch Chief Special in an ankle holster. Not sure where my badge is."

"How much good is a *wheel* gun going to do in the door of your car?"

"More good than it's going to do in an interrogation room." Pagan sighed. "Guns, badges...they're barriers between you and the truth. Do you really need the nine millimeter on your hip and the badge on your belt to assert your authority? Do you rely on them for their intimidation factor?"

"No. I rely on them to save my ass when everything hits the fan. When my *calamity* factor kicks in, I need to know you've got my back."

"Do you really think I don't have your back?" Pagan asked.

"Before yesterday, you were nothing more than a rumor I'd heard whispered about in the department's back corridors."

"That isn't what I asked you. Do you think I don't have your back?" Pagan changed into the slow lane then pulled over onto the freeway shoulder and braked the SUV to a hard stop. He turned to look at me, his eyes intense. His presence seemed to fill the car. Not threatening, but searching.

I realized he really wanted an answer to his question. I could feel his empathy probing me, a mental experience verging on the physical. My jumbled thoughts about everything that had happened and been revealed in the past twenty-four hours again raced through my mind snapping into place like pieces of a jigsaw.

I purposely popped the last piece of the protein bar in my mouth and chewed. I drained the last of the chocolate drink and set the can on the floorboard. I blew out a breath, looking out the windshield. There was no going back to yesterday before I'd met with the chief, but I knew in my heart I didn't want to even if I could.

"I trust you." As I said the words, I heard the truth in them.

Pagan smiled, then turned his head to check traffic and get us moving again.

"Where are we going?" I asked.

"Hollywood Division," Pagan said. He still hewed to the old habit of referring to LAPD geographic *areas* as *divisions*. "RHD has been called in on a child kidnapping, which occurred last night."

"Who is Arlo and how come you found this out through him?"

"We may be assigned to RHD," Pagan said, "but it doesn't mean they are going to like us playing in their sandbox. As you know, every detective assigned to RHD is there because they are very good at what they do. It's why RHD gets called in to take over major cases from divisional detectives. They are not going to give up jurisdiction easily. Thus we have to make sure we have a way of being kept in the loop."

"Arlo?"

"Arlo and the wolves. A lot of what we do at The Hacienda is on the barter system. Arlo is a tech guy who wants to be the next great American novelist. He gets a cubical in *Writers' Haven* in return for vetting all the daily crime reports from all the divisions."

"Which I assume he gets from one of your wolves in each of the bureaus."

"Nice to have friends," Pagan agreed. "Arlo's computer is also hooked into all of the department's computer systems and subscribed to all the public information sources available."

"Isn't giving Arlo access to the department's computer systems illegal?"

"He's acting as our surrogate. The chief isn't going to sweat the fine line as long as we get results."

"What he doesn't know?"

"Exactly."

"What about what I don't know?"

"All you have to do is ask."

"Is this like the red pill or blue pill choice in the *Matrix*?

"There is no choice where you and I are concerned. We're always going to choose to know."

I nodded and tore the wrapper off the second protein bar.

CHAPTER 11

**"No man lies so boldly as the
man who is indignant."**
- Friedrich Nietzsche, Beyond Good and Evil

Pagan steered the Escalade off the Hollywood Freeway at Cahuenga Boulevard before beginning a series of twists and turns, taking us higher and higher into the Hollywood Hills. Sweeping views of Runyon Canyon Park spread out below us as we drove past curvy streets boasting slick, mid-century modern homes worth well beyond the yearly combined salaries of any eighty cops working out of Hollywood Area.

These were the homes of the Hollywood elite, new money with a capital *M* mixing with old money with a capital *Old*. Blockbuster movie producers, tech-millionaires, the inherited money of La-La Land royalty, and foreign oil moguls – all being bought out at obscenely high profits by shadowy figures hiding drug cartel and human trafficking profits.

Near the apex of the hills, Solar Drive had been in the news recently. The residents of the cul-de-sac were in a pitched battle with the city council, seeking approval for the installation of gates to close the community off from the great unwashed who used the area's public access points to popular hiking trails.

Among the dozen or so houses, all with stylish, tiled and turreted rooflines, was the anomaly at the heart of the controversy – an abandoned, Mediterranean-style manse situated at the end of the street. Overrun by squatters and partiers, the house had attracted every bad element in the city, turning the once quiet neighborhood into one of the city's most popular spots to park and party.

Big money squawks awfully loud in Los Angeles, and the small community had become a thorn in the side of LAPD's Hollywood Area – a *quality of life issue* in department speak. The angry fight between the *haves* and the *want to haves* had the department caught in the middle while *not* so civil suits and countersuits crawled through the courts at a glacial pace.

When Pagan pulled the Escalade through the open security gates into the curved driveway of the mansion next door to the center of the hullabaloo, I knew life was about to get even more complicated.

There were two plain detective sedans and a black and white already parked ahead of us. Pagan had shared with me the printout of Hollywood Area's Daily Crime report, which Arlo had given him. Topping the page filled with run-of-the-mill burglaries, robberies, and sex crimes was a paragraph stating a six year-old girl had been kidnapped from her room on Solar Drive. It ended with a notation stating RHD was taking over the investigation.

While we were driving, Pagan had me send texts to

both the chief and to RHD's Captain North to say we were on the way. Now, I looked over at Pagan before we exited the Escalade. My stomach was feeling queasy as adrenaline mixed with the protein bars.

"How do you want to play this?" I asked.

"You're an experienced detective," Pagan replied. "Be yourself, follow your instincts, look at everything, and listen instead of waiting to speak." Then, he was out of the SUV.

As he strode up the cobblestoned driveway toward the open front door of the house, he pulled a lightweight black leather jacket over his black mock-turtleneck and black jeans. I was pretty sure he didn't have any problem getting dressed in the dark.

A uniformed officer I didn't recognize was at the door. Pagan approached him with his hand outstretched. The officer smiled widely as he took it to shake.

"Officer Burns, how are you?" Pagan asked.

"Fine, sir," the officer replied.

"How's that new baby?" Pagan asked, still holding the officer's hand. "I saw the photos your wife posted on Facebook."

Holy crap! Pagan was on Facebook ...

"He's great," said the proud daddy.

"So, who's inside?" Pagan asked. He'd let go of the officer's hand and had lowered his voice.

"Castano, Dodd, and two other detectives I don't know. My partner, Clark, is also there."

Pagan patted the officer on the arm and we moved past.

"Facebook?" I whispered.

"Arlo also keeps up with my social networking. Sends me a daily brief. Far more valuable than the crime summary reports."

"Is Burns one of your wolves?"

"Not everyone on the department is a wolf, but you need to cultivate everyone you can. Cultivating from the top down is difficult because everybody is looking for an edge or a favor. Cultivating worker bees is infinitely more rewarding and valuable."

As we entered the house, we heard a voice raised in indignation and anger coming from the room ahead of us.

"This all be crazy...Craziness! Smack Daddy don't be having time to sit here and answer questions. I got lawyers to answer questions. You do your freaking job and find my daughter."

A large black man in his fifties charged into the house's front vestibule. He was wearing an obviously expensive purple tracksuit, which was too tight around his ample middle, and enough gold chains around his neck to support the economy of a small country. His dreadlocks would have looked better on a man half his age.

I recognized him immediately, Theodore *Smack Daddy* Davis. His loud, brash presence as the face of the mega-successful hip-hop Smack Records label made a nuisance of itself daily in popular culture. He'd parlayed his early success as a rapper into a Grammy laden record producing career. As the now multi-millionaire founder of Smack Records, he'd embraced the attitude of the thug life with the lifestyles of the rich and tasteless. Two bouncer-sized men followed him into the hallway.

Pagan must have recognized him, too. "Smack Daddy Davis," he said.

"That's right. You another cop looking for an autograph?"

"Already have Bob Marley's from back in the day," Pagan said. "Don't need nobody else."

Smack Daddy, gave a throaty chuckle. "Old school, white boy. Old school."

"Real old school," Pagan said. "Back to *One Cup of Coffee* and the material Marley's Wailers worked with Lee *Scratch* Perry."

"Now you talkin' gospel," Smack Daddy said, his facial expression glowing.

Pagan was amazing, his brain working on a whole different level to everyone else. He'd instantaneously taken everything in – Smack Daddy's hair, his age, his known music connections – and produced an opening gambit, which changed the man's attitude in a heartbeat.

"This has got to be very difficult for you," Pagan said. "But you also have responsibilities to other people who are relying on you. How about you go take care of your business and I'll get everyone here taking care of the business of finding your daughter? I'll come to your office later today and give you a progress report."

I was struggling to keep my mouth shut. Pagan was acting as if he was one of Smack Daddy's toadies. If I didn't suspect better, I would have thought he was star struck or something? It had happened to LAPD detectives before – most famously immediately after the murder of Nicole Simpson, when two RHD detectives had O.J. in an interrogation room with a civil lawyer who'd let Simpson waive his rights. The emotions of the crime were fresh. There was no Dream Team. No, *if the glove doesn't fit, you must acquit* theatrics. Two of RHD's best against a Los Angeles icon who had been involved in every LAPD golf tournament and hosted numerous LAPD charity events.

It shouldn't have even been a contest. But the detectives were star struck and lost their focus. After fifteen minutes, they let Simpson walk out of the interrogation room without ever once asking him if he'd done the deed. Instead of a *wham-bam-thank-you-ma'am* slam dunk, the case went on to shake the LAPD to its foundations.

And now, Pagan was letting the best witness in the kidnapping of a child walk out without being asked any questions.

I started forward to interject myself, but suddenly felt Pagan push his palm discretely backward onto my hip. It brought me up short, realizing Pagan was simply in full manipulation mode.

I realized it, but Detective Dante Castano, who had entered the vestibule tailing behind the bodyguards, didn't. "Mr. Davis, please," Castano said, sounding like an aggrieved suitor, "We need your help to find your daughter."

Smack Daddy looked at Pagan. "We done here?"

"Two o'clock, your office," Pagan said, stepping back to let Smack Daddy and his muscle entourage pass and go out the front door.

"Now, wait a minute, Pagan." Castano had gone red in the face.

Pagan held up his hand. "Give it a rest, Dante."

Looking like a volcano about to burst, Castano tried unsuccessfully to swallow his anger. "Damn it, Pagan. You can't walk in and screw with my witnesses."

"Do you want to find the missing child or not?" Pagan asked.

"Of course, I do."

"Then how much cooperation do you think you're going to get by butting heads with a witness who is in a full narcissistic meltdown?"

"What do you mean?"

"Smack Daddy is a person who has to think he's in charge. Somebody has taken his daughter, taken away his control. He doesn't know what to do when demanding his daughter back doesn't work. He only knows how to assert his authority. It's how he got all this," Pagan waved his hand to encompass the totality of the garishly decorated house. "When you come in here acting all in charge, he sees you as somebody else pissing in his pool. He's going to fight you every step of the way as his insecurities force him to assert his authority."

Castano had the good sense to look a little chagrinned. I could sympathize, having also misjudged Pagan's actions.

Pagan put a friendly hand on Castano's shoulder, smiling as he did so. "Leave it to me. I'll get him to talk this afternoon."

Castano nodded.

"What have we got so far?" Pagan asked.

"Not much," Castano said with a shrug. He looked at a small notebook in his right hand. "Missing girl is Unicorn Davis. Six years old. Mother, Judith Davis, put her to bed last night around seven. She checked on her around midnight when she went to bed herself. Mother woke up at three when the house alarm went off. Front door was open and the daughter was gone."

"Any kind of ransom demand?" I asked.

"Nothing yet," Castano said. "Probably too soon."

"Any possibility she simply got out of bed and went out the front door by herself?" Pagan asked.

"Mother says the daughter doesn't know how to unlock the front door. Its also got a childproof handle. Still, we've got units out searching and doing a canvass of the neighborhood in case."

"There's a lot of open ground leading down to the

canyon," I said.

Castano nodded. "Sheriff's Search and Rescue are responding."

"Where was Smack Daddy when all this was happening?" Pagan asked.

"Out all night *paaartying*," Castano said, drawing out the word. "Got home around four, as everything was ramping up."

"Burns and Clark the first uniforms on the scene?"

"Yes. We're holding them over on their shift until we get some kind of direction. SID is on the way for prints and photos."

"You have point on this?" Pagan asked Castano.

Castano's face darkened, his barrel chest expanding within his out of date sports jacket. "Yes."

"We going to have a pissing contest about Randall or myself doing the interviewing and any interrogations?"

I was surprised, but pleased to be included.

"Captain North said you've got carte blanche," Castano said, begrudgingly.

"I'm not concerned with what North said. I want to know where you stand," Pagan said.

Castano took a deep breath. "I won't get in the way. Neither will my team. Just find the child."

Pagan nodded. "Who's back at the office to work the computers?"

"Lancaster," Castano said.

"We need a full public information rundown on Smack Records, Smack Daddy, and the mother, Judith Davis. And get him to pull the records for this house." Pagan said.

"What are you thinking?" I asked.

"Nothing specific, but there are some niggling details."

"Such as?"

Pagan shook his head cutting off my inquiries. "Just doing tactical background." He took out his phone, tapped the screen a couple of times, and then handed it to me. When I looked there was already a message on the screen – *Inside job.*

I looked up at Pagan, but kept my mouth shut.

"Please text Arlo," Pagan said. "Ask him to tap into his tabloid buddies and find out what kind of dirt they have on Smack Daddy, including anything not confirmed."

I pulled up Arlo's contact info and started texting.

"Where's the victim's room?" Pagan asked Castano.

"Upstairs. Do you want to see it?"

"Not yet. Let's brace the mother first."

CHAPTER 12

Lips that lie are sticky and dry,
the liar's palms are not.
Genuine tears can be verified,
only when accompanied by snot.
- Carl Stincelli, Reading Between the Lines

TWENTY YEARS younger than her husband, Judith Davis was a mess. She was clearly not a natural blonde, but she was definitely a natural Caucasian. Her skin was porcelain white. Her cheeks were blotched red from crying. A baggy tank top covered braless, store bought breasts, and her short shorts revealed a thigh gap you could drive a truck through. She wasn't wearing any makeup. She was barely over five-foot tall and as thin and fragile as a tree twig in December.

When I looked closely, I could see her whole face was a lie – eyelids tweaked, cheekbones raised, Botox in forehead and lips. Snot ran freely from her sculptured nose. She kept wiping it away with the twisted tissue in her right hand.

"You have to help me," she was saying. "You have to find Unicorn. She's all I have..."

There was a cynical part of me wanting to make a bad joke about searching for unicorns, but my better nature kept the words from slipping between my lips.

"It must have been one of the squatters from the house next door," Judith was ramping us again. "They hate us. They've destroyed everything over there."

"Was there anyone over there last night?" Pagan asked.

"There's always somebody there. Ever since the house went on the market, there have been nonstop raves and parties. We've tried to get them out, but they're like cockroaches."

Pagan was sitting on the oversized leather couch next to Judith, nodding his head and holding her free hand. I watched the colored streamers of her words. They didn't flow freely. Her anxiety made the streamers jerk, break, and reform, but the colors were all pale pastels.

Pagan had typed *possibly an inside job* on his phone screen before handing it to me. He had to be thinking Smack Daddy, because Judith had no deception on display. She may be mistaken, but she wasn't consciously lying.

I thought about the explanation Pagan had given Castano regarding Smack Daddy's behavior. I hadn't seen Pagan's words as total lies – I remembered them coming out as a translucent purple – yet I now realized they were only a half-truth. Whatever it was Pagan had heard or felt in Smack Daddy's behavior was something deeper than an insecure narcissistic meltdown.

The room we were in, like the rest of the house, looked as if it had been vomited up by an interior decorator. Everything was gaudy and overdone – money spent for show not taste.

The drapes in the room were heavy, too bright, red velvet. The lighting was too harsh, reflecting off heavy glass tables and adding a starkness to the oversized maroon leather chairs and sofa set next to a lime green eyesore of a loveseat. The paintings on the walls were all modern lines and angles surrounded by inappropriate baroque frames. They left you in no doubt they were wallet cleaners, but with as much connection to real art as Elvis on velvet.

"Tell me about yesterday. Anything unusual?" Pagan encouraged Judith Davis. She was no longer hyperventilating as she had been when we entered the room.

I had felt the warmth Pagan could emanate when he held your hands. I knew the calming effect it had. As I watched him, I found it impossible to tell how much of his concern was real and how much a manipulation for the sake of the case. Lines of pain creased his forehead and there was a depth of great sadness to his demeanor.

I looked over at Castano and his partner Ken Dodd, who stood in the room's entryway, and then across the room to the other RHD detective team, Livia Nelson and Johnny Hawkins. All four of them, along with Officer Donna Clark – a petite, short haired blonde, who was standing next to me – appeared enraptured. I realized my own breathing, like theirs, had slowed down as if we were all afraid to make a noise.

When Pagan had entered the room, Judith Davis had been on a crying jag, gasping for breath. Livia Nelson had been making an effort to speak softly and calmly to her, but without success.

Without hesitating, Pagan had taken two long strides across the teak flooring and wrapped Judith in his arms. There probably wasn't another detective on the planet who would have taken the same action, let alone so smoothly and comfortably. Pagan simply absorbed her into him.

An awkward two minutes followed for everybody with a badge except for Pagan, of course. He simply held Judith as if she were the embodiment of the missing child. He had his head buried in her hair. It was a strangely intimate tableau, yet there was no trace of a sexual component. When the embrace finally unraveled, Judith had stabilized enough for Pagan to guide her to the loveseat, where they both now sat.

She took a deep breath before answering. "We didn't do anything special. We went to the park in the afternoon. When we came home, Unicorn wanted mac 'n' cheese for dinner. We watched the Cartoon Network and I put her to bed around seven."

"Was she upset at all?"

"No. She's a really happy child. She would never wander away." Judith looked up murderously at Livia Nelson.

Pagan shook Judith's hand softly. With his other hand he put a finger lightly on her cheek and gently turned her face and attention back to him. "Of course, she wouldn't," he said. "She would never leave you. Like you would never leave her."

"Never," Judith said, her voice verging on keening again. She was starting to rock and more snot streamed out her nose.

"Tell me what Unicorn liked," Pagan said, centering Judith again.

"She's a Hello Kitty fanatic. Everything has to have Hello Kitty on it or she won't play with it."

"Could someone have led her away if they showed her something with Hello Kitty on it?"

"Maybe...She wouldn't have gone anywhere without her Hello Kitty pillow."

Pagan cut his dark, fathomless, eyes toward me and then returned his attention to Judith. It was a simple look, yet I knew what it communicated.

I used my cane to help push me up from the edge of the leather armchair on which I'd been sitting. I moved quietly and slowly out of the room, tapping Castano on the shoulder as I passed him.

Behind me, I heard Pagan asking, "When did your friend come over?"

"You know Steve was here?" Judith Davis said, surprised but not wary.

In the vestibule, I looked at Castano. "Steve?"

Castano sighed. "There is no denying your partner has a knack for asking the right question in the right way...We didn't know *Steve* was here, but we do now..."

"Where's the child's room?" I asked, getting back on mission.

Castano pointed up a sweeping stairway and started climbing the stairs. I stumped along behind him.

There were six bedrooms and four bathrooms on the second floor. Unicorn's room was at the opposite end from the master bedroom. It was all pink and white frills bought wholesale from an interior design catalogue. Aside from a shelf of plastic, china, and stuffed unicorns, everything else was plastered with the image of a white, cartoon, catlike creature, with a pink bow over its right ear. Its face consisted of two small, round, flat black eyes, a small oval nose, three whiskers exploding out from each cheek, and – disturbingly – no mouth. Hello Kitty.

The Hello Kitty sheets and bedspread were rumpled, but there was no Hello Kitty pillow.

I took in the rest of the room. Certainly no sign of a struggle and no obvious entry and exit point other than the bedroom door. There were windows on the room's two exterior walls. They were both closed and locked. When I opened them to look out, not only were the screens in place and secure, but the house's alarm system sounded a loud chime. I pushed out the screens. There were no obvious ladder scuff marks on the wall, no ladders lying in the unmarred landscaping below.

There were several framed pictures of Unicorn and Judith. Smack Daddy didn't appear in any of the photos. I picked up a five-by-seven studio shot of Unicorn. It was a hard thing to say, but objectively, she was not a pretty child. Not even the professionalism of the studio lights and photographer's obvious use of air brushing could help. Her skin coloring was blotchy, her features wide and round, her black curly hair thin, her eyes dull. She was only six. She had years to blossom like so many of us, but life had already been unkind to her. No doubt her mother loved her, but I wasn't so sure about her father.

I tried to look at the room the way Pagan would. What were the things he saw that others didn't see? It was frustrating to admit, I didn't know. It made me think what it must be like to *be* Pagan – his mind constantly racing ahead of everyone else's.

Since we had arrived, he'd worked the uniformed officer at the door, disarmed and manipulated Smack Daddy, managed to diffuse Dante Castano in order to get him to cooperate on what he thought were his own terms, and was even now running a game on Judith Davis. Pagan was so steeped in what he did, I'm sure he didn't even think about it most of the time. It was second nature to him. I wondered if he was even capable of turning it off.

Considering this, I realized how well he'd also disarmed, manipulated, and managed me. Giving me the tapes of his interrogation of Michael Horner – trusting me by exposing his deepest wounds to me. His knowledge and handling of my own most hidden secret.

Then there was the whole setup of The Hacienda itself. Specifically, I thought of Pagan throwing open the door to the apartment on the second floor, giving me the promise of a home – an invitation to be part of a family.

There was so much more, but – oddly – I thought of my name on a parking bumper.

I wasn't sure how I felt about it all. Was it too much? There had been no time to process. I instinctively wanted to rebel, but to do so would be totally against my own best interests. It was part of the trap Pagan laid for the unaware – he made his will your will. He blinded you with the force of his empathy, and by the time you could see clearly again your entire paradigm had changed.

I heard the buzzing vibration of Castano's phone. He'd been standing in the bedroom doorway watching me, as if expecting me to find the child hiding under the bed. He turned away from me to answer the phone while I took a last scan of the room for non-existent clues.

When I looked back at Castano, I didn't need to be Pagan to instantly read his body language. His shoulders were slumped, the muscles on his face sagging, his eyes hollowing.

"What is it?" I asked, feeding on his anxiety. "Did they find Unicorn? Is she alive?"

Castano shook his head. "Another six year-old child has been reported missing..."

CHAPTER 13

*Good lies need a leavening of truth
to make them palatable.*
- William McIlvanney, The Papers of Troy Veitch

My head was spinning again, but this was quickly becoming the new norm. I followed Castano downstairs. I knew his impulse was to interrupt Pagan, but that was a bad idea. Pagan could do nothing immediately about the second missing child and, from the sounds coming from the living room, he was in full flow – or at least Judith Davis was.

Her voice was a high rising screech verging on the hysterical. "That bastard thinks he can divorce me and pay me nothing..."

I was stumping along behind Castano, barely keeping up, but I managed to reach out and grab his shoulder. He rounded on me with a hiss.

"Down, boy," I said. "Take a deep breath."

Anger flared in his eyes, but then Judith Davis' voice began to register on him.

"Do you think I wanted to look like this?"

I edged past Castano and into the open entry. Judith had her back to me. She was as rigid as if electricity was flowing through her. Pagan was sitting with one knee up on the loveseat, his upper body fully open and turned toward her. His eyes were locked on her, allowing and encouraging her verbal tsunami, but I knew he was aware of me. Not only aware I was there, but also reading my body language, sensing the change the news regarding the second missing child had engendered in my mood.

Judith waved her hands around her face and medically sculpted body. "I did all of this to please him, but nothing I do pleases him." Judith was crying again, mucus streaming from her knife-sculpted nose. "He calls me a stupid bitch, and I must be to put up with him. He even wanted me to take Unicorn to the plastic surgeon because he doesn't like the way she looks. She's six for Hell's sake!"

I thought of the picture in Unicorn's room. My objectivity regarding Smack Daddy was in serious danger of slipping.

Pagan's question went directly to my point. "Do you think Smack Daddy has anything to do with her being gone?"

Judith slumped forward, her head crashing down into Pagan's lap, her hands scrabbling at his clothing. Pagan recovered quickly, but it was the first time I'd ever seen him startled. He tried to get hold of her hands.

"Whatever you want." Judith's muffled voice was saying. "I'll do whatever you want. Please find her."

It was almost funny to see Pagan in an awkward position, but he was my partner. Since every other detective in the room appeared frozen in place by the turn of events, I moved forward, setting my cane down as I slid onto the loveseat directly behind Judith. I wrapped my arms around her, pinning her elbows, and pulled her away from Pagan and back against my chest.

She was sobbing uncontrollably, trying to wiggle away from me. Pagan stood up, allowing Officer Clark to slide into his place and help me. After a few moments, I was able to release Judith, who flopped forward helplessly into Officer Clark's embrace. Clark held her and rocked her as if Judith was a small child.

I recovered my cane and stood to look at Pagan, who appeared to have recovered most of his composure. We moved together out of the room and into the house vestibule.

"What has happened?" Pagan asked.

"Another six year-old has been reported missing. This time in West Valley Division," I said.

Pagan shook his head. "Circumstances?"

"Same as here," I said. "Put to bed last night, gone this morning. No sign of forced entry."

"Any sort of ransom demand?"

"Nothing yet," I said. "Same as here."

"Boy or girl?"

"A boy."

Castano joined us followed by his partner, Dodd. "West Valley Division isn't Hollywood. It has some nice areas, but nothing like the money there is here," he said.

"Where, exactly?" Pagan asked.

"Sherman Oaks. South of Ventura Boulevard, east of Sepulveda."

"I know it," Pagan said. "Old residential area. Still mostly a Jewish enclave. Old money, but not flashy money."

"It can't possibly be connected," I said. "Can it?"

"Kids go missing every day," Pagan said. "But two six year-olds gone from their beds on the same day in the early morning hours...I don't know."

"It's certainly unusual, but they're miles apart," Dodd said.

Pagan looked at Castano. "What do you want to do?"

Castano thought for a moment. He turned and spoke to Nelson and Hawkins who had also joined our group. "Dodd and I will head over to West Valley and see what the hell is going on there. Can you run the scene here?" he asked Nelson. "Have taps been set on the phones in case there's a ransom demand?"

"Covered," Nelson said. She looked at her partner. "You'll coordinate the outside search."

Hawkins nodded. "I'll liaison with the search and rescue teams to check the surrounding trails and canyons. I'll also get something organized to interview whoever is squatting at the house next door."

"Search that place from top to bottom," Castano said. "These are exigent circumstances, so don't wait for a warrant."

Hawkins nodded. He understood the urgency. We all did. The longer this went on, the more the odds of finding Unicorn alive dropped.

"Can you also pull the prior reports and log entries regarding the problems with the house next door?" Pagan asked Hawkins.

"I'll get Lancaster on it back at the office, but it's going to be a ton of material to sift through. The problems up here have been going on for a while."

"We don't even know if anything about this situation is related to those problems," Nelson said.

"Agreed," said Pagan. "But we can't ignore the possibility."

"You staying here or coming with us?" Castano asked Pagan.

Pagan looked at me. I knew what he expected. I turned to Castano.

"Do you mind if we tag along with you?" I asked.

He grunted, then gave me a genuine grin. "You've been learning from your new partner," he said. "You're coming whether I want you to or not, right? You didn't want to appear like you were trampling on my dainty feelings."

I smiled back at him. "Did it work?"

"Yeah," he said, with an amused snort. "It kind of did."

CHAPTER 14

*"If you tell the truth, you don't have
to remember anything."*
- Mark Twain

We were back in the Escalade, traveling north on the Hollywood Freeway. The late morning work traffic was more stop than go as we headed toward West Valley Division and the location of the second missing child.

"We're not going to find Unicorn alive, are we?" I asked. I was looking straight ahead, but my peripheral caught Pagan turn his head toward me and then back ahead.

"Possibly not," he said. "But we both know the alternative may be even worse."

I'd been thinking hard. Trying to feel my way emotionally through what we had heard and seen. "The situation is off," I said.

"Take me through your process."

'Stranger abductions occur," I said. "But we know they

are rare in the grand scheme. Most missings are voluntary unless the victim is under eight. Then the abduction is usually parental or family related. Something like this is almost always an inside job – like you figured shortly after we got there."

Pagan was nodding his head, changing lanes to gain a little advantage as we moved up the Sepulveda Pass. "When Smack Daddy stormed off, the chance he was involved in the disappearance skyrocketed," he said.

"BPEs," I said, echoing what Pagan had told me. "Behavior, personality, environment."

"Exactly. What is predictable human behavior in a situation where your six year-old daughter has gone missing?"

"Normal people don't head off to work like nothing happened – despite how you justified Smack Daddy's actions to Castano."

Pagan grunted. "I had to cool Castano out. I also needed Smack Daddy out of the picture in order to break Judith Davis down."

"Now, there's somebody who displayed normal behavior. She's shattered."

"No purple ribbons attached to her words?"

"You know there weren't," I said. "On one level, she's still playing what she thinks is her expected role. But underneath her subconscious posing, there's real torment."

"What about Smack himself?"

"I saw what you saw. He was consciously acting a part, but nothing he said was a specific lie just bluster – so no purple." It was an odd feeling to talk openly about my ability. I'd hidden it for so long, it gave me an emotional fission to say it out loud.

"How about Unicorn's room?" Pagan asked.

"Nothing. No sign of a struggle. No sign of forced entry."

"So, the most likely scenario is Smack Daddy comes home late, after Judith has taken whatever it is she takes to make her sleep..."

It was my turn to nod. "Smack Daddy takes Unicorn from her bed and...what?"

"Either hands her off to somebody or worse."

"He doesn't have a lot of time for worse."

"Which is why her body will turn up quickly if she's dead."

"You don't think she woke up and wandered off?"

"Do you?"

"No." I sighed. "I don't like the alternatives."

"Me either, but it's those alternatives we deal with most often. Evil is unspectacular and unfortunately all too human"

"So, you're an optimist?"

"A realist," Pagan said.

"I was being sarcastic."

"Sarcastic? Wasn't he a thirteenth century explorer? Went over the Alps with Marco Polo? Attacked the Steppes with Genghis Khan?"

"You're impossible."

Pagan grinned. "So I'm often told."

We had crested the Sepulveda Pass on the freeway and were dropping down into the San Fernando Valley. As Pagan took the Ventura Boulevard off ramp, I spotted a Starbucks.

"Caffeine," I said, and Pagan pulled across the street and into the drive-thru.

After we ordered – with Pagan insisting on adding prepackaged salads to go with the coffee – Pagan took the coffee and food from the barista at the window and handed it all over to me. I took some cash out of my pocket and tried to give it to Pagan, but he shook me off. He pulled forward into a parking spot, leaving the Escalade's engine running with the air conditioner pumping.

"Let's eat this here," he said. "Give Castano a few minutes to get things organized at the scene of the other missing child."

He got out of the Escalade, opened the back, and returned with a tin foil wrapped package. It was filled with cold sliced chicken.

When he saw my questioning look, Pagan explained. "Mrs. Parker keeps the small cooler back there refilled with high protein food. Too many cops survive on burgers, fries, and other fast foods. Plus, I've got to fatten you up for Tanaka."

I shook my head. "So you keep saying. I'm beginning to feel like a Thanksgiving turkey." Still, I took my share of the proffered chicken and didn't argue. Instead, I said, "Tell me about Steve – Judith's mysterious visitor."

"Steve Stuben," Pagan said. He peeled the plastic covering off both salads. Using a fork, he pushed the carrots and sprouts off of his and onto mine. He thrust the plastic container toward me and I dumped the cold chicken on the top.

"The dynamics of the situation made it clear Smack Daddy and Judith weren't the loving married couple," Pagan said.

I took a forkful of salad, realizing I was surprisingly hungry. It had been a long time since I'd experienced an appetite. I didn't dwell on the reasons for the change, I started eating before the urge went away. "So you assumed a boyfriend on the side – Steve Stuben?" I asked, chewing.

Pagan talked through his own mouthful of lettuce and cold chicken. "I can guarantee Smack Daddy isn't faithful to the marriage bed. And with Smack Daddy always making Judith feel like she wasn't good enough…"

"All that plastic surgery," I said.

"Exactly. So, it was no great leap to figure out she had a lover."

"How did you know he'd been there last night?"

"I didn't know. I played the odds."

"You think Steve is a suspect?"

"Second tier maybe," Pagan said. "Can't rule him out. But I don't see a motivation since there is no ransom demand."

"What about the Susan Smith case?" I asked, referring to the 1994 notorious South Carolina faux-kidnapping case. Smith told police she had been carjacked at a rural cross-roads by a black man who drove away with her two young sons still in the car. Over a nine-day period, Smith made dramatic pleas on national television for their rescue and return. Eventually, however, after an intensive investigation, she confessed to letting her car roll into a nearby lake, drowning both boys. She claimed she did it in order to engage in a relationship with a rich local man who did not want children.

"You've watched videos of the press conferences where she was crying her eyes out and asking for her children to be returned. Even without your gift, you must have known she was lying."

"Sure. So did all the detectives standing behind her during the press conference."

"But, leaving your gift out of it, how did you know?"

There was Pagan's favorite question again. I thought about it, picturing the press conference.

Pagan pressed. "What was the one thing missing when Susan Smith was crying? Something Judith Davis had in abundance."

I'm my mind I saw Smith standing behind the blooming garden of press microphones, tears streaming down her face, pleading for the return of her children.

"Snot," I said, finally figuring out why I had instinctively known she was lying beyond the waves of purple streamers attached to her words. "There was no snot, no mucus, to go with the tears. Judith Davis was overwhelmed with mucus. You couldn't understand what she was saying half the time."

"Exactly," Pagan said, as if I was a prized pupil. "When people force out crocodile tears, they only engage the tear ducts in the corners of their eye-sockets. Real tears also engage the tear ducts in the nasal passages, rehydrating dried mucus and producing snot."

"You're saying Judith Davis was telling the truth based on her production of snot?"

"I bet you could give me some crocodile tears right now if you tried real hard, but I bet you can't manufacture me any snot."

I held up a spear of chicken on my plastic fork. "It's like I'm eating lunch with a six year-old. The next thing you're going to tell me is you can tell when somebody is lying because they fart."

"Absolutely!"

"What!"

"Uncontrolled flatulence is one of many responses to anxiety brought on by lying."

"So, if somebody doesn't produce snot and they fart, they're lying."

"You can't rely on any one thing alone, but those two

things are the start of a cluster – and clusters of anxiety driven behavior indicate deception. When you see them, you know you are making progress in an interrogation – specifically if the behaviors weren't present when you established a subject's *truth face*."

"Truth face?"

"Their baseline behavior when they are responding to non-accusatory, low anxiety questions."

I sipped at my coffee and ate some more salad. LAPD considers its training to be the best in the country, if not the world, but I'd never once heard interrogation techniques broken down in this fashion.

"Once you got Judith to tell you about Steve," I said, "cracking her open over her appearance and her relationship with Smack Daddy was easy."

"He's been threatening to divorce her for months, but only served her with actual papers last week," Pagan said.

"I take it this is not going to be an amicable situation?"

"Not a chance. Smack Daddy has all the lawyers and all the money."

"Does he want Unicorn?"

"No. Nor does he want to pay support for her. It might be different if she was a pretty child and he could keep her around like a trophy."

"Ain't love grand," I said.

"When it comes to romantic love, when somebody says, *I love you* – those three little words we all long to hear – it's almost always a lie. They may love their perception of you, but they don't love *you*. When they discover you don't actually fit their version of truth, they see the falseness of their claim. Living a lie is continuing to say you love someone when the detritus of two truths colliding settles."

"And I thought I was a cynic," I said.

"You have any life experience which disproves my statement?"

I shrugged. Pagan was hitting a little too close to home, so I changed the subject. "What's your immediate feeling about this second case being connected?"

Pagan took my empty salad bowl and placed it along with our other trash in a plastic bag he produced from the vehicle's door pocket. He then dumped the bag in an outside trash can. The guy was a regular boy scout when it came to being prepared.

"Unlikely, but I'm reserving judgment," he said putting the Escalade into reverse and backing out of the parking sport. "As we said, two six year-olds going missing in one night, very unusual. We'll figure it out."

As Pagan pulled out of the parking lot, I was struck by his last statement – *we'll figure it out.*

First hunger pangs and now suddenly a sense of fully being part of something. If Pagan was manipulating me, he was very, very good at it, because I didn't even mind.

CHAPTER 15

"A little inaccuracy sometimes saves
tons of explanation."
- Saki: The Square Egg

As we turned onto the surface streets, Pagan's phone rang through the Escalade's hands-free system. Pagan pressed the connect button on the steering wheel. "Hello, Arlo."

"Hi. I got your text. I don't know how quick you wanted this stuff, but I've got some preliminary info on Smack Daddy Davis." Arlo's voice sounded even younger over the speaker phone system.

"Great," Pagan said. There was genuine warmth of approval in his voice. "You're on speaker phone. Randall is with me."

"Hello, Detective Randall," Arlo said.

"Hey, Arlo," I said. "It's okay to call me Jane. I sent you the text from Pagan's phone."

"No wonder I didn't need a decoder ring to figure out the spelling," Arlo said.

I laughed. It was the first time I'd heard anyone poke fun at Pagan. I hadn't thought the emo-looking Arlo had it in him.

"What have you got for us, Arlo?" Pagan said, a feigned growl in his voice.

"It's not much, yet. You know he's filed for divorce?"

"Yes. I have no doubt you got copies of the filing. Anything interesting?"

"He doesn't want custody of their child, but he doesn't want to pay support for her either."

"No surprises there," Pagan said. "Especially if he's still having financial troubles, he wants to get out of the marriage free and clear."

"Then how about this?" Arlo sounded like he had a secret. "I talked to Davenport over at TMZ. They've been following the divorce ruckus and found out Smack Daddy paid for a paternity test."

"He wanted to prove Unicorn wasn't his? What a prick," I said.

"It gets better," Arlo says. "Turns out Unicorn wasn't related to the male DNA sample Smack Daddy provided for himself."

"So Smack Daddy isn't the daddy? He's off the hook?" Pagan said.

"Not exactly," Arlo said.

"Spill it," Pagan was getting short.

"Turns out the male sample Smack Daddy provided wasn't his," Arlo said.

"How did they know?" I asked before Pagan could jump in.

"The sample Smack Daddy provided for himself was from a Caucasian male not a black male."

Pagan and I looked at each other and then burst out laughing.

"The guy is not a freaking rocket scientist is he?" I said.

"Bad guys rarely are," Pagan said, then became serious. "That's one of the reasons why we're going to nail him if he did anything to his little girl."

Arlo jumped back in. "Smack Daddy tried to pay off the lab to keep his screw-up quiet, but one of the technicians saw a fast way to make some bucks and called Davenport at TMZ. Apparently, they've done business before."

"How come they haven't run with the story?" Pagan asked.

"Davenport says they're holding it back pending a full smear job. Smack Daddy has a bunch of skeletons in his closet about to come out and haunt him."

"Such as?"

"Mostly money stuff, dope, old gang connections from back in the day. He's made a lot of bad decisions."

"Have those bad decisions affected Smack Records?"

"I've got some preliminary stuff, but it looks like they were in big trouble up to a year ago when Smack Daddy signed a hip-hop star called Changeling, who went viral on the web."

"Never heard of him," Pagan said.

"Like I'm surprised," Arlo retorted. "Music didn't stop with jazz."

"I'm aware of Changeling, but didn't know he was a Smack Records artist," I said.

"He's not huge in the mainstream yet, but Smack Daddy was able to financially leverage Changeling's earning potential to keep Smack Records afloat," Arlo said.

"I don't know yet if that leverage money is going to Changeling, directly into Smack Daddy's pocket, or simply digging the business out of debt."

Pagan made a face like something smelled wrong. "No way Smack Daddy is going to be worried about paying off debts. He'll be too busy hiding assets from Judith. What about this Changeling character?"

"Surprisingly, there is not much on him outside his YouTube videos. He doesn't seem to be making the scene at the clubs or running around town with an entourage. Smack Daddy appears to be keeping him under wraps, building anticipation for an upcoming CD release. Smack Records has produced an EP of tracks – remakes actually of the viral YouTube songs. They've been getting a lot of streaming play, which promises good things for a full CD."

"An EP?" Pagan asked.

"Short for *extended play*," Arlo said. "Think of it as a musical download with more music than a single, but too short to qualify as a full studio release."

"And this EP is selling enough downloads to pull Smack Records out of a hole?" Pagan asked.

"Big time. If handled correctly, an artist like Changeling could make everybody involved rich and famous."

"It's still a longshot," I said. "Most of this stuff plays to a fickle audience."

"Agreed," Arlo said. "But from what I can gather on the music blogs and boards, Changeling has hit a chord and people are hungry for product. Smack Daddy has to play it right, but he could be onto the real deal."

"Can you keep digging?" Pagan asked.

"Will do."

"Thanks, Arlo. Stay available." Pagan hit the disconnect switch.

I felt energized. I couldn't wait to get a crack at Smack Daddy. "Decisions determine destiny," I said.

"Save it for a bumper sticker," Pagan said, not unkindly. "First, we've got to handle this new situation."

There was big money in the San Fernando Valley suburb of Sherman Oaks, but it was a different sort of money than in the Hollywood Hills. There were no jewelry-hung drug dealers or new wave movie directors clamoring to drive the real estate prices up. With its proximity to the businesses and restaurants along Ventura Boulevard and its quick access to several busy freeways, Sherman Oaks was a bastion of established family affluence. This was ancient money, dirty land deal money, dirty water rights money, money with secrets as old as the city itself.

Along with two city parks and a senior center, the neighborhood included eight public schools, seven private schools, and seven synagogues. In the heart of the ethnically diverse San Fernando Valley, over eighty percent of Sherman Oaks' residents were politically incorrect by being non-Hispanic whites.

The house on Sutton Street near Firmament was a solid two-story piece of 1950's Americana, a later arrival to the area. At first glance, the house wasn't overly large, but it had been painted recently. The roof was in good condition and the windows sparkled. A weeping willow dominated the landscaped and manicured front yard.

Castano and Dodd's unmarked brown Crown Vic was parked at the curb behind two black-and-whites with the new low profile light bars. In the driveway was a ten year-old Mercedes parked next to a spotless black hearse.

I glanced at Pagan, who'd stopped the Escalade smoothly next to the curb. "A hearse?" I asked.

Pagan tilted his head in a gesture I took to mean, *your guess is as good as mine.*

"How do you want to play this?" I asked.

"How do you?"

I looked at Pagan. He had turned off the ignition and had turned in his seat to face me.

"You've always done your own heavy lifting," Pagan said. "We're partners. You're up."

I felt something akin to electricity run up my spine, both hot and cold at the same time. I'd been on this job for twelve years – a lifetime – and I'd rarely had a male partner who didn't try to run roughshod over me. Those who didn't were lazy backstabbers who always found a way to grab the credit for your hard work. It was a constant battle.

I looked hard into Pagan's face. His dark eyes were each the center of a storm. I started to duck my head, but suddenly Pagan laid a gentle finger under my chin.

"I know all of this is sudden," he said. "But trust me, you've got this and I've got you. I'm your partner. I won't let you down." He slowly drew his hand back, still holding my eyes with his.

I took a deep breath. "Let's see what Castano has and go from there?"

Pagan nodded and the moment passed.

Police work relies on routine. Asking questions, sorting out the truth from the lies, asking more questions. We use *inductive* reasoning, conclusions drawn from observations of facts, to arrive at a solution fitting all of the evidence. It's the complete opposite of detectives on television and in novels, who use Sherlock Holmes style *deductive* reasoning

– arriving at a specific conclusion from a general assumption.

In real world law enforcement, *inductive* reasoning involves relying on facts – and only facts – until only one conclusion is possible.

Now was the time to gather facts.

CHAPTER 16

"Man is least himself when he talks in his own person. Give him a mask, and he will tell you the truth."
- Oscar Wilde

Pagan stayed a step behind me as we approached the residence's open front door. Seeing us coming, the uniformed officer at the door turned and spoke to someone inside. A moment later Castano appeared and walked toward us.

"It's bizarre in there," Castano said, without qualification. "This family has a majorly screwed up gene pool."

Pagan and I stood waiting, but he didn't expand.

Castano looked at his notebook. "The missing boy, Gerrard Martin, is a six year-old with special needs. Moderate to severe autism."

"Capable of wandering off by himself?" I asked.

Castano shook his head. "Not according to his mother. He would have to have been taken. Most probably while he was asleep or he would have screamed, which seems to be the only form of communicating he has."

"Who is in the house?"

"Single mother, Sophie Martin – apparently never married to the father, who split when Gerrard was born."

"The world is full of butt hairs," Pagan said.

I glanced at him, but he was focused on the exterior of the house.

"Agreed," Castano said, and then continued his briefing. "The house belongs to Harvey Martin, Sophie's uncle. He and another uncle own the Martin Mortuaries. Harvey operates the closest facility here on Ventura Boulevard. The other uncle, David Martin, operates their facility in Hollywood."

"That explains the hearse," I said. "Anyone else?"

Castano looked at his notebook again. "Sophie's older brother, Chadwick, but there's something wrong with him too."

"Autism?" Pagan asked.

"Nah, something else. Chad works with his uncle at the mortuary, but you can look at him and know he's not all there."

"Are your sensitivity classes up to date?" I had to ask.

"What?" Castano looked confused. Maybe there was something wrong with him too and I was the one being insensitive.

I felt Pagan's hand on the small of my back, gently pushing me forward. "Be kind, Randall. Be kind," he whispered close to my ear.

The inside of the house was much like the outside – solidly respectable, well-cared for, and completely unimaginative. Heavy dark wood covered in dark colored fabrics sat where it had sat for years. An open, leather bound, family

Bible held pride of place on its own podium, while Rock-
well knockoffs and collectors' plates out of *TV Guide* adver-
tisements clustered or hung in small groupings, all looking
terrified of dust.

Claw-footed chairs around a living room table were
never moved. Slightly less substantial oak chairs – naturally
matching the oak kitchen table – ventured far enough out
for somebody to sit down before being pushed precisely
back into place.

The trio waiting for us in the living room seemed
blended into the surroundings. Standing next to an over-
stuffed couch covered by a burgundy tapestry, Harvey
Martin would have dominated under most circumstances.
He was a crow of a man in an old fashioned black suit,
which he wore like a second skin. His tan face was filled
with fine sun lines cracking like a dried mud flat.

The man/boy next to Harvey was clearly Chad. Somewhere in his early twenties, his facial features laid claim to
the Down syndrome Castano had callously described as *not
all there*. Dressed in a suit similar to his uncle's, it hung on
him in bags and pokes, as if nobody had felt he was worth
the cost of a tailor. He looked agitated and on the verge
of tears.

I tipped my head almost imperceptibly, letting Pagan off
the leash. He practically bounded forward like a greyhound
after a rabbit.

"Chadwick?" Pagan said, holding out a hand, but not
moving in to touch the target of his attention.

"Yes." The inflection on the word was like that of a startled bird.

"I'm Ray. It's nice to meet you."

The non-threatening warmth in Pagan's words and
manner emanated from his whole body. The transformation

of Chad's emotions was clear on his face, moving from agitation to happiness like the flipping of a channel. He took Pagan's proffered hand and shook it vigorously.

I was startled to catch a glimpse of Pagan's facial expression, which had taken on a mirror-like quality – reflecting Chad back at Chad. Gently, Pagan guided him away from the grouping, best friends off to share an adventure.

Harvey Martin watched with distain, dismissing Pagan as being of the same lack of worth in his mind as Chad. He then turned his judgmental eyes on me, but I refused to be captured by them, turning my attention instead to Sophie Martin.

Sitting at the opposite end of the couch from where Harvey Martin was standing, Sophie was a woman worn to a nub. She wore skinny jeans and a yellow-checked blouse, which emphasized the frailty of her limbs. Unlike the sculpted and injected visage of Judith Davis, this woman was worn down like a riverbank, eroded by the relentless flow of painful emotions and difficult life circumstances.

Her eyes were red, but more from anger than tears. Before I could even introduce myself, she exploded.

"I hate autism! I hate it! I hate it!" Rage flowed out of her like lava. She put a boney hand like a tilted salute against her head at eyebrow level. She flung herself against the back of the couch, rocked forward, and then threw herself back again.

"Get hold of yourself, Sophie." Harvey Martin's voice was crisp, filled with an undertaker's complete lack of emotion. I wondered if it was so practiced as to now be his natural tone. Did it ever waver? Did it ever display excitement or pain, or was it permanently stuck in neutral?

"It's quite all right, Mr. Martin," I started.

"No. It's not," he said, correcting and dismissing me at

the same time. "Sophie has one job to do – take care of Gerrard – but she is incapable of even handling that responsibility. The boy has simply wandered off. All this fuss is for nothing."

Sophie dropped her hand and shot to her feet. "He didn't wander off! He is incapable of wandering off. He's got fuc..."

"Language!" Harvey Martin roared. "This is a house of God. There will be no blasphemy. Do you hear me?"

Sophie looked as if she'd been drenched by a bucket of cold water.

I rapped my cane on the hardwood floor, making my own exclamation. "Mr. Martin, would you please show Detective Castano Chad's room and allow him to look around?"

"A waste of more time," Martin said, looking intractable. However, he moved away without further argument.

Castano knew his role and obediently followed Martin's retreating back.

I turned back to Sophie, who had collapsed into a sitting position again on the couch and put her hand back up to cover her eyes.

"I knew there was something wrong," she said.

"What do you mean?"

"Somebody has been watching the house."

"How do you know?"

"I heard him in the backyard one night last week."

"Did you call the police?"

"Yes, but they found nothing. Uncle Martin told them it was all in my imagination."

"Was it only the one time?"

"No. There were two prior times, and the next day, I

came back from taking Gerrard for his checkup, and I found the backdoor open."

"A burglary?"

"No. Nothing was gone, but I knew I closed and locked the backdoor before we left. It had been pushed in."

"Did you call the police again?"

"Yes. They took a vandalism report because nothing had been taken."

"And you think it might have something to do with Gerrard going missing?"

Sophie sighed. "I don't know," she said. She was silent for a moment then asked, "What happened to your leg?"

If the tension of the situation hadn't been so high, I might have laughed at the non-sequitur transition. Instead, I sat down on the couch myself, placed my cane across my knees, and answered.

"I foolishly stood in front of a bullet. A real one," I said. "But I doubt its effects are much different than the metaphorical bullet you've been hit with."

Sophie began to cry. Sobs racking her body. I sighed inwardly. My days, like those of most detectives, are filled with tears and pain. Sometimes, it's hard to absorb it all. I didn't want to comfort Sophie. Every fiber in my body didn't want to open up to receive her pain, but I knew what Pagan would expect.

I pushed reluctance aside, and pulled Sophie into an awkward, yet genuine embrace, which caused my cane to fall to the floor with a clatter.

Against my chest, I heard Sophie say, "It is happening all over again, isn't it?"

"What's happening again?" I asked.

"Maybe tomorrow, he'll be run over also and die. I want him to die!"

"Sophie, what are you talking about? Why would Gerrard get run over?"

Almost violently pushed herself away from me. "Not Gerrard!"

I was confused. "Then who?"

"That bastard who calls himself my uncle."

Sophie started crying again. I didn't want to hug her, so I simply took her hands in mine.

"Tell me what you mean by *it is happening again*. Has Gerrard gone missing before?"

Sophie gulped, got control of herself. "Not Gerrard. Connor."

"Conner?"

Sophie took her hands back and pulled a tissue out of the pocket of her jeans. "Connor was our oldest brother. My parents had trouble conceiving, so they adopted Connor when he was an infant. Then suddenly my mother found herself pregnant with me and, a year later, Chad." Sophie twisted the tissue through her fingers.

"One night, ten years ago, Connor disappeared from our house. The next day, our father, Jack, was killed in a hit and run accident outside the first of the family mortuaries."

"What happened to Connor?"

Sophie shook her head. "He was never found. He was ten years old and he was just gone. I think in some ways my mother was glad."

"What do you mean?"

"Even as young as I was, I knew he wasn't the child my parents wanted when they adopted him. Today, we would realize his birth mother probably had a drug or alcohol addiction when she gave birth."

"What make you think so?"

"Connor always took care of Chad and I, but otherwise

he was a wild child...constantly in a battle of wills with my father, who frankly made Uncle Harvey seem like a liberal saint."

"And your mother?"

"Always sick and too weak willed to stand up to my father. A lot like me."

I paused as the portent of Sophie's statement settled in the atmosphere like a blanket landing on a bed of nails.

When the moment passed, I asked, "Did they find out who ran over your father?"

"It was all so long ago," Sophie said, seeming to pull herself together. "They found the car that hit him. It was still there in the mortuary parking lot pinning my father between it and his own car. It had been reported stolen. They said it must have been some kid on a joy ride, high on drugs."

"That was it?"

Sophie shrugged.

"Why do you think Gerrard going missing means whatever it was is happening again?"

"Connor wouldn't have left us. Chad shared a room with him. He slept through whatever happened. He's always said the *wee folk* took Connor."

"*Wee folk?*"

"Irish fairies. It's the only explanation Chad can wrap his head around. Connor always read to him from *Tales of the Wee Folk* before they went to bed. The fairies fascinated Chad and the stories would help him sleep. Like Connor wouldn't leave us, Gerrard didn't go missing. He would have to be taken. I sleep in the room right next door with the doors open. Gerrard wears a weighted vest at night, which comforts him. There's a movement monitor right next to his bed. It alerts if Gerrard has a night seizure or if the bed is empty. Gerrard can't get up by himself. He can't go to the bathroom by himself. He can't eat by himself. You have to understand, Gerrard's autism is completely debilitating. He needs constant care. He didn't just wander off. He won't survive twenty-four hours if somebody doesn't know how to take care of him."

"What about his other caretakers?" I asked.

"There are no other caretakers. Only me. In case you hadn't noticed, Uncle Harvey has made it abundantly clear – Gerrard is my responsibility. It's my fault for having sex outside of marriage. I sinned and Gerrard is my punishment."

"That isn't true," I said. I regretted the words the second they slipped over my lips.

"Maybe not in your world," Sophie said, crossing her arms. "But in my world it is."

"What about your mother or your aunt – Mr. Martin's wife?"

"Ha!" Sophie sort of exploded. "My mother died of cancer the year after Connor disappeared. My uncle had two wives and both ran screaming from the marriage quicker than a one term senator."

"So there's nobody else to help you take care of Gerrard?"

"Chad does what he can, but he has his own challenges with DS. It takes almost everything he has to keep up with his Bible lessons and Uncle Martin's odd jobs."

"Your other uncle?"

"Uncle David keeps clear. The mortuaries are connected in name only. On paper, they are separate businesses."

"Did your father have a separate mortuary facility?"

"Yes. The three brothers cooperated only by branding

themselves to a reputation. Otherwise, they could never work together. I know now that having the three separate branches helped with buying in bulk and other business saving opportunities, but beyond those practices everyone went their separate ways."

"Was there competition between the brothers?"

"Not on the surface, but even now Uncle Harvey and Uncle David have an underlying dislike of each other."

"Who took over your father's branch of the mortuary?"

"I think they fought over who would run it. Eventually, they sold it to the McDowells, the Irish couple who lived on the premises as caretakers, and split the profit."

"Did any of the money go to you and Chad or your mother?"

"Are you kidding? My mother was already dead by the time it was sold and Uncle Harvey was our guardian. He would never stand for me having any money of my own."

"What do you think happened last night?" I asked, changing the subject.

"I don't know. Gerrard went down early. He'd had a good couple of days. No seizures. He'd been as loving as he gets. He went off to sleep no problems."

"How much later did you go to bed?"

"As soon as he was down. Even on his good days, Gerrard is a handful. I have to sleep when he sleeps."

"And you didn't hear anything, you didn't wake up at any time?"

"Not once. I was a little amazed to wake up of my own accord this morning at five-thirty. It doesn't happen often. I got dressed and went to get Gerrard, but he was gone."

"What about the weight vest and the monitor?"

"The vest was gone. I don't know what happened to the monitor. It never went off."

"Anything else missing? Clothes or toys?"

Sophie shook her head. "He couldn't get out. He couldn't get out..."

Cops hear declarative sentences all the time...*He couldn't have...She wouldn't have...He didn't...She'd never...* You often heard it from the families of suicide victims, refusing to accept the responsibility and perceived shame of their loved one dying by their own hand. They all want it to be an accident, or like they see on TV where every suicide is a cover-up for murder. It is the natural, knee-jerk reaction of those affected by circumstances they don't want to accept. Despite what Sophie thought, the fact was, Gerrard was gone.

Like most individuals in a heightened state of emotion, Sophie was sensitive to the emotions of those around them. She immediately picked up on the thoughts running through my head.

"You're wrong," she said. "You'll see. It's happening again." Defiance settled on her face like a thick fog.

I felt somehow untethered. There was nothing here yet to grab onto to provide an explanation.

At the moment, the return of the *wee folk* was the only working theory we had.

CHAPTER 17

"As one knows the poet by his fine music, so one can recognize the liar by his rich rhythmic utterance, and in neither case will the casual inspiration of the moment suffice. Here, as elsewhere, practice must precede perfection."
- Oscar Wilde: The Decay of Dying

We tried to sort it all out in a powwow back at the RHD offices.

Pagan had surprised me when we left patrol officers and a uniformed sergeant in charge at the Martin residence. He flipped me the keys to the Escalade, proceeding to the passenger side himself. After setting our destination as PAB, the Police Administration Building, he told me he had to shut his eyes for a few minutes. Without further ado, he reclined the seat and to all appearances dropped immediately off to sleep.

I would come to find this was not unusual behavior. Turns out Pagan rarely slept more than two or three hours at night, relying on two thirty minute power naps during the day to keep him going. I would eventually get to know his rhythms, to know when he was running out of gas and needed either food or sleep, but this first time caught me off guard.

I was full of questions and a need for more information. I wanted to talk about all that had happened. I needed to find out what Pagan had learned from Chad, needed to bounce ideas off him, but that was hard to do with him virtually snoring next to me.

I felt like a spurned lover. I was aroused and he'd rolled over to his side of the bed.

I was being stupid.

I was angry.

He didn't make this being a *wolf* thing easy.

Still being a neophyte acolyte, I didn't realize I was in the midst of an unspoken lesson – things Pagan respected you enough not to explain.

We all rush into things. We overload on information. We don't take time to think and consider – to even remember – all of the little things we've seen and heard before we jump to conclusions. He was teaching me the difference between a good interrogator and a great interrogator – the ability to process and understand nuance.

Pagan's naps were his time to let his subconscious cogitate. He always woke up in a good mood and full of energy. It had to be learned behavior. If somebody woke me up after twenty or thirty minutes, I'd be a volatile crank bucket ready to snap at anyone unfortunate enough to cross my path. I had to find my own way to accomplish subconscious reflection.

That was the thing about being mentored by Pagan, he always gave you space to find your own way. He didn't expect, or even want, you to do things his way. He wanted you to find and develop the way best suited to your specific personal strengths and personality.

Pagan's wolves were not at all cookie-cutter versions of him. They varied wildly in style and temperament, connected only through the excellence they demanded of themselves and their loyalty to Pagan. They were all in his pack, but each was equally dangerous alone.

We had gathered in the RHD conference room. Coffee cups and energy drinks abounded. Captain Carl North was overseeing the briefing. He was a competent, slim, quiet spoken man given to three-piece pinstripe suits, expensive ties, and – oddly – black patent leather shoes. Nobody ever mentioned the dead raccoon of a hair-piece he wore on his head, which somehow never sat straight.

Livia Nelson and Johnny Hawkins had come in from Smack Daddy's residence in the Hollywood Hills.

"Patrol and Sheriff's Search and Rescue are still at the scene, but there's nothing further. No ransom demand. No sign of the child," Livia said. She was a black woman in her early forties. Experienced and hardened by it. Twice divorced. Her two middle-schoolers were cared for by their grandmother, who lived with them.

"What about the house next door?" Captain North asked.

Johnny Hawkins spoke up. A college basketball star not quite good enough to play in the NBA, he'd spent a couple of years playing in Italy before coming home and on *the job*. Word was he was angling to be his partner's third Mr. Nelson – a tough assignment by anybody's standard. "An expensive dump. We cleared the residence, rousted a half-dozen meth heads."

"Maybe they took the kid to sell her or some other meth-addled scheme. Maybe they killed her by accident." This was from Castano who hated meth heads.

"No way," said Hawkins. "There's not enough brain cells left in this bunch of burnouts to keep their story straight if they were lying. None of them had a record for anything beyond petty theft, forgery, vehicle burglary, or possession. Anyway, we tore the place apart, what was left of it. We even dredged the scum in the pool out back. We thought we had something there, but it was only a dead dog."

Ken Dodd, Castano's partner, made a look of distaste. "This freaking job gets more pathetic every day."

I remembered he was very active in a greyhound rescue project. He was probably more upset by the dead dog than the missing child, but that was me being unkind.

"What's the score with the other missing?" North asked.

The other missing. None of us had yet mentioned the name of either child. You kept things at a distance. You didn't let it get personal. You never promised the family you would find a missing child, or promise to get the guy that took them. You did the best job you could at the time, but that still meant sometimes you didn't *find 'em* or *get 'em.*

"Same deal as the Hollywood case," said Castano. "Zip. No ransom and no evidence. The batteries in the motion monitor in the missing's room must have been dead. No sign of forced entry."

"Anything substantial to tie these two cases together?"

We all looked at each other, except for Pagan who was staring into space.

"Ray?" North prompted.

Pagan reeled his mind back into his body and turned a flat gaze on Captain North. "They are connected," he said.

"Okay...How? Why?"

Pagan rubbed his chin. "Pattern of behavior. On the surface we have two unconnected missing six year-olds, from two different parts of the city, occurring in the same relative timeframe. If that was all we had, I'd say they were separate incidents, but the fact we have *zip* on both cases, as Castano so elegantly stated, makes them feel the same to me."

"I know better than to disregard your gut feelings, but is there anything solid?"

Pagan sighed. "Only negatives – no ransom, no forced entry, no prior history of either child wandering off, and no specific clues." He flicked his eyes over to Castano. "Did you bring in the baby movement monitor from Gerrard's room?"

Pagan would be the only one of us to use specific names for the missing children. I figured he did it on purpose, knowing it would focus everyone.

Castano dug into a brown paper bag next to his chair, pulling out the plastic movement monitor. He handed it to Pagan.

Pagan took the unit. He tried to turn it on, but nothing happened.

"Batteries are dead," Castano said. "There aren't a lot of electrical plugs in those older homes, so there wasn't one close enough to the bed to use. It's supposed to have an alarm when the batteries are getting weak, but it must have malfunctioned."

Pagan turned the unit over and opened the battery box. He popped out six double-A batteries. He looked at each of them. He selected one and held it up to the light. With everyone watching him, Pagan used a fingernail to peel a transparent piece of tape off the negative end of the battery. "Not dead," he said. "Silenced."

The malevolence of the act hit everyone. This was not a random crime of opportunity. Garrard wasn't missing. He'd been taken. Targeted.

"Why?" North asked, voicing the question in everyone's head. "What's the motive?"

There were clearly bad motives for kids being taken, but these two cases didn't feel sexual. There were far easier ways, with less logistical problems, to victimize children for sexual purposes than kidnapping them from their rooms. Also, neither of these victims fit the profile of children taken as part of human trafficking rings. Particularly Gerrard.

We were all experienced enough to know it wasn't possible to completely rule out somebody with a specific fetish involving a special needs child or an unattractive, racially specific child. However, if Pagan was right and the two cases were connected, then that particular motivation didn't make sense – the suspect would have taken one or the other, not both.

So, that left, what? Money? No ransom demand appeared to rule it out as a motive.

Revenge? Against who? For what?

The moment was broken when Detective Chris Lancaster, the unit's administrative whiz, entered the room holding a raft of papers. "I've got the scans of the reports from ten years ago when Connor Martin went missing. Also the hit and run report on Jack Martin, Connor's father." Lancaster handed copies all around. "I'm getting someone to dig the originals out of the archives, so there may be more than what records scanned to the computers."

This was a common problem. Scanned reports were okay in most cases, but *chaos law* determined the more important the reports you want, the more chance of missing pages or unscanned follow-up reports. Getting the originals was a pain, but necessary.

Pagan sped his way through his copies of the scanned reports and placed them on the table in front of him. "Apparently," he said, "ten years ago, nobody thought to connect the missing kid to his father being the victim of a hit and run."

"Why would they?" Castano asked. "The reports would have been handled by completely different units. Juvenile would have handled the missing and traffic would have handled the hit and run."

"What makes you think they are even related now?" Livia Nelson asked.

Pagan didn't bother to answer her, and nobody else jumped into the breach.

Cases have weight. Some cases are straightforward, lightweight, run-of-the-mill. Other cases are tangled masses of barbed wire, painful to dissect, yet still resolvable. Some cases are brick wall, dead end, slams to the solar plexus, filled with frustration – unsolvable, but without resonance.

Then there are the *spook cases* – those rare occurrences where you get drawn in despite yourself chasing wisps of clues. Cases where you can see tendrils of smoke stretching across the years to affect the present, yet you can't grasp a single solid lead. Cases you must solve or they will haunt you forever.

Pagan swiveled his chair and tapped some keys on a computer set on a stand behind him. The screen at the front of the room suddenly glowed with the frozen image of Chad Martin's flat facial features – small nose, upturned eyes with small skin folds at the corners, tiny ears, and the soft tip of his over-large tongue protruding between his lips.

Pagan had used a lapel camera to record his interview with Chad and had cued the feed to what he considered the appropriate moment.

"The fairies would come into our room at night," Chad said, his voice low and serious.

"The room you shared with Connor?"

"Yes."

You were nine and Connor was ten?"

"Yes."

"How did you know they were fairies?" Pagan's voice was a soft lullaby, no judgment, no disbelief.

"Connor told me."

"Like in the stories he read to you?"

"Yes." Chad turned and walked over to a shelf. He took down a book and handed it to Pagan with what appeared to be reverence. "Fairies do bad things. They don't like humans."

Pagan held the book up in front of his lapel camera. The title Tales and Legends of Ireland ran in ornate gold script across a picture of wizened male fairy spiriting away a baby. This wasn't a book about Tinkerbell. These stories would be much darker, more the original Brothers Grimm than Disney happiness.

"What did the fairies do to you?"

There was a pause as Chad clearly struggled with this question.

In the squad room, Pagan glanced over at me. I knew he was looking for confirmation of what he already knew. I nodded my head, letting him know I was in agreement with him. I could see no purple streamers attached to Chad's words. There were pastel greens, blues, and yellows, even an interesting touch of orange, but not a trace of purple. Chad was telling the truth – the truth as he knew it.

On the video feed, Pagan didn't prompt Chad. He simply waited, letting silence build.

"He didn't like it," Chad said finally, not specifically answering the question.

"Connor didn't like what the fairies did to you?"

"Not to me," Chad said, his face clearly showing his distress. "To him. Connor told me when the fairies came, I had to roll over and look at the wall. He told me the fairies would take me if I looked, but I could still hear them pinching him."

"Pinching?"

"Connor said they pinched him and it hurt, but not too bad. I didn't like it. I was scared, but Connor said it was okay. He said the fairies wouldn't pinch me or take me if I was looking at the wall."

Pagan stayed silent, letting the moment stretch.

"Then one night the fairies came, and in the morning Conner was gone...and then the fairies ran Papa down when he tried to get Connor back."

"How do you know that's what happened?"

Chad looked at Pagan plaintively, as if the answer was obvious. "I told Uncle Harvey about the fairies taking Connor, but he said there were no such thing as fairies. He said it was God who took Connor and Papa because they had been bad. But Connor said it was fairies." Chad's emotions were etched deep into the softness of his face. "God wouldn't take Connor for being bad. Connor was good. He protected me from the fairies. Uncle Harvey was wrong!"

Pagan stopped the video feed with the tap of a button.

Everyone in the room was silenced by Chad's raw emotion and innocence.

Then Castano stamped his size thirteens into the moment. "Hope you've got some teeny-tiny handcuffs available if you're going fairy hunting..."

CHAPTER 18

*"I'm not upset that you lied to me,
I'm upset that from now on
I can't believe you."*
- Friedrich Nietzsche

The Smack Records building was on a side street off Sunset Boulevard, a couple of blocks away from the once renowned *Whiskey a Go Go* nightclub in West Hollywood. The distinction between Hollywood and West Hollywood was far more cultural than geographic. *We Ho* is upscale, hip, and gay-centric. *The Viper Room* and *The Roxy*, along with the *Whisky*, regularly throbbed with nightlife.

Next door, Hollywood's stars were only on the sidewalk. A seedy tourist mecca populated by meth heads in character costumes outside Grauman's Chinese Theater, Hollywood is a worn dowager long past her prime.

We Ho had once been part of the unincorporated areas

of Los Angeles County. It's bordered by the Los Angeles City areas of Hollywood and Fairfax on two sides and the city of Beverly Hills on another. In 1984, *We Ho* became its own incorporated city and is patrolled by the Los Angeles Sheriff's Office. There has been more than one incident when a body found on one side of the boundary between the LAPD and the LASO has miraculously risen from the dead long enough to deposit itself in the other department's jurisdiction – all depending on which department arrived on the scene first.

Pagan and I had left Castano and Dodd working point on the two current cases while Nelson and Hawkins were digging into the missing child – Connor – and hit and run from fifteen years earlier. The foursome were good detectives and would find what there was to find and handle anything that came up.

Pagan believed we were best suited to staying with our mandate as interrogators, and Smack Daddy was squarely in our sights. Pagan had been anxious to hustle out of the office, but I remembered, Pagan had agreed to meet Smack Daddy at two o'clock at Smack Records. There was plenty of time to get there, but Pagan was surging with urgency.

"Predictable human behavior, Randall," Pagan said. "Think about it. He didn't want to talk to the cops at his residence, and he won't want to talk to us at his office. If we get there at two, he'll be long gone."

"What makes you think he's going to cooperate even if we do catch up with him?"

"What is the most important thing in Smack Daddy's world?" Pagan asked.

"Smack Daddy," I answered immediately.

"So, if we make talking to us a priority to keep his reputation intact..."

I nodded. "He'll talk as long as he believes it's in his best interest..."

Pagan smiled. "And I'm very good at making people believe talking to me is in their best interest."

"Even when it isn't?" I couldn't resist the jibe.

"Especially when it isn't," Pagan said.

I actually felt as if I was vibrating internally. Pagan had insisted on doing a lot of research before we left PAB. I'd never known anyone prepare for an interrogation like he did. Most cops barely take the time to read a crime report before they've formed an opinion based on prior experience, stereotypes, and personal prejudices and jump right in to asking questions.

Pagan, on the other hand, took what he called a *tactical response* to interview and interrogation, which he equated to being no different than responding to a *hot* radio call.

By the time Pagan had finished pushing Chris Lancaster for information coaxed from his computer and administrative resources, we had more information on Smack Daddy and Smack Records than I figured we would ever need. However, when you were working with Pagan, you never knew what was going to end up being relevant.

Two years earlier Smack Daddy and Smack Records had been barely hanging on. The IRS was coming down on both Smack Daddy and the business. There had been a series of bad financial decisions, verging on the disastrous. There were liens against the house in Hollywood and the building from which Smack Records operated.

Then Smack Records discovered Changeling. More specifically, Smack Records beat every other hip-hop and rap label to get Changeling signed after he went viral via YouTube videos.

Against the promise of future success, Smack Daddy

was able to get more financial backing – cash infusions to keep his company afloat while getting Changeling set to move from video cult favorite to overnight mainstream star. Smack Daddy was apparently playing it cagey, releasing streaming remixes of the viral YouTube tracks, which hit the *urban* and *hip-hop* Billboard charts with a flood of digital downloads.

Other than his real name, Benny White, info about Changeling was very sketchy. He hadn't made any public appearances, nor were there any interviews to be found online. There appeared to be a blanket of secrecy surrounding him orchestrated by Smack Daddy who, like all the snake oil salesmen before him, promised great things to be delivered. Smack Daddy was an expert huckster and Changeling was another product he had to sell.

With the lack of information on Changeling, Pagan went so far as to make me sit down with him to watch a number of Changeling's viral videos.

The ethnically blended Changeling was slight of build with a full head of wild, black dreads – a Rasta version of Michael Jackson. His looks were ethereal, matching the way his body swayed and moved to his music. His phrasing and riffs were catchy, but the music and lyrics were edgy, filled with longing and suppressed pain.

The videos were stripped down, amateur affairs. The backdrop appeared to be a marble wall, the lighting harsh. A fixed camera focused directly on Changeling's face and guitar covered torso. As each song started, Changeling could be seen adjusting a drum machine and a playback keyboard, which filled in the background behind his guitar playing with a strange eerie echo.

However, even with the basic, one man production

values, it was clear Changeling had whatever it was stars have – the special something making it impossible to take your eyes off him. His rhythm was hypnotic, his dusky features as hard as diamonds, his surprisingly blue eyes accentuated by deep pink scars across his cheekbones. His straggly dreads swished around his face with his movements, his voice a plaintive wail.

I felt old listening to his music. I felt no connection to it or to the generation who revered it. It was urban, but I wasn't sophisticated enough to say more.

Watching the YouTube video, Pagan said one word to himself in a half whisper. "Fairies."

I looked at the video playing on the computer monitor. Even though Changeling was slight and odd, he did not give off any kind of homosexual vibe. I also knew Pagan wasn't the type to use racial or sexist slurs.

Before I could ask what he meant, he was up and moving.

"Keys, Randall," he demanded. I grabbed them from the desk where I'd placed them and tossed them to him.

As I clomped after him with my cane, I realized I hadn't taken a pain pill since the night before...Surprisingly, I didn't feel the need for one.

In the Escalade, Pagan asked me to call the West Hollywood Sheriff's Station. "Ask them to send a patrol unit to meet us at Sunset and San Vincente."

"Parking lot of the Whiskey?" I asked, knowing the area.

"Perfect."

I made the call without asking questions, but once things were rolling, I had to ask, "What are you up to?"

"We need to get rid of Smack Daddy's muscle. Richards

and Tuttle will be carrying guns they don't have permits for," Pagan said. "It goes with the territory. We'll need some backup from the Sheriffs, since it's their area, to get them off the street."

More *tactical* research on the RHD computers had identified Smack Daddy's two bodyguards as little more than thugs. Both Bobby Richards and Elmo Tuttle had records for various levels of strong-arm violence, but surprisingly, nothing dope related. Both were actually real cousins related to Smack Daddy, as opposed to the *play cousins* so often claimed in *the hood*.

Bobby had graduated high school and did two years in the Army. Elmo had a GED earned before his dishonorable discharge from the Marines. Both had claimed at various times to be Special Forces, but it was a lie designed for intimidation not for scrutiny.

Conveniently they both had outstanding warrants – Richards for Assault with a Deadly Weapon and Tuttle for felony battery. Both charges were the scourge of the bodyguard trade – almost a rite of passage. However, I could see Pagan making use of the warrants to take Richards and Tuttle out of play. He was also thinking ahead, knowing they would probably be illegally armed, which would make their current legal troubles much more serious.

I frowned now, sensing a calamity in the making.

It was shortly after noon-thirty when we cruised past the Smack Records' building. It was nothing to look at on the outside – all whitewashed stucco and reflective windows. There was a small adjacent parking lot with a security guard in a wooden shack. He gave our tinted windows a hard stare as we drove past. Perhaps Pagan's high end Escalade was too low rent to be considered for a space on the lot.

"Can you get me the number for Triton Security?" Pagan asked me.

"Sure," I said, pulling it up via the Internet on my smartphone. Pagan had me punch it in to the Escalade's phone system.

When the phone was answered, Pagan gave his name and asked for Bradford Zale.

"Ray! How are you?" Bradford Zale asked when he came on the line.

"Good, Brad."

"Business or personal?"

"Business. I need a favor."

"Tell me."

"Is Triton still running all the guard contracts in West Hollywood?"

"Eighty percent."

"You have a guy working the parking lot for Smack Records?"

"Yes."

"Armed?"

"No. Is there a problem?"

"Not for you. I just need your guy to take a long toilet break."

"How long?"

"No more than an hour."

"That's still a heck of a bowel movement. Any back-splash on Triton?

"None. Everyone should be too busy to notice the rent-a-cop isn't on post."

"I'll make the call. By the way, I never did get to thank you for sending that security contract with Heller Indus-tries our way."

"You just did," Pagan said, then disconnected.

I shook my head. "You are amazingly connected."

Pagan smiled. "This job is not only about what you can find out. It's also about what you already know, who you know, and bringing it all together."

CHAPTER 19

**"Fiction is a lie. Good fiction is the
truth inside the lie."**
- Stephen King

Pagan found curb parking on the opposite side of the street facing back toward Sunset Boulevard. Parking was always an exercise in paranoia for cops. You never wanted to get pinned in, yet you wanted to be close enough to get to your vehicle in a hurry if needed.

I slid the portable *rover* out of the main radio unit under the dash. I keyed the microphone and told the RTO to show us code six – *out for investigation* – and gave our location. If I didn't clear or check back within an hour, somebody would start looking for us.

We'd already met and briefed the two LASO officers. They were happy to be on board as we were handing them two felony arrests on a platter, and maybe more if Pagan was right and Smack Daddy's bodyguards were illegally armed.

From where we were parked, we could see the Smack Records parking lot. We could also see the guard shack was now empty. Clearly, it was good to know the right people to call.

The pimped out black Lincoln Navigator belonging to Smack Daddy was parked close to a rear door into the building. Its golden spinner rims sparkled in the sun, and you knew the sound system's bass would shake your molars. It had illegally dark tinted windows and the *de rigueur* personalize plate, which in this case read SMACK 1. In Smack Daddy's world, it was important to let everybody know who you are.

The Smack Records building was anonymous by necessity. With recording artists coming in an out with their entourages, the anonymity of the building actually spoke volumes about its importance. You had to be cool enough to know it was there and what it was.

By contrast, Pagan had his own kind of cool. His Escalade had been customized on the inside only. From the outside it was a basic black with stock rims and tires, complete with the standard California license plate you could never remember. Aside from the slightly darker than normal tint on the windows it could belong to any local soccer mom late to pick her gaggle of kids up from school.

Like his Escalade, Pagan just *was* – he didn't appear to have a need to proclaim himself to anyone. He had the ability to rivet your eye or blend into the background as his needs required. Working with him was an exercise in simply keeping up.

Pagan checked the Escalade's dash clock.

1:15 pm.

"Anytime now," Pagan said.

As the words left his mouth, the rear door to Smack Records opened and Bobby Richards stepped out followed by Elmo Tuttle. Richards was smoking what looked like a home rolled spliff. Talk about your probable cause, although the outstanding felony warrants were more than enough.

I hit the speed dial on my phone. Deputy Creed, one of the LASO officers with whom we'd met, picked up immediately. The phone was faster than trying to get hold of them over the two department's incompatible radio systems.

"Show time," I said and disconnected.

Across the street in the parking lot, Richards and Tuttle had moved over next to the black Navigator. Richards took a long drag on the spliff and handed it over to his compatriot. Tuttle was taking his own drag when Smack Daddy himself walked out of the building.

He strutted up to Tuttle and slapped the spliff out of the bodyguard's mouth. We could see Smack Daddy yelling, but not what he was saying. He lived up to his name by smacking Richards upside the head to even things up.

With both large men cringing away from their employer, the Sheriff's unit chose that moment to roll into the parking lot. They had their light bar whirling, but no siren as requested.

So far so good, but I could feel calamity in my bones.

The squad car screeched to a halt and its two crew cut, muscular, uniformed deputies exited out, staying behind their doors on either side, with weapons drawn and pointed. I realized Creed had a .9mm, but his partner, Dixon, was pointing an X26 taser, which looked like something Robocop should be carrying.

Panic hit Smack Daddy and he turned to run, but found himself immediately blocked by the bulk of his Navigator.

"Hands in the air! Hands in the air!" Deputy Creed, the squad car driver yelled in a deep voice filled with command presence.

Both Richards and Tuttle were *educated* enough to recognize the difference between the LASO and the LAPD. They knew LAPD officers could be counted on to hesitate before using deadly force, or any force for that matter. Organizationally, the LAPD was drilled to the nth degree about use of force, and any application – no matter how small – had to be justified in triplicate. If a suspect actually sustained an abrasion or a scratch as the result of his own stupidity, the paperwork was endless. The Los Angeles Times, the Police Commission, the ACLU, and a whole flock of lawyers couldn't wait to jump on that bandwagon.

For reasons the LAPD could never figure out, the LASO had never suffered any such restrictions or scrutiny. LASO officers, who started their career working the county jail system, learned the hard way that you hit, kick, or fire first – and damn the paperwork.

Hands high in the air, Richards and Tuttle actually turned around of their own accord, dropped to their knees, and then went down on their stomachs, arms outstretched, legs spread. Like I said, educated – *magna cum laude* gangsters.

Smack Daddy apparently had skipped a few lectures. He turned toward the deputies, gesticulating wildly, spewing *F-bombs* and *do you know who I ams*.

I could see it about to happen. The calamity was unfolding before my eyes. I knew I didn't have a chance to stop it, but I slid out of the Escalade anyway. However, before I was able to cane my way across the street, Smack Daddy was convulsing with 5,000 taser delivered volts –

think of the effect as putting one foot in a toilet and one finger in an accessible light socket.

Smack Daddy was on the asphalt, hair smoking. His bladder had emptied down the front of his Gorgio Armani's.

As I reached Deputy Dixon on the passenger side of the LASO car, he was getting ready to pull the trigger on his taser again because he could. It would send another 5,000 volt shock down the wires attached to Smack Daddy by the darts shot into him.

"Enough," I said, putting my hand on his shoulder.

He looked at me like a toddler told it was time to leave the playground.

"You're no fun," he said.

I saw the mischievous grin flash in his eyes a split second before it reached his lips. I whipped my cane up into his groin hard enough to make his eyes water before the intent in his grin – born out of LASO/LAPD's love/hate relationship – could travel down his arm and twitch his finger on the trigger of the taser again.

Deputy Dixon doubled over from my blow, his head bowed toward me. I grabbed the taser from him with my right hand, then used the flat of my cane under my left palm to push on the crown of his head, moving him backward into a sitting position in his car.

"I said enough." I was feeling pissed. I looked over the roof of the squad car at Deputy Creed. "Get the two goons cuffed," I ordered him. "I'll cover."

I ejected the spent dart canister from the taser onto the ground then tossed the taser itself onto the roof of the squad car. I stepped away from the car. I slid my cane under my arm, drew my 9mm Beretta and then, using two hands, pointed it toward Smack Daddy's bodyguards.

"Put your hands behind your heads then don't move," I ordered them. From their proned-out position on the ground, both men did as requested without any fuss.

Smack Daddy was still groaning on the asphalt. The charge from a taser incapacitates the body's neuromuscular system like static on a telephone line. But even after the shock is turned off, it takes a while for the body to get back in sync.

Deputy Creed didn't like me giving him orders. After all, we were in his jurisdiction, and he wasn't quite sure what I had done to his partner. However, he holstered his gun and moved forward.

He crouched, dropping one knee into the small of Richards' back. Then, quickly and expertly, moved Richards' hands, one at a time, from the back of his head and cuffed them in the center of his back. Next, he grasped Richards by the left arm, turning him in order to search the suspect's left side.

Moving to the right side, Creed went through the same maneuver. This time he stopped at Richards' waistband. "Gun," he said, pulling clear a pearl handled .45. Richards must have confused himself with General Patton.

With Richards secured and searched, I maneuvered so Creed would not be in the line of fire as he moved to go through the same process with Tuttle. This time Creed located a .357 revolver in a holster under Tuttle's arm. He also found a baggie of cocaine. This was getting better and better.

A somewhat sheepish Deputy Dixon was on his feet now, helping Creed get Richards and Tuttle up and secured in the back of the squad car. I holstered my gun and looked around for Pagan.

He was crouched down by Smack Daddy. He was slipping his own smartphone into his inside jacket pocket. He'd either been recording or taking pictures. I watched as he helped a still disoriented Smack Daddy into a sitting positon, all the while talking to him in tones too low to hear.

He looked up at me. "Get the keys to the Navigator."

I was a quick learner and didn't stop to ask questions. I walked over to where Creed and Dixon had their cuffed arrestees leaning over the hood of the deputies' squad car. I thought they might give me a bad time, but Dixon located the Navigator keys in Richards' front pocket and handed them over without even a snide comment.

In fact, as he handed me the keys, he bobbed his head and mumbled, "Sorry."

It sort of startled me.

"What is your partner going to do with the video?" Dixon asked.

I got it now.

He'd caught Pagan catching the action on his phone and knew things might not look good if the Sheriff's internal affairs unit got hold of it.

"No worries," I said. "Pagan is no snitch."

"How about you?" Dixon asked. To his credit he looked directly at me.

I held my cane up slightly and waggled it. "Not exactly department issue is it?" I smiled.

He caught my grin and gave one back, knowing he was home safe – knowing I wasn't going to push anything further.

I turned back to Pagan, who had Smack Daddy on his feet.

"Open the back door," he said as I approached.

I pressed unlock on the Navigator key fob. The car's system beeped and I pulled the door handle.

Pagan approached with Smack Daddy and helped him onto the backseat.

"Theo," Pagan said to me, using Smack Daddy's real first name, "has asked us to get him clear of the area before anyone sees him in this condition." Pagan closed the car door.

I looked over toward the back door of Smack Records. I could see there was something stuck hard underneath the jam preventing it opening outward. Nobody from inside, who'd heard the commotion had been able to get out. If anyone had seen anything from the blind-covered windows and wanted to interfere, they would have to go out through the front door.

Pagan had obviously been busy while I'd been dealing with thugs, guns, and recalcitrant deputies.

"What did you do with the taser darts?" I asked. It often took a jail doctor to remove them.

"Wasn't a problem," Pagan said. "Only one hit him, and that was in his arm. His jacket slowed the impact and it popped right out. No harm, no foul, no bleeding."

He reached over and tapped my cane with a long index finger. "That's a real Tiger Woods swing you've got. I thought you were trying to drive Deputy Dixon's balls all the way to the green."

"Nah," I said in as offhand a manner as I could muster. "Just a little putting practice."

Pagan opened the Navigator's driver's door and motioned for me to get in.

"You're a natural at more than lie catching," he said. "Tanaka's going to enjoy teaching you."

CHAPTER 20

"I lie to myself all the time.
But I never believe me."
- S.E. Hinton, The Outsiders

I drove the Navigator while Pagan sat in the back with Smack Daddy – or Theo, as Pagan was now calling him.

Pagan had brought a small backpack with him from the Escalade. From it, he now produced a packet of wet-wipes. He handed them to Smack Daddy, who took them surprisingly gratefully.

As Smack Daddy wiped his hands and face, he let out a big sigh in the form of a drawn out profanity. He leaned his head back on the car seat and closed his eyes. I watched this via glances at the Navigator's rear view mirror.

Adrenaline was still coursing through my system from the parking lot confrontation, and I fought the urge to drive through traffic like a maniac. I kept my hands at eight and five on the wheel, and consciously kept easy on the accelerator.

I thought about the situation we were in and wondered if this hadn't somehow been Pagan's plan from the start. I realized how quickly a car can become an intimate space. There is nowhere to go, no way to get out while the car is moving. There is also something soothing about being on the move, a sense of safety, cocooned from the elements in a regulated temperature – ask any parent trying to put a crying baby to sleep. I turned the SUV's internal temperature up two degrees.

With Smack Daddy voluntarily in the car – I had no doubt Pagan had used a phone app to record Smack Daddy's request for us to drive him away from the parking lot...was even recording now – we had complete control over his environment. We had the ability to change it from the comfort of grandma's feather bed to a pressure cooker. At this point it was a rolling interrogation room without any need for lawyers because the situation was *non-custodial*, which removed one of the three prongs – police, *and* custody, *and* interrogatory questioning – necessary for Miranda to come into play.

Pagan took a bottle of water out of his backpack, cracked the top, and handed it to Smack Daddy.

I kept driving while Pagan waited and Smack Daddy tried to pull himself together. I could feel anxiety churning in my gut. We had two missing children and we didn't seem to be even close to uncovering clue one as to how to find them. Yet somehow, Pagan was as cool as if we were out for a Sunday drive heading for a leisurely picnic.

I confess his unperturbed countenance was beginning to irritate me. Yet, there was a dispassionate side of me realizing how my own anxiety was affecting me, and I began to understand how Pagan turned a subject's anxiety against him or her.

"How are you feeling, Theo?" Pagan asked.

I longed for a stronger opening gambit. I wanted Pagan to reach over and throttle Smack Daddy – excuse me...Theo – until he coughed up something we could use.

"Better," said Smack Daddy.

He brushed his hands down his clothes. I had no doubt he was uncomfortable in his urine damp pants, but Smack Daddy was never going to admit to it. His suit was dark blue, so if it wasn't for the slight acrid smell, you wouldn't know right off he'd peed himself. Pagan certainly gave no indication, sitting as close to Smack Daddy as was possible on the rear bench seat without actually touching him.

"I'm glad we were there to help you, Theo," Pagan said. "That could have turned into a very nasty situation for you."

"Those two idiots couldn't find their own ass with two hands and a flashlight."

"Hiring family hardly ever works out," Pagan said.

Smack Daddy looked at him, a bit surprised Pagan knew the bodyguards were actually related to him. "Sometimes you can't trust nobody else."

Pagan gently bounced his head up and down in agreement. "Theo, you owe a lot of people a lot of money. How much good do you think Bobby and Elmo would be if things got serious?"

"How do you know I owe people money? Smack Records is back on top. I don't owe nobody nothing."

Pagan didn't change the even tone of his voice. "You've got one artist. Granted he's becoming a star, but you were deep pockets in debt before he came along. In debt to the kind of people who don't ever want you to catch up with your payments."

"I can take care of myself."

"I think we both know that's not entirely truthful."

Pagan had called Smack Daddy a liar, but in such a way it didn't ignite any blustery explosions. *Liar* is a bomb word. Nobody likes to be called a liar – even if they are. Being told you're not being *entirely truthful* is somehow far more acceptable.

Smack Daddy didn't respond. Pagan didn't want him thinking too hard, so he filled the void.

"How do you feel about talking to me?" Pagan asked.

"It's cool," Smack Daddy said.

"Tell me in your own words why we're here talking."

"It's about that damn brat wandering off."

That response was very telling. Unreasonable anger coupled with the soft phrase *wandering off* – not kidnapped...not even missing...*wandering off*.

Pagan reached over and put a hand on Smack Daddy's shoulder. "Theo, if you had anything to do with Unicorn's disappearance, you need to tell me about it *now*."

Words were weapons to Pagan – emphasis and timing were imperative. If Smack Daddy was complicit in Unicorn's disappearance, he only had two choices to respond – admit or lie.

"No, man...Nothing."

The back seat of the Navigator was suddenly filled with purple streamers, but there was something odd. I usually saw lies as deep purple streamers. Those attached to Smack Daddy's words were a pastel purple. I didn't know what that meant.

Pagan did.

"Theo, Theo, Theo," Pagan still had his hand on Smack

Daddy's shoulder and was rocking it back and forth. "What do I do for a living?"

"What are you talking about?"

"It's an easy question, Theo. What do I do for a living?"

"You're a cop."

"No, Theo. I'm a human lie detector."

"I ain't..."

"Hold on!" Pagan said, throwing his free hand, index finger extended, right in front of Smack Daddy's face, cutting off what Smack Daddy was about to say. "Don't say anything else. You need to listen to me right now. I'm the one hope you have of coming out of this situation." Pagan's words were articulated clearly, clipped and delivered firmly, brooking no interruption. "Right now you are under so much pressure from what is going on in your life, you have no idea which way to turn. Your business is in trouble..."

Smack Daddy made to interrupt and disagree, but Pagan raised his finger again, effectively shutting him down.

I was stopped at a light on Sunset Boulevard. There were cars on both sides of me. I cut my eyes from the rearview mirror and checked out the other cars' drivers and passengers. None had any idea of the drama unfolding in the back compartment of the Navigator. It struck me as more than a little surreal.

The light changed and I accelerated smoothly. I had to do everything smoothly, allowing nothing to disturb the verbal and physical dynamic Pagan was building. He was dominating Smack Daddy, but the energy being generated was as fragile as gossamer.

"Your business is in trouble," Pagan reiterated. "Your marriage is crumbling. Your partners are filing lawsuits. Your wife's lawyer is on your back. You're surrounded by incompetents like Bobby and Elmo. You have to use them because you can't trust anyone else, plus they're family, and family brings with it even more pressures. You have a lot of mouths to feed. And there ain't nobody looking out for Theo." Pagan squeezed Smack Daddy's shoulder.

"Even being Smack Daddy is a burden." Pagan continued in full verbal flow. "When you're being Smack Daddy it takes constant effort...thinking on your feet... making decisions involving millions of dollars...making sure nobody gets a leg up on you. Whew! Man, you are under a ton of pressure."

Pagan had moved in even closer to Smack Daddy, into the intimate space where great interrogators operate. "But you know what the great thing is about pressure?" Pagan didn't wait before he answered his own question. "It produces diamonds. And you are a diamond, Theo."

What a crock of old cheese, but one glance in the rearview mirror at Smack Daddy's face was enough for me to see the tears in his eyes. Listening to Pagan's lulling voice almost had me believing. Smack Daddy didn't have a chance. He was a fish hooked hard on the line. Pagan only had to reel him in.

Pagan kept right on talking – *monologing*. This wasn't the regular *ask and answer* most interrogators employ. This was something else. This was Pagan defining the narrative, throwing out *themes* like bait, seeing to which one Smack Daddy would respond, which one Smack Daddy would think was a socially acceptable motivation for his actions.

We'd agreed the most important thing in Smack Daddy's life was Smack Daddy. Now, Pagan was working his patter to make everything about poor, hard-done-by, misunderstood, little Theo Davis. He was working his way behind Smack Daddy's Oz-like façade and selling snake oil for all it was worth.

People who don't understand why anyone would ever talk to the cops have never been questioned by a professional interrogator – let alone a savant inquisitor like Pagan.

Listening and watching, I began to understand what Pagan had tried to tell me about how *knowing* somebody is lying isn't enough. You have to be able to turn the lies into something substantial, something that will make a difference in the case.

I drove on and on, giving Pagan the time he needed to do the job.

"Diamonds, Theo." Pagan was digging deep. "They are clear, and pure, and hard. Nothing can dull their luster. Those people who are diamonds. They are the ones who are still standing when everyone else has fallen away." He'd been saying the same thing a number of different ways, never pushing too hard, but never allowing Smack Daddy off the hook.

Communication has been deemed to consist of fifty-five percent physical gestures, thirty-eight percent verbal tone, and only seven percent verbal content. Somebody, like Smack Daddy, who is under stress, is only hearing seven percent or less of what you actually verbalize. Repetition is key to an interrogator being able to get a message across.

But I was missing something here. I'd seen the pastel purple streamers attached to some of Smack Daddy's earlier words. I didn't know how they were different from the deep purple streamers I knew were lies. It was making me anxious about my own role in this new partnership.

I'd always been so sure before, but now it was as if Pagan was taking me with him down a rabbit hole where all the things I'd depended on before were shifting. I was being forced to pay *attention with intent* to what Pagan was doing. I knew he was leading Smack Daddy somewhere, but I didn't think it was to an admission of being complicit in the disappearance of Unicorn.

Then I got it.

I realized the difference between the purple streamers attached to words I knew were lies, and the pastel purple streamers I'd seen attached to Smack Daddy's denial of involvement was the *intent* attached to the words. When somebody intends to lie, I see the deep purple streamers flowing from the words. When somebody is attaching *unfocused guilt* – anxious, not sure if they are lying, wanting only to believe they are telling the truth – the purple becomes a lighter pastel shade.

If I was right, then Smack Daddy wasn't specifically complicit in the disappearance of Unicorn, but still felt guilt attached to whatever role he believed he *might* have played.

Pagan was way ahead of me from simply reading not only Smack Daddy's body language, but also the words he chose and the tone and emphasis he placed on them. Pagan had said he needed me to keep him from making another mistake, but clearly I needed him to teach me more about how to use my gift first.

My gift. It had been a long time since I'd looked at it as anything but a curse – a trait setting me apart. In a little more than forty-eight hours, my life had undergone a watershed of change.

I forced myself not to think about it, to let it happen. I was scared, but I knew somehow I trusted Pagan. I had to concentrate – had to think about driving...and listening.

CHAPTER 21

"We lie loudest when we lie to ourselves."
- Eric Hoffer

As I passed the entrance to the UCLA campus on Sunset Boulevard, I realized one of the main perks of being teamed up with Pagan was *focus*.

Right now, RHD detectives were working two missing children cases – one involving a high profile individual. They were being run ragged by parents, relatives, family friends, the police brass, and the press.

Each detective was also responsible for an array of other cases, and cases don't get to RHD in the first place unless they're high profile, each one with its own high mainte-nance demands. The daily juggling act often spiraled into a stress filled nightmare.

Working with Pagan meant none of that was my worry. Per the chief's mandate, we could cherry pick not only

investigations but *parts* of investigations. I had no doubt
Pagan's brain was working ahead, but right now, our only
focus was Smack Daddy.

The lack of distractions was liberating – intense, but
liberating.

I pulled into a campus parking lot and turned around. I
exited east on Sunset Boulevard, back the way we had
come. Traffic was still dense, but moving. Keeping my speed
steady at thirty-five miles per hour helped coincide with the
traffic lights turning green. I was covering ground on the
wide surface street with very few stops, keeping our moving
interrogation room on a smooth even keel without any
distractions – a perfect, protected bubble, completely separated from the world outside the Navigator's tinted
windows.

Pagan was still talking, but one quick glance in the
rearview mirror was enough to see Smack Daddy wasn't
listening.

However, I knew this was a good thing.

Smack Daddy was not employing the deliberate non-
listening of mental *escape* – checking his brain out to a
beach in Hawaii. This was something very different. Smack
Daddy was in what interrogators call *transition*.

His head was bowed, the crown of it showing to Pagan –
a sign of submission – and I knew he was literally experiencing a change of chemicals in his brain. His mental
processing was moving from, *I can't admit to anything*, to
*what is the best way for me to give up the information I'm
hoarding*.

"I feel for you," Pagan kept talking, not letting Smack
Daddy's lack of response deter him. This was not a conversation or a dialogue. Pagan was not asking questions. It was

still a monologue – Pagan verbally leading Smack Daddy down the path to the truth.

"You're scared of what you think might have happened to Unicorn. You're worried it might be your fault. You don't want to think about it, but we have to think about it. We can't deal with it if we don't talk about it. I can't help you if you don't help yourself."

In an *interview*, you are attempting to get information somebody *wants* to give you. In an *interrogation*, you are trying to get information they *don't* want to give you. Pagan clearly believed Smack Daddy had information he didn't want to divulge. Whether it was significant to the disappearance of Unicorn, or related to something else in Smack Daddy's self-centered world, would only become clear if Pagan could pry it loose.

"I know at least two things you're worried about," Pagan continued, his voice had dropped an octave and was filled with an intonation both comforting and assured. "You're worried about your reputation. In your business, everything is about reputation. If you let your guard down for a second, your competitors are going to smell weakness like blood in the water and come after you."

None of what Pagan was saying had anything specifically to do with Unicorn's disappearance, but it had everything to do with opening Smack Daddy up on a psychological level. Two of the main keys to any interrogation are finding a socially acceptable way for the subject to confess, and *becoming the person the subject needs you to be in order to confess.*

For the first key, the subject needs to believe the explanation you're offering for his or her actions is a socially acceptable excuse the interrogator will accept without judgment. The interrogator doesn't actually have to *believe* it is socially acceptable, but the interrogator has to be able to *sell it*.

Pagan clearly didn't think anything having to do with Smack Daddy's reputation could justify his attitude toward his missing daughter. However, in Smack Daddy's self-centric world, Smack Daddy might feel protecting his reputation was an acceptable excuse for being a total jerk. *Reputation* was a *theme*, another fishing lure thrown out to see if Smack Daddy would bite.

Through his demeanor, Pagan was also turning himself into a shoulder for Smack Daddy to cry on. Pagan was becoming an intimate confidant, somebody with whom Smack Daddy could share his deepest secrets.

Pagan had been talking non-stop for over thirty minutes. You had to admire his gift for gab. He relied a lot on repetition, saying the same thing over and over in slightly different ways. However, I could tell he was now getting to the heart of the matter.

"I want you to know," Pagan was saying, "I know what going through a divorce does to a person. I've been through it twice and it's a nightmare."

I was glad I could see the royal purple streamers attached to Pagan's words. He was lying his ass off, but if I couldn't *see* the lies, I'd believe him in a heartbeat.

"You have to protect yourself because you know the bitch you're trying to escape from is going to take you for every cent she can get. When somebody you love turns on you it is frightening. They turn on you in an instant. One second it's all hearts and flowers and the next minute they are out to destroy you."

"I loved her," Smack Daddy said quietly. Then more loudly. "I picked her out of the gutter. She was another crack whore, but I saw something in her. I gave her every-thing. Made her what she is today."

Smack Daddy had taken the verbal bait. His words were all pastel streamers. I had to take in a deep breath, but Pagan just nodded his head.

"She took advantage of everything you had to offer her, and then gave you a child she wanted to pass off as yours. Who knows who that child's *baby daddy* really is?" Pagan was in full flow – taking advantage of the information he had obtained from Arlo and his TMZ contact to manipulate and twist the facts to his advantage. He was keeping it impersonal, not using Unicorn's name at the moment, turning her into an object – *that child*.

It didn't matter whether Unicorn was or wasn't the fruit of Smack Daddy's loins. Pagan was saying what Smack Daddy wanted to hear, what he needed to hear in order to be pulled further and further into Pagan's whirlwind of words.

"Anyone looking at that child would wonder if she was actually yours," Pagan said, continuing down the dark path he'd chosen.

I felt it was a horrible thing to say, but Pagan was feeling his way through the situation, saying the things he felt he must in order to connect on a base level with Smack Daddy.

"She's not mine...she's not mine." Smack Daddy was blubbering now, but suddenly I could see royal purple streamers. He was knowingly lying.

I opened my mouth to alert Pagan, but he looked up at that exact second and caught my eyes in the rear view mirror. I snapped my mouth shut and gave a slight nod. Pagan was way ahead of me.

I watched Smack Daddy rocking back and forth while Pagan rubbed his back, as if comforting a distressed child. It was both a brilliant and disgusting performance at the same time.

I turned down a quiet side street. After about a block, I eased the Navigator to a stop at the curb under a spreading oak tree. I'd done it smoothly enough Smack Daddy wasn't even aware we'd stopped. I caught Pagan glancing at me again in the rear view mirror and saw him nod his approval.

I sat as quietly as I could, not wanting to shatter the fragile, intimate, almost tangible texture of the world Pagan had spun.

It was weird, but I could see Pagan literally shifting gears. Smack Daddy's statement about Unicorn not being his had been tinged with the tone of desperation. Pagan had heard it and interpreted not what the words literally meant, but what their tone and intonation indicated they meant.

Smack Daddy didn't hate Unicorn. He loved her. She was his child. Pagan was untying the knot of raw emotion a strand at a time.

"Unicorn may or may not be yours," Pagan said softly. "But you still love her."

Using Unicorn's name at the right moment, with the right inflection, broke whatever reserves Smack Daddy had left. He began to cry with full, body wracking, sobs.

Smack Daddy was bent fully over now, rocking, his face buried in his hands. Pagan kept gently rubbing a palm over Smack Daddy's back, the human touch a powerful bonding technique.

Pagan didn't speak, just let the pent up emotions flow. If he felt any embarrassment or revulsion, you couldn't tell. Instead, compassion flowed out of his expression, his body language, his gentle movements.

I couldn't believe it was all an act. This was Pagan's gift as an empath – the ability to feel the pain and emotion of others, to channel and respond to it in kind. Pagan had transformed himself. He actually believed, for this moment, everything he was saying. I knew the words coming out of his mouth would no longer have even a tinge of purple streamers attached.

I suddenly realized I had never thought much about truth. As Pagan had said, like most cops, I would have said truth was a fixed point. I would have turned to cultural platitudes: You can't hide from the truth; the truth will set you free; it has the ring of truth. Even after all my time on the job, from rookie to experienced detective, I had simply gone through the expected motions in the pursuit of *truth*. After all, wasn't the truth simply the truth, plain and guileless, black and white? Truth and lie? If doubt ever entered the picture, it was just the truth becoming more evasive. Cynicism took the place of objectivity.

It doesn't take long for any detective, especially one who is cursed with the ability to actually *see* lies, to begin believing everybody lies about everything...all the time. We begin looking for only lies and forget to look for the truth.

However, Pagan was different. He didn't look for lies. He looked for truth. He had the ability to see truth through perspective. As he'd said, the truth wasn't a fixed point for Pagan. In his world there wasn't one truth – there were as many varied *truths* as there were perspectives of those involved. His gift was in finding which truth carried the most weight. His was a gift of the subjective, a constant balancing act on the edge of a razor blade.

I didn't quite know how Pagan managed to keep his own perspective. If he truly felt the pain of others over and over again, and I could see he did, it had to be a soul sucking experience. He might be the best at what he did, but at what price?

And what price was I expected to pay while working with him? Right now, I was riding the lightning of my own emotions. My own truth had changed, channeled through Pagan, but would this emotional high last...would there be a crash?

Looking in the rear view mirror, I realized I needed to stop worrying about my own crash for the moment and concentrate on Smack Daddy's.

"You've got to be in so deep you can't see up," Pagan said still rubbing Smack Daddy's back. "What if I could tell you *they* don't have her?" Pagan asked.

Smack Daddy immediately raised his face from his hands, looking askance at Pagan, his eyes bloodshot and wide.

Who the hell were *they*, and how did Pagan know *they* didn't have Unicorn? I'd lost the thread somewhere, but Pagan and Smack Daddy still appeared to be tied together.

I thought Pagan must be winging it, but that didn't feel right. Pagan had put something together I had missed. The question was when did he put it together? Since he'd been in the back of the car, or earlier? If earlier, why hadn't he shared his thoughts?

Maybe because he expected me to keep up.

They? They? Then I got it. *They* were organized crime. In this case black organized crime. Not street gangs, but what had evolved from street gangs. I remembered the example of Death Row Records – hip hop as fueled by drugs, guns, and gangsters. Hundreds of millions of dollars had flowed in and out, tempers had flared and the bullets had flown. The black mob had risen from the ashes, eschewing street level violence for something more sinister and more deadly.

The LAPD even found itself unwillingly in the mix

when a federal informant provided testimony that Los Angeles police officers David Mack and Rafael Perez – both implicated in the Rampart scandal – had worked as security for Death Row when off-duty. Things had gotten very ugly, very fast.

If black organized crime had their hooks into Smack Records, then Smack Daddy was in a world of hurt.

Pagan had been talking levelly and calmly, without hesitation or pause, to Smack Daddy for almost forty minutes. All that time, he'd been subtly probing, looking for some kind of solid reaction from Smack Daddy – and now he had it.

"How do you know *they* don't have her?" Smack Daddy asked. There was a pleading tone to his voice.

Pagan had hit a nerve. I hoped he had something he could use to drill down.

For his part, Pagan maintained his calm exterior without even the flicker of an eyelid – he kept talking, monologing, moving Smack Daddy along to a point where he would spill whatever information he was concealing.

"The music business is as cutthroat as the movie business – as any business where millions of dollars can be made or lost," Pagan said, explaining the obvious, but with a purpose. "When you're up, everybody wants a piece of you, but when you're down the only place you're going to find the money to keep going is by making deals with very dangerous people. People who expect you to not only repay them on time, but with heavy interest."

Smack Daddy was nodding his head. "They never let go. They keep tearing at you until there's nothing left."

"I know. I've seen it before," Pagan said. "But then Changeling came along and suddenly you have an artist who gives you a chance to dig your way out, even get back on top."

Changeling? We were suddenly back to the artist who could change the fortunes of Smack Records. I'd discarded him as somewhat irrelevant, but Pagan hadn't.

"But that's not how it works, is it?" Pagan said, then went on to answer his own question. "The people you owe don't want to let you off the hook. You're a cash cow, or a money laundry, or a legitimate front. You're too valuable. They threatened your family, didn't they?"

Tears were streaming down Smack Daddy's cheeks. Pagan handed him a tissue he pulled out of nowhere, like a magician.

Smack Daddy blew his nose, nodding his head at the same time. "I finally cut a deal. Five million. Do you know how hard it is to get that kind of money in cash? The freaking banks are impossible to deal with and report everything over one hundred thousand to the feds. Getting that much cash is a nightmare."

Talk about your first world problems.

I had turned slowly in my seat to watch the fascinating tableau in the back seat of the Navigator.

"But you knew it would take more than cash," Pagan said. "You had to make them think their threat to your family wouldn't work. You began trash talking your wife and your child."

Smack Daddy seemed to startle, but Pagan shut him down.

"It's okay. It's us. I know Unicorn really is your child. I know how much you really love both Unicorn and Judith, but you couldn't even let Judith know what you were trying to do. You had to sell it. You needed them to think Unicorn wasn't your child, that you didn't want her. That's what this has all been about. You were sacrificing everything you loved, tearing them both down, to keep them safe."

This was a completely different tangent than the one Pagan had taken earlier. Before, he'd been agreeing with Smack Daddy that Unicorn couldn't be Smack Daddy's child. That he was right to not want to support her, that Smack Daddy's wife had betrayed him.

Smack Daddy had originally responded in the affirmative to these statements, but Pagan must have seen something in Smack Daddy's body language, which made it clear he was being deceptive. Following his instincts, Pagan had changed the tune. Now Pagan was giving the situation a completely opposite spin – and giving Smack Daddy a much more socially acceptable out.

Smack Daddy started, stammered, and started again. "I had the money, but they took it all when they took Unicorn. They took my baby girl..." Smack Daddy began drowning in his tears again.

Pagan was calm. "I need you to breathe, Theo. Breathe with me." Still rubbing Smack Daddy's back, Pagan began taking slow deep breaths. I found myself breathing in unison with him and, eventually, so did Smack Daddy. His crying stopped and he became much calmer, almost docile.

"Let's look at this logically," Pagan said. "You were going to give your business partners the money." Pagan's inflection put quotes around the term *business partners*. "They didn't need to take it from you. And even if they did, they wouldn't take Unicorn. There has been no ransom demand. No threats to harm her if you don't come up with more money."

"Then who took her? Who took the money?"

I was concentrating so hard, I almost missed the mottled colors in the streamers coming from Smack Daddy's mouth.

I was so used to seeing colors, I sometimes didn't even notice them. I needed to go back and see them again – I'd missed something – but it was too late. The streamers faded almost as soon as they appeared. There was no instant replay.

"Ah," Pagan said, with a surprising smile on his face. "That's the question, isn't it?

CHAPTER 22

"Lying to ourselves is more deeply ingrained than lying to others."
- Fyodor Dostoyevsky

Livia Nelson was scowling at Pagan. "A camera?" she asked.

"A camera," Pagan replied calmly.

"How big?" Livia asked, scowling even deeper. It was clear she didn't like Pagan's unstated assertion she may have missed something.

We were again standing in the living room of Smack Daddy's house. For me, the surprise bigger than Pagan's theory about cameras was Smack Daddy and Judith Davis holding each other on the couch like long lost lovers. In an amazingly short period of time, they had gone from tabloid divorce fodder – with an unwanted child caught in the middle – to, *I'm so sorry, darling. I can't live without you.* They were even appropriately concerned about Unicorn.

Pagan's breakthrough in the back of the Navigator –

that Smack Daddy had been trying to lessen the threat to his family from his dangerous creditors by making out Unicorn and Judith weren't important to him – had been on point. Or at least as on point as it needed to be to clear up much of the mystery surrounding Smack Daddy's actions. It remained to be seen if his theory about cameras would be similarly inspired.

Then there was the money. The five million dollars Smack Daddy said went missing along with his daughter was somehow a detail Pagan had failed to mention to Livia Nelson, or anyone else connected to the investigations of the two missing children.

My silence made me his accomplice.

Pagan hadn't told me not to say anything about the money. But he didn't say anything, so I didn't. It was a *partner* thing. Right or wrong, I trusted him. Partners backed partners. It didn't mean you condoned illegal behavior or violence. There was a line, but I couldn't tell you where it was until I reached it.

Not saying anything about the money didn't even need thinking about. If Pagan tried to pocket the money, that would be another thing. But I instinctively knew that wouldn't ever be an option for Pagan. It wasn't part of his being.

If he wasn't saying anything about the money, I knew the reason would have something to do with furthering the investigation – something to do with finding the missing children. I'd either figure it out along the way, or Pagan would eventually explain.

Clearly, the things Smack Daddy had done to get five million in cash were not things of which the IRS or the LAPD would approve. However, in the intimate setting of the interrogation room Pagan had established in the rear seat of Smack Daddy's Lincoln Navigator, whatever the crimes committed to get the money together were of negligible importance. What was important was the bond the kept secret had established.

Pagan now smiled at Livia. It wasn't the full wattage charmer he could turn on and off at will. It was more that of an innocent cherub about to pull the rug out from under you unless you played nice. "I'm talking about something like a hidden *nanny cam*. Nobody would notice it at first glance."

"Those things don't have a long transmitting distance." This was Johnny Hawkins' contribution to the conversation. He wasn't saying anything Pagan hadn't already considered.

"At the Martin house in Sherman Oaks, they'd made a series of prowler complaints and a break in where nothing appeared to be taken," Pagan said. "I believe there is or was a camera there as well. The prowler was most likely the suspect getting close enough to download the video remotely."

"How far can they transmit?" Livia Nelson asked. "Through walls? From upstairs." She was smart enough not to challenge Pagan further at this point. Probably had been burnt by him before. However, she was a good detective and was immediately trying to narrow the field.

From where he stood in the middle of the room, Pagan turned a full three-sixty. "Not upstairs," he said. He turned completely around again. "Probably placed against the inside of an exterior wall...A wall easily accessible from outside...most likely near a window..." He began turning around again.

"Or a sliding glass door," I suggested.

Everyone turned to look at me. I was standing next to

the sliding glass door leading to a back garden patio. On the other side of me was a fireplace with an ornate plaster mantle. Nothing looked out of place.

"Needs a power source," Pagan said.

I looked down at the electric plug outlet in the small space of wall between the fireplace and the start of the sliding glass door. There was what looked like a six outlet surge protector plugged in and completely covering the standard two plug outlet. I unplugged it and took a close look. It was a disguised camera.

"You make my brain hurt," I said to Pagan, holding the device out toward him.

Pagan reached for it, but Livia Nelson stepped in front of him and grabbed the item from my hand.

She turned it over and around and touched a little round hole on the front. She swore softly.

Pagan was already on his phone talking to Dante Castano, who was still at the Martin home in Sherman Oaks. Pagan described what we'd found then disconnected.

He took the device gently from Livia.

"How much does something like that cost?"

"A few hundred dollars," Pagan said.

"Easily available?"

"Online, Best Buy, Walmart."

"No way to trace the purchase?"

Pagan shook his head and handed the device back to Livia. He turned toward Smack Daddy and Judith. "I take it neither of you bought nor installed this?"

Smack Daddy looked a little shell-shocked.

"I never even noticed it before," Judith said. "What is it?" She was having a little trouble keeping up.

"A remote recording device."

"Somebody has been watching us?" Judith's already pale face turned chalky.

Pagan's phone vibrated. He accepted the call and spoke his name into the phone, "Pagan." He listen for a moment, nodding. "Okay. Thanks."

He disconnected and looked at me. "Same device as here. In Gerrard Martin's room. A plug right beneath a window."

I sighed. I didn't know if we were any closer to finding the missing children, but there was now no doubt they were connected, even if we still didn't know why.

CHAPTER 23

*"The truth is always an insult or a joke,
lies are generally tastier. We love them.
The nature of lies is to please. Truth
has no concern for anyone's comfort"*
- Katherine Dunn, Geek Love

I sat across the table from Pagan and watched him savor the last morsel of what had been an amazing *ossobuco alla milanese*, which was a fancy way of saying cross-cut veal shanks braised with vegetables, white wine and broth. I knew it was amazing because I'd finished my own portion moments before. We were back at the Hacienda in Sophia's, the Italian trattoria. Apparently, there was always an open table kept for Pagan. One of the perks of living at the Hacienda he told me.

The restaurant itself verged on kitsch, the painted murals on the wall almost obscured by grape vines and framed photos of the Italian goddess who provided both namesake and inspiration. However, the red-checked tablecloths over rough wood tables and candles stuck in Chianti bottles were offset by the amazing food and the warmth of the family who ran the business.

In her late teens, Ciara, one of three daughters who acted as waitresses, was clearly infatuated with Pagan. For his part, he was smiling and friendly without in any way being encouraging. I appreciated him after having worked with too many preening males who would have taken advantage.

Pagan accepted an espresso, which was provided without his asking. Somebody knew I couldn't stand the stuff as I got my own pot of regular coffee delivered, again without asking. Life with Pagan was a constant surprise. Apparently, there was no check either. Another perk.

"What's your take on the case?" Pagan asked me after his first sip of espresso.

I made a production of pouring out coffee into the provided mug, giving myself a second to think about my answer. My bad leg ached a bit and I had it stuck straight out along one side of the table. I took a swallow of my own coffee, thankful for its warmth. I'd chowed down more calories today than any two days in recent memory, but when Ciara delivered tiramisu, I found I still had a little room. Pagan's plan to fatten me up was obviously working.

"I think we've still got two missing kids, not to mention a missing five million dollars, which we didn't *actually* mention to anyone."

Pagan gave a low chuckle.

The two crime scenes had been turned over to the PM Watch detectives from the respective areas. There was a patrol unit stationed at both residences, but everything appeared to be on hold.

"Frustrating, isn't it?" Pagan said.

I chased the last trace of tiramisu around the small bowl it had been served in. I swallowed the captured delicacy and indelicately licked the spoon. I sat back in my chair and readjusted my leg using both hands. "Still no ransom demand, which seems a moot point if you factor in the five million dollars. If this was about money, there would have been no reason to take the kids, but there are no other indications of why these two kids were targeted. It's clear they are connected, but who would want these kids?"

"Exactly, Randall. The precise point," Pagan said. "Good for you."

I must have looked confused.

"Think about your last statement," Pagan said.

I tried to remember. "Who would want these kids?" I said tentatively.

"Look at it from the opposite angle..." Pagan urged.

"Who didn't want these kids? I don't get it."

"Yes. Who *didn't* want these kids? Come on, Randall. I need you to work it through so I don't sound crazy," Pagan pushed.

"You always sound crazy. You sound crazy right now." I was stalling for time, my brain whirling.

Pagan rolled his eyes. "You can see my words. You know I'm being sincere. Humor me."

I picked up my coffee mug. Set it back down without drinking from it. I took a deep breath to clear my head, then closed my eyes, blew the air out slowly through pursed lips, and started talking.

"Smack Daddy didn't want Unicorn," I said, eyes still closed, making my way slowly through the mental maze Pagan had posited for me. "At least he wanted everybody – or at least the bad guys to whom he owed money – to believe Unicorn was unwanted. It's why he set himself up to be ridiculed by leaking the screwy DNA tests. That was deliberate. He was willing to suffer the scandal in order to completely distance himself from his child."

I opened my eyes to see Pagan's cool grays staring at me steadily. "And..." he prompted.

"And..." I hesitated, and then continued. "From their body language and the color of their words, it is clear both Harvey Martin and his daughter Sophie considered Gerrard a huge burden, but for different reasons."

"Did they want him?"

I shook my head. "Harvey definitely not. Sophie is a different situation. She's carrying a huge burden of guilt. Harvey Martin denies her any kind of help, any outside life. He is punishing her for Gerrard's condition. As a result, Gerrard is a huge responsibility weighing Sophie down."

Pagan nodded. "Crushing her."

I sat and thought. "You're saying the commonality between the two children is they were unwanted by those who are supposed to care for them."

"Yes."

"Okay, but why only these two kids? It's a harsh world. Aren't there many unwanted children?"

"*I am only one, but I am one. I can't do everything, but I can do something. And because I cannot do everything, I will not refuse to do the something I can do.*"

I was confused again. I hated when Pagan did this.

"A quote from Edward Everett Hale," Pagan said. The colored ribbons attached to his words showed only slight exasperation. "But passing over the attribution, the homily applies."

I got it. "Somebody decided to do something about these two children in particular because he or she could. But it has to be somebody who the two children have in common. Somebody who is familiar with both situations."

"Somebody with a plan," Pagan said. "Opportunity."

"And money," I said.

"Five million dollars is a lot of money. It may be the key to the timing."

"Somebody who knew Smack Daddy was gathering cash," I said.

"Somebody who would care deeply about both these children." Pagan said.

"Somebody smart," I said. "Which would leave out Richards and Tuttle, Smack Daddy's bodyguards."

Pagan chuckled. "Those two might be sharing a jail cell, but not a brain cell."

"Then who else? Who do these two kids have in common? There are no mutual caregivers. The families are from completely different worlds."

Pagan leaned back in his chair and ran his hands through his hair. He looked thoughtful.

"You know something," I said. "Don't you?"

"I suspect," Pagan said.

"What? Who? Give..."

Pagan held up his hands. "Not yet. It's only a glimmer of an idea. Let me gnaw on it. I don't have it yet."

"Come on ..." I was exasperated.

"It's no good, Randall. I can't get the words out yet. The idea is unformed. It has no substance. I've got to think more about it."

"And what am I supposed to do while you cogitate?" I folded my arms across my chest.

Pagan leaned forward, put his right hand on my left forearm and pulled my arms loose. "Don't get angry with me..."

"I'm not angry..."

"Arms crossed high and tight across your chest. Classic anger. Plus, never forget, I can hear it in your tone."

He was right, of course.

"This is my process." Pagan said. "I can only explain something to somebody else after I've worked it through sufficiently for myself."

I tried a smile. "That way you always sound like the smartest person in the room."

"I am not always the smartest person in the room, Randall, but I am always the most sensitive. And despite your attempts to soften your delivery I can still hear the underlying rancor."

I threw up my hands then recrossed my arms. I tried not to do it high and tight, but the end result was not exactly low and loose.

Pagan smiled. "Please try to understand." Sincerity colored every ribbon attached to his words. "Isn't this why we both have trouble sustaining any kind of social relationships? Please be the smartest person in this room. Please understand me."

CHAPTER 24

"Things come apart so easily when they have been held together with lies."
- Dorothy Allison, Bastard Out of Carolina

Fifteen minutes later I was in a daze of a different nature. It had been very odd sitting in Sophia's and realizing my living quarters had been changed without anything more than me turning over a key to my own apartment.

Leaving Pagan to his ruminations I'd made my way up the Hacienda's bell tower stairway to the second floor and turned left to the doorway Pagan had shown me earlier in the morning.

So much had happened that *earlier in the morning* seemed almost a lifetime away.

The day had been filled with emotional scenes and there was yet to be a resolution to most of them. I hesitated outside the door, not willing to go in and face a space filled with moving boxes containing my life, none of which I would have packed myself.

I finally used the key pad beside the door to gain entry. I led with my cane and stepped in with my head down, but when I looked up I was flabbergasted. The whole loft area had been transformed. Yes, the hanging, flying carpet bed was still there, as was the wall of electronics, but several explosions of colorful flowers had been added along with a white lace mosquito netting, which fell from a point on the ceiling and draped down over the bed like something out of Scheherazade.

There were no packing boxes. I moved to the closet and found my clothes all arranged on matching hangers. Next to the closet, the drawers of an antique dresser I hadn't seen before were filled with my sweaters, workout clothes, and more personal items.

Two bookcases had been moved in. One held my books and the shelves of the other displayed my father's collection of antique cameras – each placed with more care than I had ever shown them. Hell, I hadn't had them out of their storage box in years.

Tears sprang to my eyes as I ran a finger over the battered Leica, which had been my father's personal favorite when he was photographing in combat zones. It all felt weird and other worldly. Who had done this? Certainly not Arlo, to whom I'd given my apartment keys. It was almost a violation, yet everything appeared to have been done with such care it was hard to be upset.

I wandered through my new space. There was a fresh comforter on the bed with pillows in crisp white cases. A nightstand and lamp had appeared from nowhere, the lamp plugged into a conveniently placed floor socket by the bed.

The book I'd last been reading in my apartment had been placed on the nightstand's polished surface.

There was a knock on the door, which I'd left open.

"Are you alright, dear?"

It was Rose Parker. She stood in the doorway with a warm smile looking maternal and understanding.

I tried to stop the tears from streaming down my face, but the dam suddenly burst. Rose stepped forward and gathered me into an embrace. My cane slipped from my grip and I clung to this woman I barely knew, an emotional tsunami sweeping through me.

"I'm sorry," I blubbered, "I'm sorry. I don't know what's wrong with me."

Rose stroked the back of my head. "There is nothing wrong with you," she said softly. "At least nothing wrong with you that isn't just as wrong with all the rest of us here at the Hacienda."

"What do you mean?" I still had my face buried against Rose's shoulder.

"The Hacienda is about second chances. It's about a home and a family of our own choosing. Mr. Pagan chose you, just like he chose the rest of us. And we chose him."

"Why do you all insist on calling him Mr. Pagan?" I asked, gulping to get control over my emotions.

"It's a bit of a tease, dear. A nickname, which we know embarrasses him a bit. But he has been so kind to all of us here, it is really a term of endearment."

I pulled back, disentangling myself from Rose's embrace, a little embarrassed myself. "Who did all this?" I asked.

"Arlo and a number of others who are part of the Hacienda. Many hands make short work of a task, but I supervised and took care of all of your more personal items.

A woman needs to keep certain things private." Rose smiled.

It wasn't like I had a drawer full of Victoria's Secret underwear, or the array of icky plastic phallic items we uncover every time we serve a search warrant, but I was unreasonably grateful for her gesture.

"Thank you." Tears welled up in my eyes again. "I'm sorry," I snuffled. "This is so silly."

"Not silly at all, dear," Rose said, handing me a tissue from a stash in the sleeve of her light white sweater. "I'm sure you've had a very long day. Mr. Pagan can be a hash task master. Why don't you take a shower and see if you can get some sleep."

"I'll do that, Rose. Thank you."

When Rose left, closing the door behind her, I took her advice. There were fresh, fluffy white towels in the bathroom, along with a light terrycloth robe. It was long enough to hide the scars on my thighs when I wrapped it around me.

With my hair still slightly damp, I propped my cane against the three box steps leading up to the hanging bed. I then scrambled up and dropped down onto the soft wonder of it all. It was like being surrounded by Heaven.

I was exhausted, but I took a quick mental inventory and found I was feeling something odd and alien – happiness. In the middle of everything – shot in the leg, mental aberrations, two missing kids, and so much more – my default setting for the first time in forever was happiness.

I held the joy of that realization for a second, then two, and then fell into unconsciousness rather than sleep.

"Rise and shine, Randall..."

What the hell!

I sat bolt upright in bed, totally disoriented.

Where was I?

"Pagan?" My voice came out via a croak, my heart pounding.

Where was he?

"If you are talking to me, Randall, I can't hear you. You have to press the intercom button. It's right next to your front door."

I plopped back onto the bed pillows.

"Randall..."

I sat up again, angry. I swung my legs out of the bed, and almost killed myself tripping down the three box steps. I finally steadied myself, grabbed my cane, and limped over to the front door. On the wall to the left was an intercom panel to which I hadn't paid any earlier attention.

I flipped down the speaker button. "I swear I'm going to kill you, Pagan." Anger and disorientation fizzed through me.

"Good morning, Randall." Pagan's voice was filled with sunshine and bluebirds. I might just actually kill him. "It's five-forty. You've got twenty minutes to get to the dojo. Don't be late. Tanaka hates it when people are late."

There was a flat click as Pagan hung up.

I flipped the talk switch on my end again. "Pagan?" I was incensed. "Pagan? I swear, I'm going to rip this thing out of the wall." I slapped the intercom panel with the flat of my hand. "Aarrrgh!"

I dropped my cane, turned my back to the wall, and slid down until I was sitting on the floor with my knees up. My heart was pounding.

I didn't want to go to the dojo. Pagan couldn't make me

go to the dojo. I ran my fingers through the tangle of my hair.

The robe I was wearing dropped open and I could see the livid scar on my thigh.

I looked up and took in the surroundings of my new home.

Despite the rude awakening, I'd slept better than at any time since the shooting. I sighed. Last night, climbing into the hanging bed, I'd felt like a child again. Maybe this was home. Maybe Pagan was nothing more than the pain in the butt older brother I'd never had.

I groaned and worked my way to my feet. Limping into the kitchen, I hit the button on the prepared coffee maker and headed to the bathroom.

Fifteen minutes later I walked out the door wearing sweats, and made my way to the dojo.

———

Tanaka was a surprise. I'd expected a traditional if grueling workout. What I got was a lot of one-on-one attention from Tanaka as he placed me in balanced positions and had me hold them. It all sounded so simple, but within minutes I was sweating up a storm.

I had expected Pagan to be there, but he wasn't anywhere to be found. It was just Tanaka, who kept talking in a reassuring voice as he assessed everything I did, moving my limbs with his one calloused hand from position to position. His round face was placid, concentrating.

At one point, Tanaka moved my left foot slightly beneath me. He made me bend my left knee another few degrees. My right leg was extended, but also bent to maintain balance.

Tanaka stood behind me, his hand cupping my left hip bone. Suddenly, he pulled my left hip backward, twisting it behind me. There was a split second of intense pain. I lost my balance and fell clumsily to the padded mat covering the floor of the dojo.

The pain passed as quickly as it came, but the relief was amazing. It was as if my back had been set free. Pain I hadn't known I was harboring had fled like the night. I gasped with relief, feeling sweat break out on my forehead in huge droplets.

"What did you do?" I asked.

"You favoring hip too much since shooting. Spine completely out of alignment," Tanaka said. "Better now, but still work to do."

"Yes. Better," I agreed. "But how about warning me next time.

"Warning not work. You tense up. Surprise best." Tanaka held out his hand. I grasped it and he pulled me up. I knew it couldn't be true, but my left leg felt stronger, longer even.

"Muscles have atrophied," Tanaka said, beginning to put me into another balance position. "Still too skinny. Need to build up strength and speed. Need to eat."

After about thirty minutes, he let me take a water break.

"Let me have your cane," he said after I'd gulped down a half bottle of water.

I handed it to him without question.

He examined it briefly. "Any sentimental value?" he asked.

"I hate the thing," I said.

Tanaka tested its heft then trapped it at an angle between the floor and his hand and snapped it cleanly in half with his opposite foot.

"Hey!" I was genuinely surprised. "I said I hated it. I didn't say it wasn't expensive. And I need it."

Tanaka grunted. "For now," he said. Seemingly out of thin air, he produced another cane. It was black and looked very similar to the cane now splintered on the floor. He offered it to me.

Taking it, I could immediately feel the difference. It was lightweight, but balanced with a heavy silver knob in the shape of a crown on the top and a similarly weighted ferrule tip on the other end.

"More expensive," Tanaka said, a silly smile splitting his face.

"Is there a sword inside?" I asked, jokingly. I gave the cane a tentative baton twirl.

"Twist crown," Tanaka said.

I looked at him, then did what he asked. A wicked two-inch blade shot out of the ferrule tip. "Holy crap," I said.

"Titanium cane. Very light. Never break," Tanaka said. "When you learn to use it, it will help you balance. I will teach you to fight with it. It is a weapon, not a tool or a toy."

I twisted the heavy silver crown back the other way and the blade slid back into hiding. I hefted the cane. It made a wicked nightstick.

"Not exactly department approved," I said.

"Neither am I," Pagan said, his voice coming from the front door of the dojo as he stepped inside. He looked grave despite his jibe.

"What is it?" I asked.

"We have to go," he said. "Harvey Martin has just been killed in a hit and run outside his mortuary."

CHAPTER 25

"The man who lies to the world, is the world's
slave from then on. There are no white lies, there
is only the blackest of destruction, and a white
lie is the blackest of all."
- Ayn Rand, Atlas Shrugged

It had taken thirty minutes after Pagan interrupted my
workout with Tanaka to just grab a shower, pull my wet hair
back into a ponytail, drag on slacks and a blouse, a pair of
comfortable flats, buckle on my gun, and grab my new cane.
Pagan was too impatient to wait while I messed with
make-up.

Since I didn't carry a purse, keeping my driver's license
in the same flat wallet with my ID card, I realized I was
going to have to stash a back-up bag of necessities in Pagan's
Escalade. It was either that or go through my days looking
both underfed and pale.

Pagan was again dressed in contrast to the accepted
detective uniform of suit and tie. Black jeans over Cuban-

heeled black boots, a tucked in dark blue tee-shirt, another wide silver bangle on his right wrist, a white watch on his left, and a holstered Glock, flaunted his disregard for department conventions. With his straight black hair and sharp angled face, he looked more gypsy than cop. He caught me looking at him.

"This is just a costume, Randall."

"What?"

"You were looking at the way I dress and wondering how I get away with not conforming to the department's detective standards."

Damn him. How did he do that?

"Now you're wondering how I knew what you were thinking."

"Stop doing that," I yelped.

"Can't," he said. "It's second nature. Being an empath helps me do my job, but in normal circumstance most people find it disconcerting and irritating. Like you, though, I can't turn it off."

"Fair enough," I said. "But what did you mean about a costume?"

"We all wear costumes. Sometimes we call them uniforms, or protective equipment, or fashion, but everything we wear is a costume. How we dress declares who we are within the world where we operate. We dress to send a subconscious message to those with whom we interact."

I fought the urge to look down and take in my own sartorial choices. I didn't want to know what kind of message my costume was sending.

Pagan's face was a complete blank, but I knew that was because he was reading my mind again and didn't want to specifically hit my nail on its head.

Instead of rising to the bait, I said. "You dress specifically to throw off people's expectations of cops?"

"Exactly. To be successful, I have to take every advantage, no matter how small or inconsequential. I read people by how they dress, by how they carry themselves, by how they talk, how they move. But those people are also reading me, albeit on a much more subconscious level. If they read me as a stereotypical cop, it's just another barrier I have to overcome to get to the truth."

"So, it's a manipulation?"

"Absolutely. I'll wear whatever costume, whatever facial expression, whatever physical stance is needed in order to get to the truth."

I thought about that for a second as Pagan weaved through traffic. "Then who is the real Ray Pagan?" I asked.

Pagan shrugged. "All of them and none of them," he said quietly. Twisting the Escalade's steering wheel sharply, he suddenly cut off a semi-truck and trailer and sped into an open lane.

I dramatically grabbed the plastic panic handle above the passenger door. "Can we cool the engines on this jet a bit? I need you to talk to me."

"I am talking to you," Pagan said, but his foot eased up on the accelerator and we dropped down to a respectable speed.

"About the case," I said. "What do you know that I don't?"

"I don't *know* anything..."

"Then what is it you *suspect*? Clearly, you've gone down some kind of twisted path."

"I spent most of last night going over the reports on the ten year–old LAPD missing person's case for Connor Martin and the hit and run report on his father, Jack Martin."

"How much sleep did you get last night," I asked.

"Sleep is inconsequential."

"How do you keep that attitude long term?"

"Do you want to know what I think about this case, or do you want to discuss my sleep patterns?"

"Both," I said. "But let's stick with the case," I said, relenting now that Pagan was no longer driving at warp speed.

Pagan sighed. "Before I go way out on a limb, tell me your impressions of the case. What is the first thing to come to mind?"

I'd been doing some thinking myself and replied immediately. "All that stuff about pinching and fairies and making Chad turn and face the wall was simply Connor trying to protect Chad from what was really happening. Connor Martin most likely ran away ten years ago because he was being molested by the man who had adopted him, Jack Martin."

"Agreed," Pagan said.

It was silly, but his approval gave me a warm feeling. I was an experienced detective with one of the highest clearance rates in RHD, but somehow Pagan's opinion of me was more important. It was a bit ridiculous, but there was a part of me that recognized it as truth – my truth, at least.

"Do you tie Connor going missing to the hit and run involving Jack Martin the next morning?" Pagan asked.

I thought for a moment. "If Jack Martin *hadn't* been killed, and Connor was never found, then I would be looking at Jack Martin as a suspect in Conner's disappearance."

"Given those circumstances, I'd agree again," Pagan said. "It has always disturbed me that only humans tolerate same-species predators."

I kept my train of thought going. "However, Castano was right earlier. Ten years ago Juvenile Division would have handled the missing, and Traffic Division would have handled the hit and run, and clearly nobody bothered to put the two cases together."

"A much different time in the Department's history. Not only that, but ten years ago we didn't handle missing kids under twelve as *critical missings*. We did nothing more than we did for any other missing kid – put their name in the system and handled them as if they were a runaway until they came home, got arrested for something else, or turned up dead. However, even today, the connection could have fallen through the cracks."

I nodded. "With hindsight, I think it's pretty clear, Conner was behind the wheel of the car that killed his adopted father and abuser."

"Revenge?"

"Partly, but there's a much more likely reason."

Pagan produced a sad, but knowing smile. "Conner probably believed Jack Martin was getting ready to turn his sexual attentions to Chad, who Conner would protect at any cost."

"It happens in families all the time," I agreed. "As one victim ages out, the abuser turns to a younger family member."

"Conner must have known having his brother turn and face the wall was no longer going to be enough to protect him from also being *pinched by the fairies*," Pagan said.

"But how does a ten year-old, even if he's a wild child, learn to hot wire and steal a car?" I asked, following the thought process. I could see where Pagan was leading me, but I wasn't ready to go there just yet.

"No mystery. The report states the keys were in the vehicle when it was stolen," Pagan said.

I finally gave Pagan what he was waiting for. "You don't think Jack Martin was the only one of the Martin brothers who was an abuser, do you?"

"Statistics show the majority of sexual child abusers victimize their direct or extended family members."

"And it can be perpetuated from generation to generation," I said.

"Which means, the Martin brothers were very likely abused by their own father," Pagan said.

"But there is no way Gerrard Martin is capable of running his uncle down. Even if he understood the abuses his uncle was possibly perpetrating." My head was beginning to hurt.

"Probably, not possibly," Pagan said. "But, no, not Gerrard," Pagan paused, then continued. "Conner. Once a protector, always a protector."

"What?"

"Think about it."

I ran my hands through my hair. "Conner Martin? If he's still alive, he'd be twenty now. Where has he been for ten years, and how do you connect him to both missing kids?"

"Fairies," Pagan said, and pulled in to the crime scene before he explained further.

―――

The scene at the Martin Mortuary and Funeral Home was a hive of police activity. Yellow crime scene tape had been secured around stacked orange pylons, which outlined the area of the hit and run in the parking lot. There was a slight breeze, which fluttered the loose ends of the tape giving everything the feel of a church fête.

Between the pylons sat the hearse used by the business. Harvey Martin's body had been caught as he was getting out of the driver's side. It had been mangled and pinned there by the impact of an ancient white Ford pick-up truck, which was still at the scene – its own driver's door left open, the cab abandoned.

An ambulance, a fire truck, and a phalanx of paramedics and firemen all went about their various tasks. The detritus of their useless first aid work was scattered around the dark pools of blood on the parking lot tarmac.

"Any witnesses?" Pagan asked Dante Castano, who was already on the scene with Ken Dodd.

"Not to the actual incident," Castano said. "There was another employee already at the mortuary who heard the crash and came out to see what happened."

"See anyone leaving the scene?" I asked.

Dante snorted. "We're never that lucky. No video in the area either."

"We on the same page that this is a deliberate act?" Pagan asked.

"Absolutely," Castano said. "We've got a full forensic crew on the way. If there's any trace evidence in the pick-up, we'll find it."

"Who owns the pick-up?" I asked.

"It's an all-purpose vehicle, which belongs to the mortuary. It's usually kept in the back with the key in it."

"Common knowledge among the mortuary staff?"

"Apparently. The key is supposed to be kept on a hook in the main office, but nobody seems to have followed that protocol in years."

I nodded. "Premeditated. Suspect was clearly lying in wait and knew the victim's routine."

"Also made absolutely sure the victim didn't survive," Castano said. "From my prior experience working traffic, I'd say the impact was made at the fastest speed possible when mashing down the gas pedal from one end of the parking lot to the other. Victim had turned to reach back into the vehicle. Impact crushed him to a paste."

Both Pagan and I turned and looked from one end of the parking lot where it exited to the street, to the other, which led around to the back of the mortuary. The lot ran the full length of the mortuary building, which seemed a little excessive for the type of business, but then some viewings and funerals could be very large.

"Anybody check on Sophie Martin?" I asked. I remembered what she had said about wishing somebody would run down her uncle, Harvey Martin.

"She's at home with her brother Chad," Castano said.

"They alibi each other?"

"For what it's worth," Castano said. We all knew the worth of a familial alibi was low, but it would hold for the moment.

Livia Nelson and her lap dog partner, Johnny Hawkins, pulled up and parked. They walked over to join us.

Livia took one look at the body still trapped in the mass of steel waiting for the tow truck to pull the vehicles apart and release it, and then turned to look at me.

"You look a bigger wreck than he does," she said, jerking her head toward the mass of crushed metal, bone, and flesh.

"I feel it," I said with a smile. Her words were tied to yellow streamers, which I knew held no poisonous harm despite their biting sound. If they had been red, or I hadn't been paying attention, I might have reacted differently.

Being around Pagan was making me spend more time in the moment.

Livia smiled back and laughed. "You've got a good one there, Pagan," she said. "No getting under her skin."

Pagan looked pointedly at Livia. "Do we need to have a lesson about glass houses?"

Livia laughed again then cursed when she realized a news camera was capturing our frivolity at the crime scene on video.

"I'll just make sure that doesn't end up on the next newscast," Johnny Hawkins said, moving away toward the independent cameraman.

"Better behave," Pagan said. "The network and cable people will all be here soon."

Livia grabbed a roll of yellow tape. "I'll just go expand the crime scene. Keep the cameras at bay and give the brass somewhere to stand and make themselves feel important."

Having a two-tiered crime scene was a good idea. The outer ring kept the public at bay. The inner ring was where police supervisors and brass could feel separated from the *hoi polloi*, yet not step all over clues on your crime scene.

A loud sound made us all turn toward the emergency rescue personnel. They were starting the *Jaws of Life*, which were misnamed in this case, to cut what was left of Harvey Martin out of the wreckage.

Over the racket, Pagan turned to me and asked, "What do you think?"

I thought back to the conversation we'd had in the Escalade on the way over. Pagan's left field explanation for what was going on.

"I think somebody was mightily pissed off at Harvey Martin," I said.

Dante Castano's ears perked up like a horse scenting water. "You two got some kind of lead?"

Pagan remained silent, so I stayed quiet also. This was Pagan's show.

"Come on," Castano said. "We've still got two missing kids, now this meat bag explosion, and we got nada in the clues closet. Tell me you got something."

"Maybe," Pagan said.

"You want to share?"

Pagan shook his head. "Not yet. It's too tenuous."

Too crazy was more like it.

"Then go make it more *tenuous*," Castano said, exaggerating the last word. The maroon and black intertwining ribbons on his words showed how frustrated he was. "Find the kids and solve this freaking case already."

I thought I saw a split second smile flash across Pagan's lips. It was there and gone. A micro expression. What had it been? Contempt or satisfaction. Was it Pagan's ego showing a crack in his unflappable façade?

He turned and walked away without saying a word.

"What's with him?" Castano asked me.

I pondered that micro expression for a moment longer. Not contempt or satisfaction. Not ego either. It had been guilt.

"He thinks he could have stopped this."

"How?" Castano's word ribbons matched the genuine look of shock on his face.

"Because he thinks he is responsible for everyone and everything."

"That won't kill him as quick as a bullet," Castano said. "But it's a slow poison and he'll be just as dead in the end."

Pagan honked the Escalade horn and I turned on my new cane and went to join the impatient bastard.

CHAPTER 26

"Fiction was invented the day Jonah arrived home and told his wife that he was three days late because he had been swallowed by a whale…"
- Gabriel García Márquez

Climbing into the Escalade I asked, "Where first?"

"Sophie Martin," Pagan said.

"That's going to be a fun interview?" I asked.

"Has to be done," Pagan said. "Her special needs son has disappeared. Her abusive, demanding uncle has just been killed. She's the one who has been carrying the crushing load, which makes her a suspect."

"But not our suspect," I said, seeing the message in the color of Pagan's words. "You think she knows Connor is alive, maybe even knows where he is?"

"No," Pagan said. "But Smack Daddy might, although I doubt he knows him by the name Connor Martin."

"What? I'm confused. How do you make that leap?"

"Fairies," Pagan said.

"So you keep saying, but I'm still not getting it."

"Do you know what a changeling is?"

"Something out of a horror film franchise or something, isn't it. A good kid replaced by a bad kid."

"A changeling is what's left behind after a human child has been stolen by fairies."

"Fairies again. And this applies how?"

"Remember, I come from a culture lumped together by the song as *Gypsies, Tramps, and Thieves*. We are taught to lie to everyone except our own, and our history is full to the brim with folklore. We know all about fairies. As children we're taught fairy women find birth a difficult experience. Many fairy children die before birth and those who do survive are often stunted or deformed creatures. The adult fairies, who are aesthetic beings, are repelled by these infants and have no wish to keep them.

"To make us behave, our parents told us the fairies will try to swap their ugly babies with healthy, but naughty, children who the fairies steal from the mortal world. The wizened, ill-tempered creature left in place of the human child is called a changeling and possesses the power to work evil in a household.

"It is their temperament, however, which most marks the changeling. Babies are generally supposed to be joyful and pleasant, but the fairy substitute is never happy, except when some calamity befalls the household. For the most part, it howls and screeches throughout the waking hours and the sound and frequency of its yells often transcend the bounds of mortal endurance."

I shook my head trying to make sense of what Pagan

was saying. "You want me to believe Chad and Gerrard are changelings left behind by fairies? Come on..."

"No. That's not what I think."

"Wait..." I made the mental leap. "You think Smack Daddy's rap artist Changeling is actually Conner Martin? That he chose the name Changeling because of all the fairy tales he told Chad? That he thinks the child he became after the abuse was a changeling...that he became a changeling?"

"I can *feel* it when I think about him. He feels he was stolen away by what his adopted father did to him."

"How can you *feel* something like that? We don't even know for sure Conner is still alive."

"I listened to a lot of Changeling's music last night. It's all there behind the poignant words. The tone and intonation of how he sings speaks volumes about the pain he has experienced, about how he feels."

"But how can you *feel* that enough to be sure it's what he's feeling?" I still didn't want to just roll over and submit to something that sounded so suspect.

"How do you see colored streamers tied to people's words?"

That brought me up short. "But isn't Changeling's real name Benny White? And why would he take Gerrard and Unicorn?"

"One mystery at a time, Randall. But we're going to have to hurry. I'm empathically aligned, and I know if we don't unravel this fast, Gerrard and Unicorn are going to be beyond our reach. If we don't get to Connor soon, something very bad is going to happen."

Sophie Martin was not happy to see us, but then who is ever happy to see the cops? We only turn up when we've caught them doing something wrong, or when they've been the victim of something and want to blame us for not doing our job by stopping whatever it was from happening.

Sophie met us at the door to her house wearing a bright sundress in a blue paisley pattern. Perhaps she hadn't had time to pull out her black mourning clothes. As the daughter and niece of funeral directors, she should have something more appropriate, but perhaps she had an aversion to black.

The bright dress accentuated what curves remained on her frail frame and her hair was brushed. Light makeup accentuated her eyes, but the effect was spoiled by the misaligned slash of too pink lipstick across her thin mouth.

"Why are you here and not looking for the person who murdered my uncle?" Her arms were crossed in front of her and she clearly wasn't about to let us in.

"There is a whole team of detectives at the crime scene working this case," I said.

This was apparently the wrong approach because Pagan somehow eased himself in front of me and waved at someone I couldn't see.

"Hi, Chad," he said.

"Hi, Ray." The voice from behind Sophie was filled with the excitement of a child seeing a new friend. "Can they come in, sissy? Please." Chad's voice was now plaintiff. I didn't need Ray's skills to hear the underlying whine indicating an emotional storm if he didn't get his way.

Sophie put her head down, but she moved out of the doorway.

Pagan and I stepped in. Ray moved immediately to

Chad, giving him one of those *bromance* handshake and hug things, which I've never understood.

I looked at Sophie. There was going to be no sisterhood bonding with her, so I plunged right in.

"I'm sorry about your uncle."

"I told you it was happening all over again. I told everyone, but nobody listens to me." The streamers attached to her words were in colors indicating fear, not anger.

"I listen to you," Chad said. The blue hue attached to his words was beautiful, the color of innocence.

Pagan had released him, but was still standing close to Chad as if offering security. Some people with mental disabilities can't stand to have their space invaded, while others don't understand normal social boundaries and seek out closeness. Pagan had obviously read Chad correctly. I wasn't surprised in the least.

Sophie's face softened. "I know you do," she said to her brother, older than her chronologically, but mentally years behind her.

"You did tell us," I said to Sophie. "I'm sorry." It was better to diffuse her with agreement, than arguing about what she had or hadn't told us making sense at the time. "I need your help to figure this whole thing out." Even though Pagan was with me, I was trying to get through to Sophie on a one to one level.

Something flashed across Sophie's face and was gone. A micro expression, too fast to interpret. "What do you want?"

"Do you have any photos of Connor?"

"Surely the police were given a photo when my parents reported him missing."

"I'm sure they did," I said. "But that was ten years ago. The report was digitized, but the photo wasn't added.

We've requested the original file, but it hasn't yet been retrieved from the bowels of the police archives."

Sophie shook her head as if this incompetence was only to be expected. "I don't think there are any photos of him after all these years."

"Why not?" I asked gently. Most families would treasure photos of a missing or deceased child.

Sophie shrugged. "I was too young at the time to understand and everything was in such upheaval after Connor went missing. With father being killed and mother being sick, it's all a blur."

"What do you remember?"

The shrug came again as did the micro expression crossing her face. This time, I caught it – *embarrassment*. That was odd.

"There was a lot of drama over Connor being adopted. I heard my parents arguing one time. Father was furious. Connor's birth mother was white, but as Connor grew, it became clear there was some *mud in the water*, as my father so crudely put it."

"How old were you?"

"This was just before Connor went missing. I was nine, but just because you are young doesn't mean you don't hear and remember things."

I agreed. "Words like that can leave a lasting impression. So, your father believed Connor was of mixed race?"

"Yes. He accused my mother of lying to him about Conner's father because she wanted a baby so badly."

"Do you think that was true?"

Sophie shrugged. "Maybe."

"Clearly, this made your father very angry."

Sophie nodded this time. Unfolding her arms then, not knowing what to do with them, refolded them. "The mortuary business has made my uncles very comfortable financially, but it has also made them very, very conservative in their view. My father was just like them. I don't think he could abide the thought the son he adopted wasn't pure. That's what he said to my mother – Connor wasn't pure."

"Do you think he was abusing Connor?"

The tears rolling unashamedly down Sophie's face were more of an answer than any words.

"Where is Gerrard?" She suddenly gulped for air. "What has happened to Gerrard? Uncle Harvey hated him because of his condition, just like my father hated Connor. Where is he? Please find him." Sophie started to sag to the floor, but I caught her and guided her to a chair.

She was sobbing when Chad stepped forward and put his arms around her. "It's okay, sissy. Ray will find Gerrard." He looked over at Ray. "Won't you?"

Pagan was obviously uncomfortable. It was a promise he couldn't make. I knew it, Pagan knew it, and Sophie knew it.

But Chad didn't. And he knew just what he could do to help.

He suddenly released Sophie and ran out of the room like a hyperactive five year-old. He was back in less than a minute holding the book of Irish fairy tales.

"I still have a picture of Connor," he said. "I kept it."

Opening the pages of the book, he reverently pulled out a four-by-six photo. He handed it to Pagan.

Standing next to Pagan, I could see the photo was of a seven or eight year-old Chad standing next to a slightly built boy, their arms linked across shoulders. Chad was smiling sweetly.

Conner was taller, but he could have been taken for the same age or even younger if it wasn't for the haunted almost feral look of a stray cat in his eyes. If it wasn't a trick of the camera, or the light, this was a child either possessed or wise beyond his years. Even in the faded colors, it was clear the slighter built boy had a darker skin tone. His head was buzzed, nothing but a fine covering of black fuzz.

"That's Conner," Chad said proudly. "My brother."

I looked beyond the figures to the background of the picture. "Where was this taken?" I asked.

"At the cemetery," Chad said.

"The cemetery?"

"Valley of Olives," Sophie said. "We played there all the time as kids. It was part of the first Martin Mortuary owned by our father."

"This is the one your uncles sold?"

"Yes. I found out in later years they sold it because complying with all the state regulations of having a private cemetery attached to a mortuary was cutting into the prof-its. Uncle Harvey and Uncle Dave never really got along, so it made sense to sell and invest the proceeds into their own mortuaries. The businesses are completely separate except for the shared names."

"Do you know who bought Valley of Olives?" Pagan asked.

"The Krugers. They were employees of our father. They were caretakers for the cemetery and lived on site."

"They would give us cake and lemonade," Chad said. His smile was soft, but the memory clearly gave him plea-sure. "Connor was the best at hiding."

I looked at Sophie. She took the photograph from Pagan and looked at it. "We always played hide and seek in the cemetery after it was closed when we were waiting for father. We could never find Connor. It drove my father mad because sometimes Connor wouldn't come out when called, and he would never tell where he'd hidden."

"I assume Valley of Olives is still in existence," I said.

Sophie shrugged. "Sure. I don't know how full the cemetery is, but the mortuary still operates. Uncle Harvey often complains about them stealing business from him. He hated the Krugers because they were German Jews and he thinks Uncle Dave, who was our father's executor because our mother was too sick with cancer, sold the business to them too cheaply."

"Do you know anything about Connor's birth parents?" Pagan asked.

"I don't think even the mother really knew who the father was, that's why his being bi-racial was a surprise."

"What about the mother?"

"I came across some papers a few years ago amongst some other legal things my mother had set aside. They adopted Conner when he was still an infant through a lawyer who the mother hired to find a home for her baby."

"For a price?" I said.

"No doubt," Sophie agreed. "The mother's name was Gretchen White and she'd originally named her baby Benny, but father had it legally changed to Connor Martin as part of the adoption."

CHAPTER 27

*"When truth is replaced by silence,
the silence is a lie."*
- Yevgeny Yevtushenko

I was driving the Escalade with Pagan lying back in the passenger seat. My head was a whirl of colliding information. Even though his eyes were shut, I could tell by the tense lines of his body that Pagan was having the same mental experience.

Before we'd left the Martin residence, Pagan used the department radio to contact the uniformed officers still outside Smack Daddy's house. After verifying the record executive was still at home, Pagan told them to ask Smack Daddy to meet us at Hollywood Area station.

"Ask him politely," Pagan had told them. "I want him there voluntarily. If he gives you a bad time, tell him I have information on his daughter."

"You want the wife?"

"Not if you can get him there without her."

Next Pagan called Arlo while I'd jabbered at Chris Lancaster – RHD's resident computer geek. We asked both of them to find anything solid on Benny White, a.k.a. Conner Martin, a.k.a. Changeling.

Arlo was the first to call back. Pagan sat up and punched the Escalade's phone button to accept the call.

"We have a mystery here," Arlo said without preamble.

"Meaning?" Pagan asked.

"There are a ton of articles about this guy, but no personal interviews. Everything says the same things, which looked to have been coordinated by Smack Records."

"What about before he was signed by Smack Records while his videos were going viral on the web?" I asked.

"Everybody and his mother have viral videos these days. Nobody really pays any attention until something like an actual record deal comes through."

"Does he have an agent, a lawyer, some kind of representative?" I asked.

"I checked with Davenport at TMZ again," Arlo said. "He found out a couple of the television singing contests tried to track him down to get him to audition, but got turned down. He's making more calls to find out who turned them down."

"This guy is a freaking ghost," I said, after Arlo disconnected. My adrenaline was pumping, rubbing against the endorphins in my system. I felt I was heating up from the inside out.

"Not too many people can fly under the radar like this," Pagan agreed. "He had to have help."

"He's not a superspy. He was a ten year-old boy when this started. Where does he get that kind of help?"

"Clearly he's a street survivor. Sophie Martin said he

was a wild child. No telling how the connections in his brain worked after everything he'd been put through."

"Still, he was ten. Somebody had to take him in."

The phone went again. It was Chris Lancaster calling from RHD.

"I've been able to track one juvenile arrest for a Benny White from nine years ago. I can't say for sure if it's the guy we're looking for, but from the circumstances I'd say it is."

"Tell me," Pagan said.

"I put a fire under the clerk working the report archives and he faxed me the original paperwork. White was spotted at two o'clock in the morning walking on the street a block over from the Martin residence. He took off running and the officers went into pursuit. He got away for a while, but another unit called into the area spotted him again and cornered him."

"What was he arrested for?" I asked.

"That's the point," Lancaster said. "They had nothing substantial on him and he refused to talk. He finally gave up his name, but not where he lived or anything further. They booked him into Juvenile Hall for *evading*."

"No way was that going to stick," Pagan said.

"It didn't. I made some calls to the Hall. Because he refused to give anything other than his name, he was turned over to Child Protective Services."

"Don't tell me," I said. "I can guess the rest. They put him in an unsecured foster home from where he immediately ran away never to be heard from again."

"End of story," Lancaster agreed. "But it's still a surprise he's never been contacted again."

"Do us a favor," Pagan requested. "He must have been printed when he was booked for evading. Can you get those prints pulled and run them through the system to see if they match up with any other records?"

"Sure, but it will take time."

"Thanks, Chris," Pagan said, and disconnected.

"Are you thinking he might have been arrested under other names?"

"I don't know. I think he slipped when he used the name Benny White. This was only a year after he'd originally run away. Maybe he was back in the area because he was homesick, or wanted to check up on Chad or Sophie. When the cops nabbed him, he didn't want to use Connor Martin in case they connected the dots. Benny White was safe, but it was too close to the truth for him to feel comfortable using it if he got popped again."

"How did he even know the name Benny White?"

Pagan shrugged. "Maybe he found the adoption papers, maybe Jack Martin taunted him with it while he abused him. I don't know...yet."

I connected some dots of my own. "He's probably been checking up on Chad and Sophie when he could over the years."

"Probably wondering if his uncle was doing to them or to Gerrard what Jack Martin had done to him."

I kept following the train of thought. "And if he suspected Harvey Martin was molesting Gerrard..."

"He'd want to do something about it."

"And Unicorn?" I asked. I'd never before had this wavelength lock with a partner. A lot of *good* detective work is kicking over the traces of the case to see what turns up, but doing it with a partner like this was new for me. It was exhilarating.

"Smack Daddy lied," Pagan said.

"To us? Come on..."

"What we do is not a science, Randall. It's an art – an imperfect art. Think about how you've changed your perspective on your gift in just the past couple of days."

"Point taken," I said, realizing the truth of what Pagan said. "It's always been with me, a burden, something to ignore. Now, I'm paying precise attention to it and finding out I don't know what every nuance of color actually means. It will take a while. But I still don't see how or about what Smack Daddy lied about."

"Lie catching is not just preparation, manipulating anxiety, and asking questions. It's also asking the *right* questions and catching lies of omission – what *isn't* said."

I thought about omissions and flashed to the last encounter we had with Smack Daddy. "When we discovered the recording device in Smack Daddy's house," I said. "You asked if either he or Judith had bought or installed it. Judith answered, but Smack Daddy didn't say anything."

Pagan nodded. "Actually, I screwed up. I didn't ask it as an effective question. I just said, *I take it neither of you bought nor installed this.* It was lame. I gave Smack Daddy an easy out. I didn't even wait for him to respond, just let Judith's answer stand."

"Don't beat yourself up. It's such a little thing."

"There have been a lot of little things. In the back of the Navigator, I gave Smack Daddy a way to keep his self-esteem, but it was only in thinking about it later that something he said struck me as off-kilter."

I suddenly remembered that exactly as well. It was when I missed the mottling of the colors in the streamers attached to Smack Daddy's words. "When he asked, *then who took her? Who took the money?*"

Pagan eyebrows shot up. "Yes. You knew?"

"Only in retrospect. When he spoke, I wasn't concentrating. I missed something in the colors attached to his words. They were mottled, muddied up. It was only for a second. Sometimes colors linger, but usually they appear and disappear as fast as the words themselves. I've seen the mottling of colors before, but never thought about what it meant."

"It was put on," Pagan said. "He doesn't know for sure who took the money and his daughter, but he's got a very strong idea."

"Changeling?"

Pagan nodded again. "If we're right, Changeling is the connector between the two cases. And Smack Daddy is our connection to Changeling..."

"Because, since he signed him to a contract, he must know how to contact him," I said.

Pagan nodded. "It's time to peel Smack Daddy like a grape."

Pagan put his seat back again and closed his eyes.

I left him to nap and concentrated on fighting traffic. My own subconscious was going over all I'd heard and seen, trying to put it all together.

There comes a point in every investigation where everything either unravels or ties itself into a hopeless knot to be tossed aside as an unsolved cold case.

This case had reached that point, and I was bound and determined we weren't going to lose two children to a knot of bad leads, lies, and greed. This case was going to unravel if Pagan and I had to pull it apart thread by thread.

CHAPTER 28

"There are only two people in your life you should lie to. The police and your girlfriend."
- Jack Nicholson

Hollywood Area station is an institution. In the span of a day, the whole spectrum of the human experience usually walks through its doors. *Hollyweird.* The nickname is more than appropriate. If you work Hollywood Area long enough, you can legitimately claim to have seen it all.

On Wilcox south of Sunset Boulevard, the sidewalk outside the station is itself surreal. A little further north, Hollywood Boulevard sports the well-known tourist attraction of stars implanted into the sidewalk sporting the names of Hollywood's entertainment heroes – and more recently, any celebrity with the ego and cash to make it happen. The sidewalk outside Hollywood Station sports the same stars in the sidewalk, only these bear the names of real heroes –

those officers assigned to Hollywood Area who gave their lives in the line of duty. There are a lot more stars for dead cops than there should be.

As I pulled the Escalade into Hollywood Station's *official vehicles only* secured parking lot, Pagan sat bolt upright in the passenger seat. He appeared to have the ability to go from sleep to hyper-alertness in an instant.

"What is it?" I asked. Clearly Pagan was experiencing some kind of revelation.

He looked at me, eyes clear yet distant.

"We are running out of time," he said. His word streamers were an intense red. Blood red. Not the pastel red I was used to seeing attached to his words. There was so much about my condition to which I had never paid attention. I inwardly cursed myself. How could I stop Pagan from making another mistake as he insisted, if I didn't even know what all my colors meant?

"Okay," I said, unsure of where his statement was leading.

"No," Pagan insisted. "I can feel him."

"Who? Changeling?"

"Yes." There was no purple tinge to the deep red attached to his words, nothing to indicate he wasn't telling the truth.

Pagan's eyes focused on me. "Don't ask," he said. "Just believe. We have to get to Changeling fast."

He got out of the SUV with purpose and I scrambled after him, my new cane feeling curiously smooth and natural as I prodded it along.

"What are you planning?"

Pagan opened the backdoor to the station. "Nothing. Just a little parlor trick to grease the truth along."

The first thing Pagan did was head into the station's video room. We checked the video and sound equipment for the interrogation room we chose to use. The room was currently dark. Once we started the video running, I went to the room, opened the door and turned the lights on. I then made a show of searching the room by checking under the small table anchored in one corner, turning over both chairs to show there was nothing underneath, stood on one of the chairs and checked the drop ceiling tiles for any concealed contraband left behind by a prior suspect. When all was clear, I exited the room leaving the lights on.

I'd learned early the value of doing a *lights on to lights off* check of the interrogation room to make sure a defense attorney couldn't claim anything had been planted on his client or that improprieties took place in the room before or after the video was turned on or off.

When we were done, I followed Pagan as he scooted through the back corridors of the station and out the doors leading to the station lobby, where Pagan had asked the patrol officers to bring Smack Daddy to meet us.

The lobby, usually filled with a bright array of *Holly-weird* citizens, was surprisingly empty except for two desk officers and the two uniformed officers standing on either side of Smack Daddy. The record producer was wearing dark sunglasses, a de rigueur tracksuit, and too much bling. He was looking particularly disgruntled.

"What's this about?" he asked as soon as he spotted us.

I was watching Pagan closely. He had a wide smile slapped across his face and he seemed to glide as he closed the distance to his quarry.

He stopped just to Smack Daddy's left and extended his right hand. Predictable human behavior caused Smack

Daddy to extend his own right hand. Pagan's hand engulfed Smack Daddy's, but he didn't shake it.

Instead, at the same instant his right hand grasped Smack Daddy's, Pagan raised his left hand and touched the tip of its extended index finger just below his left eye.

Pagan spoke softly, "I hope you had a goodnight's..." In a smooth movement, he moved his finger from below his eye to touch a point on the top of Smack Daddy's right shoulder. At the moment his finger touched Smack Daddy's shoulder, Pagan gave a short, sharp, pulse-like tug to Smack Daddy's right hand, and finished his sentence with the word, "...sleep," delivered more sharply than his other words.

The tug on Smack Daddy's hand had been almost imperceptible. I was sure neither of the patrol officers on either side of Smack Daddy, or the desk officers, even registered it.

However, the effect of the tug caused Smack Daddy's head to nod forward in a narcoleptic movement. I even saw his eyes snap shut.

Keeping hold of Smack Daddy's right hand, Pagan moved in close. He smoothly moved his hand from Smack Daddy's shoulder to the back of Smack Daddy's neck, pushing the man's head down to rest on Pagan's right shoulder. To anyone watching, the movement looked like a variation on a *bro-hug* shared by two good friends.

Pagan's mouth was now positioned next to Smack Daddy's right ear. I saw a short burst of color slip out of Pagan's mouth. He had clearly spoken, but too softly for me, or anyone else, to hear.

He then dropped his left hand from Smack Daddy's neck, stepped back, and shook Smack Daddy's sharply.

Smack Daddy's head jerked up as if on a puppet string, and his eyes flew open.

A second later, Pagan was thanking the patrol officers for bringing Smack Daddy to the station and asking them to wait to take him home again.

Without losing physical contact, Pagan used his left hand to encircle Smack Daddy's right wrist and led him away as if Smack Daddy was a child following his mother.

Pagan led the docile Smack Daddy to an interrogation room and opened the door. Inside, the ghastly yellow walls welcomed us home. I moved to stand very still in a corner to one side. Pagan guided Smack Daddy to one of the chairs and allowed him to sit down.

The chair was positioned so Pagan was able to rest Smack Daddy's right forearm on the small table beside them. Pagan still held Smack Daddy's right wrist, turning it slightly so the back of Smack Daddy's right hand was also flat on the table. I could see Pagan's left index finger was pressing firmly to the central point of Smack Daddy's inner wrist.

Pagan used his right hand to pull his own chair in behind him, sitting on its edge. His right leg was between Smack Daddy's legs, his left leg to the outside of Smack Daddy's right leg.

"Theo," Pagan said gently, using Smack Daddy's given name. "I want you to know you are not under arrest. You are free to leave at any time. Do you understand?"

"Yes," Theo said. Surprisingly there was a twist of a smile on his lips.

This was known as a Beheler admonition. Miranda warnings are not appropriate in every situation where police question an individual, not even if the questioning takes place in the station house, or because the questioned person is someone whom the police suspect. However, use of a Beheler clarified the situation when Miranda was not required. Too many detectives, not sure of their legal standing, misused Miranda and often caused themselves to shut suspects down unnecessarily.

"Do me a favor, Theo, take off your sunglasses," Pagan said.

Smack Daddy complied almost instantly, taking off the sunglasses with his free left hand.

Pagan took the glasses with his right hand and set them on the small table. Then, still cradling Smack Daddy's upturned right hand, Pagan tapped his left index finger several times on the center of Smack Daddy's right wrist. I was surprised Smack Daddy wasn't questioning the contact, but it was as if he was completely unaware of it.

"Theo, I don't think you've been completely honest with us have you?"

"What do you mean?"

Pagan tapped his finger on Smack Daddy's wrist several more times. "You were worried about the people to whom you owe money, but you didn't really think they took the money or Unicorn. Did you, Theo?"

Smack Daddy remained silent, the small smile still on his face.

"Tell me about Changeling," Pagan said. As he finished his sentence, he lifted Smack Daddy's wrist enough to raise the attached hand off the table and then released it.

Smack Daddy's hand hit the table and he blurted out, "He ripped me off! He was my ticket back to the big time, and I was his ticket to stardom, but he ripped me off! Everybody is so damned greedy." Smack Daddy shook his head.

"Do you have any idea how hard I had to work to find this guy? Nothing but a gutter kid with a laptop, a sound machine, and a microphone. You'd think he'd jump at the first chance of a record contract."

"How did you find him?" Pagan asked.

"Tracked him through the IP address attached to his YouTube channel. Found the lawyer who was paying his bills. He eventually set up a meeting."

"Where?"

"My house. The kid was shut down. There was something not there about him, but the lawyer tried to help him understand the chance I was offering him."

"But he wasn't interested?"

"Didn't want to do anything but play his music. Liked the anonymity of the Internet and YouTube. He had no idea how big a star he was becoming – how big a star I could make him."

"What happened next?"

"Unicorn came into the room and the kid lit up like a Christmas tree. Thought I could show him what signing with Smack Records could bring him, but he was only interested in playing with Unicorn. They made each other laugh. Thought I was dealing with another Michael Jackson. Changeling was childlike, just like Unicorn. It was like they had instantly bonded."

"But you needed the money he could bring in," Pagan stated, his tone nonjudgmental.

Smack Daddy's face became animated. "He opened the vault, man."

"Did you know he took Unicorn?"

"Who else?" Smack Daddy said. "He took my money and my little girl."

"Why?"

"Because it was five million dollars!"

Smack Daddy was being Smack Daddy – thinking it was all about the Benjamins.

"But why take Unicorn?" Pagan pressed.

"How should I know? Maybe he's a creep, a pervert, likes little girls. You should have seen him playing with her – like two kids on a playground."

"Why didn't you tell us you thought Changeling took her?"

"Because I didn't want to lose the money. You guys weren't getting anywhere. I thought I could find him. Get the money back. Have you seen him? He's nothing but a scrawny street kid. I'd crush him and get my money and my daughter back."

Again his priorities – money first, then Unicorn.

"Did you find him?" Pagan asked.

"Tried calling him. No answer. Tried calling his lawyer. No answer. Left messages, but no response."

"Did you go looking for him?"

"Didn't have anywhere to look. Only had phone numbers. The lawyer doesn't have an office listed. Was waiting for him to make contact."

"Did he?"

"No."

"Tell me what went wrong with making Changeling a star?"

Smack Daddy looked taken aback, a little scared. "Nothing went wrong."

"Theo, you know you want to tell me the truth, don't you?"

Smack Daddy now looked confused. "Yes," he said, but it was like he couldn't stop the word from escaping his mouth. The streamer attached to it was the pastel blue of truth.

"Then tell me what went wrong," Pagan said.

"How do you know?" Smack Daddy asked. It was as if he was fighting with his words, the colors of the streamers tightly intertwining.

"Because of the way you've been manipulating the media," Pagan said. "Nobody has been allowed access to Smack Records' new star. Every press release has been handled and manipulated by you. Even the tracks you've released have been nothing more than reworked versions of his YouTube videos."

"Had to get money somehow otherwise I was going to sink." Smack Daddy looked chagrinned.

"So you released remixed tracks stripped straight off of the YouTube videos."

"Told you," Smack Daddy insisted. "Had to create a streaming revenue. The videos were going viral. Three of them over two million views. It was a pot of gold just sitting there. I needed it to get out from under."

"But you didn't give any of it to Changeling, did you?"

Smack Daddy smirked. "Just kept stalling. His lawyer just did wills and trusts, had no idea how entertainment law worked. I turned the tap on and filled the buckets."

"Did Changeling ask you for money?"

"Sure. Had some sob story about his nephew needing special care. Man, I've heard it all in this business. Smack Daddy needed special care before some sad sack kid who doesn't know up from down."

This was the real Smack Daddy. His words were pastel blue, but had taken on a vivid shine. I realized I was beginning to see not just colors, but all the various shades of meaning they could convey.

"Did he know you were putting the five million dollars together?"

Smack Daddy nodded. "I told him. Tried to explain he'd get his money once Smack Records was free and clear of the leeches. Told him and told him. He just needed to be patient."

"He ever see the money?"

"Once. He was at the house playing with Unicorn. Came into my office when I wasn't expecting him. It was costing me thirty cents on the dollar to get everything in cash, but I was almost there. I'd just taken a payment and was stashing it away when he walked in. You should have seen his eyes."

"What did he say?"

"Nothing. Just walked out."

"How long ago was this?"

"Two weeks ago. Still needed a couple more payments to get the full amount in cash."

"Did he ever hear you call Unicorn ugly? Did he ever hear you say you didn't want her?"

"Of course," Smack Daddy said. "I made sure everybody knew. Had to keep the men with their hooks in me away from my family. Couldn't let them know my family was my weak spot. Had to keep them away until I could get the money to pay them off. Then I'd make Changeling knuckle down and work. We both would have made more money than he'd ever need to take care of a hundred messed up nephews. Smack Daddy knows how to make money if he has a product, and Changeling was just that – a product."

Pagan waited a beat, letting Smack Daddy's statement settle on his ears.

"Have you had any contact with Changeling since your daughter and the money were taken?" Pagan asked softly.

"No."

Pagan cut his eyes to mine. I'd seen nothing but pastel blue attached to the word, so I nodded in the affirmative.

Pagan dropped his eyes to Smack Daddy again. "How do we find Changeling?"

Smack Daddy shook his head. "I got nothing man. Only his lawyer. And like I said, he ain't picking up his phone."

CHAPTER 29

*"Art is the lie that enables us to
realize the truth."*
- Pablo Picasso

Turned out Smack Daddy had something other than the
lawyer's phone number – and it was a huge gold nugget.

He had the lawyer's name.

Myron Kruger.

Kruger – as in the Krugers who first worked at, then
bought, Jack Martin's mortuary and connected cemetery,
renaming it Valley of Olives.

We were headed there now, but I had to get something
off my chest first.

"What did you do to Smack Daddy in the lobby?"
I asked.

Pagan was taking his turn behind the wheel of the
Escalade, but I sure as hell didn't feel like taking one of his
catnaps.

"I told you we don't have a lot of time. If we don't keep moving and crack this open, bad things are going to happen."

"You didn't answer the question."

Pagan shook his head. I got the feeling he was a little irritated I'd noticed his actions. Either something was wrong or he wasn't used to being questioned.

"I just planted a subconscious suggestion for him to tell the truth."

"Hypnosis is out of policy."

"You think Internal Affairs – pardon me, Professional Standards Bureau – is going to believe I have the ability to instantly hypnotize people into telling the truth?"

"Do you?"

"What color were Smack Daddy's words? Did he tell us the truth?"

"Yes." I didn't like admitting, caught myself folding my arms high and tight across my chest in anger.

"Then what is the issue?"

"I don't know."

"Was I not playing fair?"

"There's a difference between fair and legal," I said, feeling petulant.

"Semantics," Pagan said, calling me on my statement.

"You said you need me to stop you from making another mistake." I wasn't ready to concede.

Pagan shot me a look. "Are you going to play the mistake card every time we have a disagreement? Shouldn't you save it for special occasions?"

"Don't be a jackass."

"Listen to yourself," Pagan said. "What colors are attached to your words? What color is disapproval? Censure?" Pagan's tone had turned edgy, rough. His voice had changed. "Would you feel better if it had taken us several hours to wring the truth out of Smack Daddy and then not being sure we had it all?"

Suddenly, I registered the colors of Pagan's word streamers. Like his voice, they had changed. The usual red hues I associated with him had blurred. There was a harsh bright yellow intertwined around them as if trying to contain the red in a stranglehold.

I had an epiphany. "Are you channeling Changeling?"

Pagan shook his head and took a deep breath. "Not him, his emotions."

I didn't question him. I could see it in his words.

"Changeling is not a master criminal," Pagan said. "Everything he's done, starting with the hit and run murder of Jack Martin, has been fueled by opportunity."

I changed gears mentally and caught up. "The kidnappings – they wouldn't have happened if not for the opportunity of five million dollars in cash."

"Exactly. He sees himself as an avenger and a protector, willing to kill to do both."

"Do you feel he's a threat to Gerrard or Unicorn?"

Pagan shook his head. "No. But if he's used the five million dollars to hide them away somewhere..."

I picked up the thread. "...He might do something to himself so nobody will learn his secrets."

"It's in the name he chose for himself. A changeling is a force of destruction and chaos."

It was my turn to nod. "And he'll use chaos to steal away and protect other children, so what happened to him, won't happen to them."

"All you have to do is listen to the tones in Changeling's voice when he sings – there is a deep rage and an equal and opposite depth of compassion," Pagan said. "I can feel them both."

"Literally? Is that what it means to be a true empath?" I needed to know how he really ticked.

"Yes."

The truth wasn't just in the color of his words. I could see the pain etching itself into his face.

"Holy crap."

"Yeah," Pagan said.

We were silent for a moment. Pagan changed lanes and sped down the freeway off ramp, turning north onto Sepulveda Boulevard. Almost immediately, I could see a sign for the entrance to Valley of Olives Cemetery and Mortuary on the west side of the street.

Pagan was becoming more and more agitated.

"What else are you feeling?" I asked.

"Despair," Pagan instantly replied. "Changeling knows time is running out. He knows we're coming, and he will protect the children at any cost to himself."

CHAPTER 30

"People would lie less, or learn to deceive more skillfully, if they understood how easy it is for a trained investigator to detect lying."
- Ruth Rendell, Harm Done

The actual gates leading to the Valley of Olives entrance were off Sepulveda on Morrison Street. The cemetery was old, but tidy and appealing. It was nestled in a natural basin, bordered by the Ventura Freeway on the south, the San Diego Freeway on the west, and the concrete channel of the Los Angeles River on the north. The traffic noise from the intersecting freeways was a constant. I wondered how any of the interred could rest in peace.

Still, there was a charm and a calm to the area with recently tarmacked drives winding through buzz-cut grass expanses filled with ground level memorial plaques and dotted explosions of cut flowers. In another section, head-stones and statues proliferated.

There were enough mature palms, cypress, and pine

trees to give the area the feel of a park. That wasn't including the rows of olive trees, which gave support to the cemetery's name.

Several twenty-foot-long by eight-foot-high internment walls, for the keeping of ashes, helped to act as dividers for different areas of the cemetery. Far in the back, I could see a number of marble mausoleums rising up to proclaim the high financial standards of the families who owned them.

The large building housing the mortuary offices had a profusion of colorful bougainvillea spread from one end to the other, as if holding the walls together.

I'd looked at a satellite view of the area on my phone and knew there were several outbuildings behind the main offices. Two appeared to be residences. The other was a long rectangle, most likely discreetly hiding away those things needing to take place at a mortuary none of us like to think about.

There were three cars parked in the lot outside the main building. Pagan added the Escalade to the line-up. Before we got out, I used my phone again to download the information on Myron Kruger and his parents, which Chris Lancaster had scanned and emailed over from RHD. I read it quickly to Pagan. There was nothing really of note, but I didn't know how much Pagan was taking in.

When we got out of the Escalade, his face was taut and drawn.

"You okay?" I asked.

He took a deep breath and forced out a smile. "Can you feel it?"

"Feel what?"

"He's waiting."

I frowned and shook my head. "How do you know?"

Pagan shrugged. "As I told you, ever since I was a child,

I've been able to put myself in somebody else's place – literally feel what they are feeling. It's an instinct. I have to think consciously about it to turn it off."

"You turned it off when you were dealing with Michael Horner?"

Pagan looked down then back up at the sky. "I was just so damn tired."

"But you've never met Benny White, Changeling. How can you feel him?"

"I've seen him, I've watched his videos, I've heard him sing. I know where his pain comes from. I don't need to meet him to feel him."

After another moment passed, I asked. "Is that what it's like, being an empath? Feeling everybody else's pain? What about their joy, their excitement?"

"I can feel those things, but they don't linger. It's the negatives that are absorbed into my psyche."

I considered the implications, then said, "I'm glad being an empath is your gift and not mine."

Pagan seemed to come back into himself. "Sure you don't want to trade?"

Before I met Pagan, I would have given anything to not see colored word streamers – not to know when people were lying. Now I realized there could be more...*difficult* gifts.

"Not a chance," I said.

We continued to stand by the car in silence for a moment. Pagan was scanning the area, almost sniffing the air like a hunting dog.

I laid my free hand on his arm. "No more parlor tricks, okay?"

He looked down at my hand on his arm and gave me another tight smile. "Won't need them," he said.

He led off and I followed. I was using my cane, but was so juiced with adrenaline, I hardly needed it.

As we walked, Pagan asked, "Where would you go if you were ten and needed to hide?"

I immediately remembered what Chad and Sophie had said about the cemetery, and I clicked into Pagan's thought process. "Somewhere familiar. Somewhere where nobody had ever found me. You think he had a bolt hole here."

"When they played hide and seek here, nobody ever found him."

"What then?"

Pagan shrugged. "Let's find out." He pushed open the mortuary door.

As we stepped into the cool interior, I did feel something. It was like a soft blanket, or a cone of silence had been lowered, as if talking in a normal voice would shatter the walls.

The carpeted lobby area was partially filled with a round polished wooden table with a tall vase of real flowers in the center. The fragrance of the flowers was an assault on the senses, as if covering up the scent of constantly hovering grief and pain. On the back wall, a huge Star of David hung over a closed door. On a side wall was a smaller simple cross. Door-lined hallways escaped down either side of the lobby.

Our entrance caused a soft *bong* to resonate. I caught movement out of the corner of my eye and turned to see a man emerge from the first open door off the left hallway. He was probably in his thirties, but short and heavyset, with mud colored eyes and a shock of finger-combed hair as black as his ill-fitting suit.

He took us in with an uneasy assessment, but delivered a professional smile. "Can I help you?"

Pagan smiled. "Myron?"

"Yes?" he answered in the positive, but there was a question still in his tone.

Pagan stepped forward and extended his hand. I went on high alert, but Pagan did nothing more than grasp Myron Kruger's hand and shake it.

"Ray Pagan," he said. "I think you've been expecting us."

"Expecting..." The color of Myron Kruger's word belied his attempt at witlessness. It was the color of fear.

"Detective Ray Pagan and my partner, Detective Jane Randall," Pagan said, putting the emphasis on *detective*.

The color drained from Kruger's face.

"Please come this way," he said. With an ushering hand, he showed us into the office from which he had appeared.

Inside, an older man and woman stood up from a flowered upholstery couch set against the back wall. The family resemblance to Kruger was clear.

The woman took one look at Pagan and burst into tears. The man beside her, obviously her husband, put his arm around her. He, too, looked on the verge of tears.

I wasn't shocked when Pagan stepped forward and gathered both of the older folks into an embrace. The three of them held onto each other as if they were standing on the deck of the Titanic.

Myron looked at me and blinked. I blinked back at him. We both stood there awkwardly while grief poured out of the trio. I had a tentative grasp of what was going on, but there was no way I was hugging Myron – no matter how pathetic he looked.

I did try out a smile, which caused him to offer me access to a chair in front of a paper strewn desk. I slid into it with as much grace as I could muster. Myron sat in another chair opposite me. Progress of a sort.

"My parents," Myron finally said. "Isaac and Abi Kruger."

"They own Valley of Olives?" I asked. I knew the answer, but was just searching for something to say.

My stilted question had the effect of breaking up Pagan's group hug with the older Krugers.

"Yes, we own it," Isaac Kruger said, handing his wife a big white handkerchief to wipe her eyes. "One day, hope-fully not too soon, it will belong to Myron. He's a good son. He will bury us here."

"You bought the business from Harvey and David Martin after Jack Martin was murdered?" I asked, watching closely and seeing Abi Kruger give a slight wince at my harsh use of the word *murder*.

"A terrible hit and run," Isaac said.

People who are innocent have no issue with the use of harsh words. Suspects who are guilty, or who have *guilty knowledge*, will use softer words. Money is *missing* not *stolen*. *Touchy-feely stuff* not *child molest*. *Hit and run* not murder.

Pagan spared me a glance. "Why don't we all sit down," he said to Isaac and Abi. Pagan sat with them on the couch. It was a tight fit for three, but nobody complained. Abi was in the middle between the two men. Isaac held one of her hands. Pagan took the other and looked at her directly.

"You have another son, don't you?" Pagan asked her gently.

Tears immediately returned to Abi Kruger's eyes.

"He is not our son," Isaac answered for his wife. "But he has been like one."

Myron Kruger cleared his throat. "You've come for

Benny, haven't you?" The statement was spontaneous, driven by anxiety. "I knew dealing with the record company was a mistake, but I just thought..." He tapered off.

I saw the pain for his parents' predicament in the color of his words and wondered if there was pain there also for Benny. His words certainly let us know we were closing in on Changeling...Benny White.

"It's not like we needed the money," Isaac said. The look he shot Myron was right out of the *I told you so* playbook.

"He's not a bad boy," Abi Kruger said. "He was...is... just...different."

"Please explain so I can understand," Pagan directed gently. "He needs someone on his side right now."

"You are on his side?" Isaac Kruger scoffed.

"We both are," Pagan said, indicating me with his free hand.

I wasn't sure I was on the side of somebody who had most likely committed two murders and kidnapped two children. However, I arranged my facial expression appropriately remembering a great interrogator *becomes the person the subject needs you to be in order to confess*. If the Krugers had been harboring Changeling, helping him hide the children – for whatever reason – they were suspects, too.

"How can that be?" Abi asked. "You are the police."

I doubted the police in Germany, from where the Krugers immigrated, were exactly paragons of forgiveness.

"We are truth finders," Pagan said, purposely softening and redirecting the harsh word, *police*. "We know the truth comes in many different shades. If we can understand the truth then we can help others to understand. Things happen for a reason. I know you have always helped Benny. I know you want to help him now."

"He was so damaged..." Abi said, tears flowing slowly down her cheeks.

"He came here to hide ten years ago, isn't that right?" Pagan said.

Abi and Isaac stared at him silently.

"Please. It's not like you were helping a criminal," Pagan said, "You were just protecting a child."

He'd fashioned his phrase as a negative/alternative question. The design of the question was to give a suspect the choice of the lesser of two wrongs: *It's not like you did it for this bad reason, it's like you did it for this less bad reason.* So you would us a phrase such as, *It's not like you stole the money to buy drugs and alcohol, you just took the money because you had to feed your family, isn't that right?* It was a way of providing a *socially acceptable* explanation for their criminal actions.

"That's right, isn't it?" Pagan persisted, his voice soft and low.

Abi nodded her head.

It was an admission. A start.

"Abi," Isaac said softly.

She took her hand out of his and patted his leg. "It's alright," she said. "There is nothing else we can do. I trust him."

Isaac Kruger looked like a man who checked his spare change every time he went to the store, but he, too, nodded his head. The tension in his shoulders visibly relaxed.

Trust. How could Pagan achieve trust in such a short span of time? He must emit some kind of trust pheromone.

Isaac took the reins. "I spotted him going into one of the oldest family crypts at the back of the cemetery."

"When was this?" Pagan asked.

"A few weeks after Jack Martin was rundown. We had lived here since it was opened as caretakers. Raised Myron here. We were negotiating to buy the business. We were very lucky. Unlike so many others from the old country, we had hidden money away and it was never found. It was enough to give us a start in America." Isaac gave what amounted to a bobble of his head paired with a one shouldered shrug and a twist of his lips. "We also had friends who were willing to help."

"We knew Benny as Conner then," Abi said. "He was slight for ten, but willful, almost wild, and it was clear Jack Martin begrudged him."

"We saw him hit the boy on more than one occasion," Isaac said.

"He didn't just hit him," Abi said, her voice full of scorn. "He thrashed him. It was because he was blacker than he was white. We know what it is like to be targets. All Jews know."

"Did Sophie and Chad see the beatings?" Pagan asked.

"Yes. Jack Martin would threaten to do the same to them, but he never did. Just Conner."

Myron suddenly chimed in. "I was away at university and then law school. They were lonely." He said it in defense of his parents, but with no censure.

Isaac gave a shrug and Abi gave several little nods.

"Had Conner been sleeping in the crypt?" I asked.

Isaac nodded. "He had become almost feral, scavenging for food, becoming lost in his mind."

"We waited until Isaac saw him go into the crypt again," Abi said.

"Nobody has visited it in years. The family who owned it were either all dead or had moved away. It had settled badly into the ground causing a small gap in the locked doors. He'd only made it a little bigger. Because he was so small, he could wriggle in."

"We went down there together," Abi picked up the thread. "We called to him and coaxed him out. We promised to take care of him, not to turn him over to children's services."

Isaac took his wife's hand gently again. "I knew she'd already made up her mind. She wanted so much to help him when Jack Martin mistreated him."

"He was just a lost little boy," Abi said. "A broken child. I couldn't not take him in."

"Did he tell you anything about the hit and run of Jack Martin?"

There was a pause, then Abi said a simple, "No."

"We didn't ask either," Isaac said with some salt in his tone. "There are some things best left alone."

Before working with Pagan, I would have been suspicious of their motives. They had been in the process of buying Jack Martin's mortuary business. They wouldn't want anything to disturb the process. However, now I was watching the colors of their words closely. I was also concentrating on their tone and intonation. I couldn't hear or see deception in anything they said.

I looked at Myron Kruger. There were tears of affection in his eyes.

"How did you feel about all this?" I asked him, using the same coaxing tone of voice as Pagan. It was unusual to interview three witnesses together, but the family dynamics were working in our favor.

"It was what they needed to do."

"Were you resentful?"

Contempt for the question washed over Myron's

features. "Not at all. My parents loved me. They loved Benny. There is never *not* enough love. My parents would never turn away someone in need."

That was quite a testament. I probed further. "How did you come to call him Benny?"

"It was the first thing he told my parents."

I switched my attention back to Isaac and Abi.

Abi had taken her hand back from Pagan and now had them clasped in her lap. "I think it was the reason he came out of the crypt. He couldn't stand being called Connor. He kept telling us Conner was dead. Told us his real name was Benny White. He wouldn't calm down until we agreed."

"You home schooled him?" Pagan asked, bringing us back on track.

"There really wasn't any other way," Abi said. "He was too damaged. He wasn't the best learner, but we got him through the basics."

"And nobody asked you who he was or where he came from?"

"People who come here are too wrapped up in their own grief to ask questions about others."

"What about your friends?"

Isaac shrugged and did the bobble head, twist of the lips, gesture again. "We are German Jews. Our friends understand secrets and how to keep them."

"It was music he loved," Abi said softly. "He learned to play the piano by ear. We bought him a guitar one year and he was playing it within a couple of weeks. He would watch video things on TV and his computer, then play them."

"What about the equipment he used to make his videos?" Pagan's voice was soft, non-judgmental.

"He worked for us," Isaac answered. "We paid him. I drove him to a music store and he bought the things he needed. I don't understand it all, but Benny seemed to know all about the things he needed."

"Did he never want to leave? To get a driver's license? Hang out with other kids or, eventually, older peers?" I asked.

Isaac and Abi looked at each other as if this was something that had never occurred to them.

"Sometimes, he would go for long walks at night, but he was calm here. He felt he had what he needed," Abi said.

"Did you know he was checking up on Chad and Sophie Martin – his adopted siblings?" Pagan asked.

Isaac shrugged. Abi looked down at her hands.

Myron came to their rescue. "He was happy here. When I graduated, I came back to help my parents. I do some will and estate planning work for customers, but mostly I helped run the business. Benny was younger than me, but he was my friend – as much as you could be a friend with Benny. He was disconnected, struggled with relationships. He was at peace playing his music and making his videos inside the crypt where he first hid. He said he liked the echo."

"And then Smack Daddy Davis contacted you," Pagan said.

"A bloodsucker if ever there was one," Myron said.

"Were you surprised?"

"Certainly. I had no idea the impact Benny's videos were having. I almost didn't recognize him when I saw them. It was as if this Changeling persona was a totally different personality."

"What did Smack Daddy promise you?"

"He wanted to sign Changeling to an exclusive deal. I didn't trust him from the start, so we kept Benny's real name from him. He had to deal through me only. He promised money. Lots of money."

"And Benny was interested?"

"It surprised me. He'd never shown interest in money before. I took him to Smack Daddy's house. Benny kept playing this role of Changeling. It appeared the only way he could interact."

"And he met Unicorn at Smack Daddy's house?"

"Yes. I took him back several times. Smack Daddy kept trying to get Benny to make public appearances or go into a real studio to record, but Benny would simply refuse and go to play with Unicorn."

"You knew Smack Daddy was streaming remixes of the Changeling songs from the videos?"

"I did some research into how streaming worked, how music downloads were paid for. I knew there must be big money coming in, Benny's Changeling character was continually *trending* all over the Internet. I could see the number of hits his videos were getting."

"Did Benny tell you ahead of time what he was planning?"

"No!" Myron was emphatic.

The blue of truth was attached to his words, plus a good, strong, immediate denial is a sign of truthfulness. Somebody who is lying will give a weak denial, sometimes after several beats of silence, and then will get weaker and weaker in their denials. An innocent person's denials will get stronger and stronger.

Myron continued, "I had no idea what was in his mind. No idea he had been watching what was happening to Gerrard Martin, or was worried about how Unicorn was being treated. No idea, until he turned up here with the children, that he was going to try to stop it...or how."

It was amazing. In that second, it all became clear to me. Everything Pagan had done since he stepped into the mortuary offices had been tactically staged to get to this point.

His total assumption of the Kruger's involvement with Benny made them think we knew so much more than we did. He had held them and cried with them, made them trust him, and cracked open their deepest secret, their deepest fears, simply with the power of his presence. The man wasn't a parlor trick magician, he was a fully-fledged wizard.

"Is Gerrard safe?" Pagan asked, his eyes hypnotically boring in to Myron's.

"I...I..." Myron stammered. "There is a trust. I wrote it. I filed it with the court. Benny is my client. I can't talk about the trust or what's in it."

"I don't want to know about the trust," Pagan said. "I don't want to know about the money."

That statement went off like a bomb in the room. Myron had *forgotten* to mention Benny turning up with the kids and the *money*.

"It was his money," Myron said desperately, his tone totally different, his word streamers filled with the color of guilt. "He earned it. He just had to take it because Smack Records would never have paid what they owed him."

There is always a justification, always an excuse for wrong actions. It doesn't matter if the justification is valid if the act is still wrong.

Pagan ignored the outburst. "Is Gerrard safe?" he asked again, softly but with a sharp edge to his inflection. The red of his word streamers was so bright it hurt.

Conflicted with emotion, Myron nodded his head once in the affirmative.

"And Unicorn?"

There was a beat, then Abi said, "She is with us. Such a sweet child."

"Benny brought her to us," Isaac explained. "Asked us to take care of her like we'd taken care of him."

"How did he bring her here?" Pagan asked.

There were several beats of silence.

"Please," Pagan said.

Isaac spoke up. "I taught him how to drive a few years ago." He tossed his hands around. "He loved going for drives in the car. I thought it would be okay. He often drove an old pickup truck we have for errands and moving equipment. I knew he sometimes took it out at night."

"You knew and you didn't stop him?" This came from Abi, who obviously hadn't known. "What were you thinking?"

Isaac gave another *what can you do* gesture with his hands. "Who thinks about these things? He'd go. He'd come back. I didn't tell him I knew. He had so little joy in his life. What's a little driving?"

It explained how Benny got to Smack Daddy's house to bug it and to steal the money. He would have also needed it to transport Unicorn and Gerrard.

Pagan finally asked the big question. "Where is Benny?"

The Krugers all shared a look. Pagan was patient, letting the moment stretch. I felt my own anxiety making my heart pound.

Abi sighed, tears returning to her eyes yet again. "He is in the back courtyard playing with Unicorn."

CHAPTER 31

**One may sometimes tell a lie, but the grimace
that accompanies it tells the truth."**
- Friedrich Nietzsche

And there she was...

I let out a deep breath I hadn't known I was holding.
Relief at finding a kidnapped child apparently unharmed
washed over me.

And then I realized...

There she was...

Happily playing with some anonymous toys on a patch
of grass near a tinkling fountain...

Alone...

I quickly scanned the courtyard, knowing Pagan was
doing the same.

"Call it in," he said. "Get back-up rolling."

I didn't argue, dialing my phone while Pagan checked

anywhere in the courtyard where Benny might be concealed.

He knew where to hide where nobody would find him.

He'd had years to make a series of secret bolt holes. He could be anywhere in the cemetery.

I disconnected my call to communications asking for uniformed units to respond to our location *Code 2.*

Pagan had gone back inside the mortuary offices. He came out with Abi Kruger, who gathered Unicorn into her arms. As she did so, I had the uncharitable thought that Unicorn was indeed not a pretty child. I was disgusted with myself for the knee-jerk reaction. She laughed as Abi tickled her, and the noise was magical. No child deserved to be judged by an adult's standards of beauty.

"Randall?" Pagan said. He was practically vibrating.

I knew waiting for back-up wasn't going to happen.

"I'm with you, partner," I said. And I was. I was tapped in to Pagan. I believed I knew what he was feeling. Changeling was a protector first before all other things. Somehow, he managed to take advantage of an opportunity – a boatload of cash and a family lawyer – to protect somebody he had been wanting to protect for years, but couldn't.

Now he perceived Gerrard was safe, protected by some sort of trust created by Myron, and he wouldn't want anyone to be able to get the information from him.

I *felt*, and I knew Pagan absolutely felt, Changeling was done being a danger to others and was now a danger to himself.

Waiting for backup was not an option.

"The Escalade," Pagan said.

I didn't argue, just turned and followed him. Moving as fast as I could, my cane was more of a hindrance than a help. I grabbed it in the middle and ran as best as I could on my bad leg.

"Northwest corner," Pagan said, as we scrambled into the Escalade. "The crypt where he first hid."

He spun the wheel and reversed out of the parking spot, then hit the gas and we sped forward.

Twice we made wrong turns on the streets meandering through the cemetery. Pagan pounded his hand on the wheel in frustration. We could see the area where the crypts were, but were having trouble getting there.

"Calm down," I said to Pagan, just as he turned the Escalade and went over a curb onto the grass. He cut a swath directly to the area where the crypts were gathered like a murder of gothic crows. I didn't want to think about what we had driven across.

We bailed out of the car, guns in hand. I'd brought my cane with me out of habit, still holding it in the middle as I jogged after Pagan with my uneven gait. I'd been free from pain since Tanaka had apparently popped everything into place, but I was beginning to feel fatigue in the leg itself.

Pagan pointed toward a black marble monstrosity rising like something out of a Frankenstein movie. It was surrounded by other above ground monuments with crypts beneath them, like a condo complex for the dead.

We spread out as we approached, but still weren't prepared for a huge bang and a black smoke-spewing fireball of red streaking toward us. We didn't have time to move as the flaming projectile hit the ground in front of us, bounced up, spun in the air hit the ground again and streaked between us.

"What the hell?" Pagan yelled, spiked adrenaline making his voice quiver.

"Flare," I said. I'd once had a Coast Guard boyfriend

who had fired one off in frustration when I'd caught him in a lie. Some relationships are more volatile than others.

"Where did he get a flare gun?"

I took the question as rhetorical. "He missed us on purpose."

"He didn't miss by much." Our voices were unnaturally loud.

"He's trying for suicide-by-cop," I said.

"He might just get his wish," Pagan said harshly, displaying yet another side of his personality. There was indeed the blue steel of a hardcore cop under all his emotional, empathetic guise.

Smoke drifted away showing a scorched strip of grass torn up by the flare as it had rocketed past. The smoke was heavier by the crypt and a small body seemed to float out of it toward us.

"Gun!" I yelled.

The warning was unnecessary as the flare gun Benny was pointing at us looked like a cannon. Benny said nothing as he came to a stop. He had the gun in both hands pointing it at us, but even through the smoke it was easy to see he had no idea of a shooter's stance. The gun wavered as if it was too heavy for him to hold.

Pagan had his gun up in a two-handed grip, his body turned sideways in a Weaver stance, his weight slightly forward. "Put it down, Benny," he ordered, command presence coming off of him in waves.

"Pagan," I said. "Flare guns only hold one round."

"He could have reloaded."

I desperately needed Benny to say something. I needed to see the color of his words. I didn't need another *calamity* on my record. I didn't want anyone else to die.

"What's he feeling?" I asked Pagan, trying to cool him down.

"Fear." Pagan paused for a beat and then added, "Anger."

The barrel of the flare gun wavered back and forth again.

Neither Pagan nor I moved.

"I'll kill you," Benny said, his voice high. And there they were, the purple streamers of lies.

"Easy," I said to Pagan. "Easy. He's lying."

"I'm not lying," Benny said. "I'll kill you both." The gun swung toward me sweeping through smoke and purple streamers.

"No you won't," I said, stepping forward.

"Randall..." Pagan said off to my side.

"I got this," I said. "Shooting him will be the mistake you wanted me around to save you from."

"I'll kill you!" Benny screamed. Purple, purple, purple.

"Randall..." Pagan said again as I took another step forward.

"Remember Michael Horner," I said. "Don't make another mistake here." I didn't know who I was more concerned about – Pagan or Benny.

As I took another step forward, I let my cane slip through my hand until I was grasping the ferrule tip – the heavy crown on the top pointed down.

I was close enough now to see Benny was vibrating. His whole body trembling.

"Put it down, Benny," I said softly.

"Kill me," he screamed, stamping his feet up and down like a child throwing a tantrum. "Just kill me!"

"Not that easy, Benny," I said.

"Benny is dead," he screamed. "Conner is dead. I am

Changeling!" As he said the words, I saw the color of his words change from purple to blue.

There was a moment I felt I might have misjudged everything. I saw the huge barrel of the flare gun in infinite detail as it swung toward me. I could hear nothing. My mouth had gone dry. The autonomic systems in my body were shutting down one by one to concentrate on the threat.

I began to raise my gun, but then Benny moved the flare gun to point at the right side of his head.

Instead of firing my gun, I swung my cane one-handed in desperation. The crown tip hit Benny's right elbow just as he pulled the flare gun trigger, the flare bursting skyward instead of into his head. Fire from the ignition of the flare exploded from the barrel and caught Benny's shirt on fire.

I was off balance and fell sideways, but Pagan barreled past me. He knocked Benny to the ground, then rolled him over and over until the flames were out.

Then he wrapped him in his arms.

My hearing came back. I heard sirens. I'd ordered the back-up Code 2 – meaning get here as fast as you can without using your siren – but some cops just love to make noise.

I picked myself up using my cane and made my way over to Pagan.

He looked up at me from where he was sitting on the ground holding Benny.

"Thank you, Jane," he said.

CHAPTER 32

**"You can't find the truth,
you just pick the lie you like the best."**
- Marilyn Manson

Waiting for the dust to settle can take a while and try your patience, but eventually the path is clear to move forward.

Paramedics had been called to the scene and treated Benny for superficial burns. He was silent during the entire procedure. In fact, he hadn't said a word since I'd stopped him from blowing his brains out.

Dante Castano along with Ken Dodd arrived only minutes before Livia Nelson and Johnny Hawkins. After checking in, Castano and Dodd went to search the crypt Benny used for a bolt hole on the off chance Gerrard would be there. All they found was Benny's keyboard, guitar, and computer. The tools he had used to communicate his pain to the world via Internet music videos. They also took the flare gun to book it into evidence.

Nobody knew yet what was evidence and what wasn't, so the rule was book everything. There could be DNA or other microscopic scientific evidence the wizards at SID could use to tell us something.

Livia and Johnny started the arduous process of paperwork documentation and taking statements from the three Krugers after transferring them to Van Nuys station.

There was some talk and speculation about charging Isaac and Abi, but attempting to file harboring or criminal conspiracy against either of them seemed over the top. They were treated as gently as possible, but the process was still harsh and taxing. Right now, they would be feeling like their world was falling apart.

Myron, however, was a different story. He hadn't called a lawyer, but was still hiding behind the legal mumbo jumbo of Benny being his client. He refused to talk further about the trust he had established for Benny or how it pertained to Gerrard.

Specifically, he refused to tell us where Gerrard was being kept. And that was the kicker. Despite everything, we still had a missing child to find. The longer Myron refused to tell us what he knew, the more likely he'd be facing charges of conspiracy and obstruction.

He eventually agreed to tell us everything if Benny would agree to let him. The problem was, Benny still hadn't uttered a word.

Peter Simmons, the district attorney who had prosecuted the Arthur Howell murder case, came to the station at Pagan's request. We wanted him getting in on the case earlier than a DA normally would in order to provide a deeper legal take on what charges we might file and what evidence we would need to establish their validity.

It was a smart move on Pagan's part as it gave Simmons

a stake in the outcome of the case. He was more likely to file charges if he was brought in as early as possible.

"The circumstantial evidence for the kidnappings is strong, but we're on much weaker ground when it comes to the hit and run murders. Can you get Benny to sing?" Simmons asked.

I didn't know if he was trying to be inappropriately funny or simply trying to sound cool and failing by using old fashioned jargon. The color of his words showed no malice, but he went down a notch in my estimation.

"Possibly," Pagan said, then asked me, "What do you think?"

I sighed. "The issue isn't just getting him to talk. The bigger issue is even if we can get him to talk to us, how we prove he is competent to waive Miranda."

Despite regulations, we had not put handcuffs on Benny at the cemetery. He was so docile and frail, it seemed like a cruelty. He was twenty, but still appeared closer to the ten year-old he had been when he fled the Martin residence. Pagan sat with him in back of the Escalade when we drove to the station.

Currently, Benny was sitting quietly in an interrogation room. The irony of it being the same interrogation room where Michael Horner had killed himself wasn't lost on either Pagan or me.

"He needs an advocate," I said.

"If you bring in anyone from the Public Defender's Office, they are going to shut you down before you get a word out of him," Simmons said.

There was no arguing with that logic.

"An advocate from the rape treatment center?" I suggested.

"You'd have a better chance with a public defender,"

Simmons said. "At least most of them don't have a private agenda."

"He has a lawyer," Pagan said thoughtfully. "Myron Kruger."

"He's a civil lawyer, not a criminal lawyer," Simmons said.

"When detectives questioned O.J. the first time, he had a civil lawyer with him who let him waive his rights," I said, not wanting to think how that disaster had played out.

"Myron Kruger is a co-suspect," Simmons said.

"Not if you don't charge him," Pagan said. "Do you really think anything you filed against him would stick? Isn't finding Gerrard and getting a statement about the hit and runs far more important?"

I could see Simmons weighing the options in his mind. Like any DA, he'd prefer a slam dunk, high-profile conviction in hand as opposed to two weaker cases in the bush.

"Okay," he said finally.

Pagan smiled at me, "I'll get him."

I looked at him suspiciously.

"No parlor tricks," he said, his hands palms-up and open. He knew I would see purple word streamers if he was lying. His words were true blue.

I went to the women's locker room to use the bathroom – first rule of detective work, *go when you can, not when you have to*. When I was done, I washed my hands and splashed water on my face. I thought about taking a pain pill, but decided my leg was doing okay.

I looked at myself in the mirror. I took the scrunchie off my pony tail and let my hair fall forward. I had a small folding brush in the pocket of my jacket. As I was using it, a muscular black woman in workout gear came into the bathroom. She had a patrol uniform in a dry cleaning bag, which she hung from a stall door. She stepped up to the sinks where she peeled off a padded pair of fingerless weightlifting gloves and began washing her hands. She caught me looking at her in the mirror.

"Tough day?" she asked.

"They're all tough," I said.

"Preach it, sister," she said, smiling.

As she dried her hands, she took in my cane. "Are you the detective who got shot taking down that human trafficking ring? The one they call Calamity Jane."

"Yes," I said flatly, angry someone I didn't know would use that moniker. What right did she have?

"Well, ain't you something?" she said. "Tough as they come, I hear," she said, then gave me a genuine smile taking any sarcasm out of the words. "You make all us sisters in blue proud. It's an honor to meet you." She reached out to shake my hand.

I swallowed, feeling deep emotion. It was not just what she said, but the sincerity in the colors attached to her words. I took her hand in mine. "Thank you," I said.

The boost had come at just the right time. I felt invigorated. I knew I wanted the ball. I wanted this interrogation.

For the first time being known as Calamity Jane seemed like a good thing.

CHAPTER 33

> *"People think a liar gains a victory over his victim. What I've learned is a lie is an act of self-abdication, because one surrenders one's reality to the person to whom one lies."*
> -Ayn Rand

I sat close to Benny, on the edge on my chair, my feet flat on the floor, knees together, hands open and on my thighs. There was no more than two inches of space between my knees and Benny's.

There was no table in the interrogation room. I had placed Myron in a chair behind Benny and off to one side.

When I had come back into the squad room, Pagan looked up at me and I saw the expression on his face change – moving from introspection to observation. I knew he was reading me. It was second nature to him.

He handed me a bottle of water and a power bar. A half-eaten duplicate of his offering was on a desk next to him. I took the bottle of water, cracked the top, and drank down half of it in one long swallow.

I ripped the packaging off the power bar with my teeth and took a bite of the goo inside.

Hydrate. Balance blood sugar. Get game face on. Standard procedure.

"I'm going in *the box*," I said to Pagan.

His pleasant expression didn't change. "It's all yours."

"Just like that? No argument?"

"At the cemetery you said, 'I got this.' And you still do. The box is yours."

He saw me watching the color of his words.

Quietly, he asked, "Are you learning what all the colors mean?"

It was my turn to give a rueful smile. "Yes. I've started paying acute attention. It *is* a gift not a curse."

"A gift that has consequences."

"I think I'm finally ready to accept them."

For the next half-hour, we discussed and planned, deciding the specific point of the interrogation would be to find Gerrard. I'd have to adjust to things on the fly, but Gerrard first, then nail down the hit and runs.

Now, sitting across from me in *the box*, Benny stared at me with dull eyes. What we do as detectives can be hard. Personally, I thought Benny had been through enough. I didn't see what prosecuting him and locking him up would achieve. He was a victim as much as he was a suspect, but we are objective enforcers of the law. This had to be done. And if it had to be done, I wanted to be the one to do it with as little damage as possible.

Myron had been briefed that he would be acting as Benny's advocate. I knew Pagan had told him privately to only to refer to the money we were assuming Benny had given him for the trust as royalties from Smack Records, and not to say how much it was. We were hedging our bets a bit, trying to adjust one possible outcome.

I could tell Myron really wanted to tell us about the trust – to tell us where Gerrard was – and we could probably find a legal way to force him to do so. However, I didn't want to break him if there was another way. I just hoped I didn't break Benny.

With Myron in the room acting as Benny's lawyer, Miranda became a moot point and did not need to be administered. Some DAs would freak out if you didn't read an *in-custody* suspect the Miranda Admonition, but Peter Simmons was up on his current law and agreed we didn't need it.

I still wanted Benny to answer some simple questions to establish competency. These would be low anxiety questions, nothing accusatory, just establishing a baseline behavior.

"Benny," I said. "My name is Jane."

I saw a flash of contempt in Benny's eyes and a minute twitch of his upper lip. He turned his head away from me and crossed his arms. I knew from experience it was something I'd said that caused him to barrier up. But what had I said? I'd just told him my name.

I sat in silence thinking before proceeding. What did I know about Benny? The only face to face experience I had was the encounter in the cemetery. I tried to clear my head and remember what was said, how he had acted.

Pagan had said Benny was feeling fear. Then he'd added anger.

This was anger I was seeing from Benny in the interrogation room. Everything is emphasized in *the box,* becomes larger, more apparent.

Anger.

At the cemetery, Benny had spoken in anger. He'd said, "Benny is dead. Conner is dead."

Then he declared, "I am Changeling!"

Maybe the only way left for Benny to interact with the world was through the character of Changeling.

"Changeling," I said. "My name is Jane."

Benny turned his head to face me. His arms unfolded. His fingers started tapping out a beat on his knees.

"Changeling," I said again, confirming I'd got the message. "Can you tell me in your own words why we are talking today?"

Tap, tap, with his fingers. Silence.

I knew this behavior in most suspects would be a sign of bleeding off anxiety. In a standard interrogation, I would shut the behavior down. But this interrogation was far from normal.

"How do you feel about being here?"

Benny remained silent, but his face took on deeper lines, his eyes almost pleading. The tap, tap of his fingers stopped and suddenly, he was playing air guitar – strumming with one hand, fingering invisible frets with the other.

He rocked forward, locking his eyes on mine, and strummed another invisible riff.

Before language, man communicated strictly through gestures. Even now, the majority of our communication still happens via gestures.

Benny was silent, but Changeling was communicating.

I reached out and touched his knee. "I understand," I said. "I'll be back."

I left the interrogation room, closing the door behind me. Pagan came out of the observation/video room. He was replaced by Dante Castano. We were not leaving Benny unobserved.

"I need his guitar," I said. No doubt Pagan was picking up on the urgency in my voice. "Castano and Dodd brought it in to book as evidence."

Pagan nodded and headed into the detective squad room where the evidence had been sequestered prior to actually being booked into the secure property room on the first floor.

He was back in under a minute and handed me the guitar. I took it with me back into the interrogation room. I sat down across from Benny, knees touching now.

I extended the guitar toward him.

Benny smiled, his face looking like the sun coming out after a storm. He took the guitar gently, put the strap over his head, and strummed it once. He fiddled with the turning keys and strummed it again.

Apparently satisfied the guitar was in tune, he looked directly into my eyes. There was a hardness to his face, but no guile.

"Changeling, in your own words can you tell me why we're talking today?"

Benny strummed his instrument gently and began to softly sing his words. He was like a person who had a heavy stutter while talking, yet can sing without a hitch. Changeling communicated through his music.

"Because I had to protect them. Had to protect them. Had to protect...them," He sang, drawing the last two words out with a Gaelic lilt. "I am the Changeling. Conner was taken to the land of the fairies, Bennie too."

"How do you feel about talking to me?"

Bennie plucked the strings of his guitar, his hands moving on the frets.

"You're pretty and sweet and quite complete," he sang, with a laugh. Then his face closed down, darkening, and the sounds on the guitar became a haunting refrain. "Unicorn, Unicorn, where does she go? Back to the monster? No, no, no, no!"

It sounded as if he was singing a Dr. Seuss book, but his agitation was clear in his body, and anger was in the color of his words.

He had given me a type of *mercy* question, something a suspect will ask in preparation to admitting culpability. It comes in the form of a concern the suspect wants addressed: *How much time am I going to get? What's going to happen to my family? Am I going to get fired?*

A mercy question meant I was making progress in the interrogation, even if it didn't seem like much at first.

"There's a group of other people who are going to decide what happens to Unicorn." There's always a *group of people* who make the tough decisions. "We have to make them understand why you took Unicorn, why you needed to protect her. But, what's important right now is we find Gerrard."

"No! Not find, never find." The music was now harsh and staccato.

I'd hit a hot button and would have to let it go for now, come at it from another angle.

Benny strummed his guitar hard. "Poor little boy all alone, fiddled with and touched, just like Conner. Never going back, never happen again."

"You made sure of that, didn't you, Changeling? You stopped the man who did it in order to stop him from molesting anyone else, just like you stopped the man who was touching you, so you could protect Chad."

More harsh angry melodies flowed from his hands and

through the guitar. "Every night he came, never leaving me alone. I sung with the fairies while he pinched me...and touched me...and had his way. The fairies took Conner away, left a changeling in his place." His voice rose with his anger, the colors of his words mixing and twisting to his music. "The changeling knew, Chad was next. The man was laughing like a clown. Didn't laugh so much when I ran him down." It was all a mix, part melodic, part rap, part pure pain.

"And you had to run down another bad man, to protect Gerrard."

Myron suddenly spoke up. "Perhaps he shouldn't answer that..."

Benny swung to one side in his chair so he could see Myron, and then he sung. "Brother, brother, brother, you were always kind to me. Let me tell the story like the ones you read to me." Benny's voice was now light and ethereal, the colors of the word streamers golden – love.

Benny swung back to me, his face doing another rapid change and his playing more strident.

"I saw him through the window, and I listened to him, too. Another wicked touch and pincher. Changeling take the baby to the fairies. Never harm no more."

"What about Sophie?" I asked. "Is she wicked?"

Benny slowed his playing, seeming to calm, seeming to think about my question.

"She loves Gerrard. She is his mother. She is worried... misses him," I said.

Benny continued to strum his guitar slowly and softly, but he said or sung nothing.

I continued working the theme. "I can't imagine how hard it was for you knowing what was happening to Gerrard and not being able to do anything about it."

Strum, strum, strum...

"Then your videos took off and Smack Daddy promised you lots and lots of money. Money you could use to help Gerrard."

Benny played several strident chords under his singing words, "He promised. He promised. Money, money, money. He promised the world and delivered only pain."

"And he was mean to Unicorn." I said.

Benny's playing changed again, now lilting and soft. "So pretty, so fun. He was the ugly one. He would have started touching, would have started pinching, but the fairies wouldn't let him, told me what to do. Izzy and Abi would take care. Love her and protect her, even if I wasn't there."

Izzy must be Benny's name for Isaac.

"So when you got your money, you knew you could rescue both Unicorn and Gerrard." I said, working on finding that socially acceptable way for Benny to tell the truth.

I had to be careful, dance around the money issue. Pagan and I were the only official sources who knew where the money came from. Smack Daddy knew, but he was in no position to prove the money was his. It had all been gathered under the table and off the books.

There was no argument Benny's song streaming revenue provided the cash, nothing to say it wasn't rightfully his. Pagan and I believed there might be a better way for the money to be used than to haul Smack Daddy's butt out of the gator swamp he'd made for himself. Still, we had to play things very close.

Strum, strum, strum...

"All you wanted to do was protect the children," I said, keeping my monologue rolling, keeping to my theme. "And you have protected them. Jack Martin is dead. Harvey

Martin is dead. Changeling ran them down, made sure they wouldn't hurt children again."

Tears welled in Benny's eyes, trickled down his cheeks, mucus covered his upper lip.

Strum, strum, strum...strum, strum, strum...

I was getting there, making progress. Had to keep at it.

"Gerrard is safe," I said. "We will do everything we can to keep him safe, but we'll need Sophie's help to do it. She loves Gerrard. She wants to keep him safe. You helped her. You helped Chad. They aren't like the men who touch and pinch. They love you. They love Gerrard. They will help us keep him safe." I just kept talking. Benny kept strumming slowly and softly.

"There are a lot of people, good people, who will make sure Unicorn is safe, that nobody touches or pinches her. You made sure we knew Unicorn was in danger. You saved her."

"Not ugly...Beautiful..." Benny's words were soft, spoken over the notes from the guitar instead of sung.

"You had to do a bad thing to stop a worse thing from happening, didn't you?" I reached out and placed my hand in a comforting manner on Benny's knee. "You had to run them down to stop them, didn't you?"

Benny's hands dropped from the guitar. "Yes..." The word was spoken, not sung.

"Would you let Myron tell us about the trust, about Gerrard?"

"Yes."

"Is it okay if Sophie knows?"

"Yes."

There it was in glorious Technicolor...Truth.

CHAPTER 34

"When you tell a lie,
it becomes part of your future.
When you tell the truth,
it becomes part of your past."
- Skip Rogers, Reading Between the Lines

The rest of the interrogation was enlightening, but uneventful. Benny was primed to talk. He spoke about both hit and runs, his intentions to kill Jack and Harvey Martin as the only way he had to stop them from molesting again and again.

He told me about getting his money from Smack Daddy – a subject I did not let him get specific about. He told me about hiding and watching Harvey Martin molest Gerrard with the same anger and frustration, the same pinching and violent touching Jack Martin had used on him.

Benny related how once he knew Smack Daddy had gathered the money Benny believed was owed to him, he planted the listening devices at both residences in order to eavesdrop and figure out what the best time would be to rescue both children. I had carefully led Benny through this part of his explanation. I wanted to make sure it didn't appear as if Benny had stolen the five million dollars, but had only taken money *owed* to him.

Benny then re-counted how he used the mortuary pickup truck on the night he rescued – the softer word for kidnapped – Unicorn and Gerrard and bringing them to Isaac and Abi and Myron.

Benny was exhausted by this time so Myron filled in the rest. He related how Benny had turned up at the mortuary with the money and the children, and his asking Isaac and Abi to care for Unicorn as they had cared for him.

Gerrard was a different story. Gerrard needed specialized care, and fast. Myron wrote a trust incorporating the money Benny earned from royalties and placed Gerrard in a private care facility with the money being managed to pay for his care in perpetuity. Myron then quickly filed the trust to protect what Benny had been trying achieve.

Bad things being done for good reasons.

Depending on how you sliced the ethical pie, it was slightly different than doing bad things for bad reasons.

Pagan was very busy during all of this. It was clear Benny would be booked and charged, but he wouldn't survive in a holding cell.

Despite possibly giving a defense attorney a built-in diminished capacity defense, Pagan twisted the arms of not only the DA Peter Simmons but also of anyone else who objected, in order for Benny to be held at a private lock-down mental facility. The man was a superstar when it came to getting his way. I had no doubt Pagan would personally make sure Benny was kept safe. So would I.

All the brass, captains and above, who needed to make themselves seen, had checked in. They tried to assert their authority, were made to think they had, and then were ignored when the chief arrived and told them all to butt out.

It became mine and Pagan's call. The chief had asked us to do a job, we'd done it, and done it fast. He would revel in handling the press while letting us get on with clearing up all the loose ends.

Livia Nelson and Johnny Hawkins took care of reuniting Unicorn with her mother. Smack Daddy was served with a restraining order keeping him away from the house and Unicorn until the Department of Children's Services could make an assessment. I had no doubt Pagan had wolves in the LAPD's Child Abuse section of Juvenile Division who would make sure the Department of Children's Services took care of business properly.

Castano and Dodd handled all the paperwork.

Being relieved of those duties made all of this a stressful, but ultimately, a pretty great gig.

However, you're only as good as your last case. I knew the next call out could be a disaster, but I also knew it wouldn't be a calamity – even though I was going to wear my moniker proudly from now on.

At the end of the day, Pagan looked at me and said the three sweetest words I've ever heard, "Let's go home."

EPILOGUE

*"Lying is the most fun a woman can have
without taking her clothes off."*
- Natalie Portman

Home.

I loved my new digs at the Hacienda. I loved everything about the Hacienda. People I already thought of as close friends were here to greet us when we return. Rose Parker was a delight, and Tanaka laughed and laughed when Pagan told him about how I'd used my cane before falling over.

"We work on balance," Tanaka said with a smile.

It was all good. Better than good. It was wonderful.

However, it was two in the morning and I was still pacing back and forth in my loft. Even the wide open floor-plan couldn't contain me as I tried unsuccessfully to come down from the high of the case.

I looked out my window. There was a light coming out

of the door of the red and gold Airstream parked below. I saw Pagan through one of the coach's windows.

I blew out a deep breath, pulled on a sweatshirt and made my way down to the carpark. As I approached the Airstream, I could hear jazz playing on a CD, but I didn't know enough to say who or what it was. I did know I liked it. It was rhythmic and soothing. The piano was obvious, but there was also a bass and drums in the background, and an occasional foray by a saxophone.

I moved toward the inviting sound and warm light. As I got closer, I could also smell something...chocolate.

I knocked on the open door and looked in. The space was larger than I expected, but Pagan had made the interior his own with his choices of fabrics and furnishings. There were bookshelves filled with tattered and odd sized books. There was even a fairly large flat screen TV and a shelf of various other electronics. The music I'd heard was playing softly out of surround sound speakers.

Pagan was sitting at one end of a built-in table. He was reading and had a mug of hot cocoa in front of him. There was a second mug set out next to a warming pot on the table.

He looked up at me and smiled. "Couldn't sleep either?"

I almost dropped my head to let my hair fall forward, but remembered I was done with hiding. "You were expecting me?" I said, ruefully.

"Of course." Pagan gestured with his hand to the clean mug and the pot of what I assumed was more cocoa. He used a remote to turn the music down low. He then picked up the pot on the table and poured into the waiting mug.

I stepped up into the coach and gratefully took the proffered offering. I sighed heavily, feeling more relaxed already.

"What's with the Airstream?" I asked.

"Gypsy roots," Pagan said. "Sometimes, you just have to ramble."

"You're a piece of work, Pagan."

"So I'm repeatedly told." He sat back down, relaxing into his chair.

I sipped the cocoa. It was rich and creamy. I'd expected no less.

"Who's playing on your stereo?"

"Dave Brubeck Quartet, *Complete Storyville Broadcasts*."

I must have looked blank.

Pagan shook his head in mock dismay. "We're going to have to do something about your jazz horizons."

"I know *Linus and Lucy* when I hear it."

"Vince Guaraldi," Pagan said.

"Who?"

Pagan shot me a look.

I laughed. I paused and then asked, "How do you do it?"

Pagan gave me a quizzical look. "Do what?"

"Keep searching for the truth when we are surrounded by lies," I said.

"It's what I do," Pagan said. "What we do."

I shook my head. "Doesn't seem like there are a lot of happy endings. Even if we do the best we can to protect Benny, the system still has him."

"Gerrard is safe," Pagan said. "He's getting professional care through the trust, and his mother can still be involved without being crushed by the responsibility."

"But who knows how Unicorn will grow up," I said with a shrug.

"At least we've given her a better shot," Pagan said. "Or maybe it was Benny who gave her the shot."

He sipped from his mug and pushed his book across the table toward me.

I picked it up. "The Razor's Edge," I said, looking at the title.

"I read it once a year. It reminds me there is no destination, only the journey."

I put the book down and wrapped my hands around my mug of cocoa.

"Are you religious?" Pagan asked.

I sighed again. "Not so you'd notice."

"Yes you are," Pagan said quietly.

I looked up at him. "What do you mean?"

"Lie catching is our religion. It's what we're here to do."

"Lie catching is a religion?"

"It's our religion. Ego does not exist anywhere else except in human beings. Ego surrounds intelligence like a dark veil. Intelligence is light, ego is darkness. Intelligence is fragile, ego is diamond hard. Ego tells us to survive, to become like a castle built of rock, strong and immune from outside attack – impenetrable. To remain alive we must remain in constant flow. If we become stagnant, we die even though we still draw breath."

"Whoa," I said. This was heavier than I had expected.

Pagan continued. "Ego won't allow us to conceive of nothingness or accept we just end when we die. If we never end, then we must always have been. Therefore, this time, this now, is only part of the journey."

"How does any of that make lie catching a religion?"

Pagan poured himself more cocoa. "I don't spend a lot

of time trying to look past the veil and see where we came from or where we're going. We have no control over those states. We can only do something about the state we find ourselves in now. Lie catching is my gift. It's your gift. It doesn't matter where we came from. Where we're going will take care of itself, but when we get there we're going to have to justify what we did while we were here. Did we help others? Were we honest? Did we make the best use of our talents?"

"You really think any of this matters?"

"Only on Mondays and every other Wednesday. Ask me on a Tuesday and I'll give you a different answer."

"You are so full of crap," I said with a soft laugh.

"Probably," Pagan said. "But do you have a viable alternative?"

I raised my cocoa mug. Pagan leaned forward with his mug and we clinked in a toast.

"To the high priest of lie catching," I said.

"And to its new priestess," Pagan said.

And then the nonsense caught up with us and we fell about laughing.

Home.

A LOOK AT HOT PURSUIT:

A CALICO JACK WALKER / TINA TAMIKO L.A.P.D. NOVEL

It's 1977 and veteran L.A.P.D. cop Calico Jack Walker and his rookie partner, Tina Tamiko, are planning to make Calico's last shift on the job something special - but plans, as they do, come apart because Walker and Tamiko are good cops no matter what the cost . . . even if they're L.A. cops, in uniform, in their patrol car, on duty, and way out of their jurisdiction on the Las Vegas Strip...When a major crime is going down, good cops never hesitate...

AVAILABLE NOW FROM PAUL BISHOP AND WOLFPACK PUBLISHING

ABOUT THE AUTHOR

Paul Bishop is the author of fifteen novels and has written numerous scripts for episodic television and feature films. A novelist, screenwriter, and television personality, Paul is a nationally recognized behaviorist and deception detection expert.

A 35 year veteran of the LAPD, his high profile Special Assault Units produced the top crime clearance rates in the city. Twice honored as LAPD's *Detective of the Year*, he currently conducts law enforcement training seminars across the country, is an adjunct professor at the University of California Channel Islands, while also focussing on numerous writing projects.

Find Paul online:
www.paulbishopbooks.com